SPITFIRE

SPITFIRE

A Livy Nash
Mystery

M. L. HUIE

NEW YORK

Copyright © 2020 by Michael Huie

Published in the United States by Crooked Lane Books, an imprint of The Quick Brown Fox & Company LLC.

Crooked Lane Books and its logo are trademarks of The Quick Brown Fox & Company LLC.

Library of Congress Catalog-in-Publication data available upon request.

ISBN (hardcover): 978-1-64385-245-4
ISBN (ebook): 978-1-64385-246-1

Cover design by Mimi Bark
Book design by Jennifer Canzone

Printed in the United States.

www.crookedlanebooks.com

Crooked Lane Books
34 West 27th St., 10th Floor
New York, NY 10001

First Edition: January 2020

10 9 8 7 6 5 4 3 2 1

To Brook, for Paris and everything.

Though those that are betrayed do feel the treason sharply, yet the traitor stands in worse case of woe.

—Shakespeare, *Cymbeline*

In fact as foreign manager of The Sunday Times and Kemsley newspapers I am engaged throughout the year in running a world-wide intelligence organisation . . .

—Ian Fleming

Chapter One

London, June 1946

Livy Nash couldn't open her eyes. The lids felt like bricks. Her head pounded in rhythm to the throb of traffic outside. Where had she ended up last night? She had no idea. The inside of her mouth tasted like curry and vodka, the realization of which sent a pang of nausea through her body. God, she needed a loo. No choice but to open one eye. Ever so slightly.

The light smarted. She recognized a watch with a cracked face on the bedside table next to an almost-empty bottle of Polish vodka. She was in her flat, at least. Then she heard the bells chiming from St. Michael's down the street, and she remembered.

How long would she need to look suitable for Buckingham Palace?

Calculations raced through her brain as she dragged herself to the edge of the bed. Ten minutes to properly dress. Thirty by train to get to Charing Cross. Probably another fifteen to walk. She needed an hour—give or take. She had forty minutes.

Plenty of time for one more drink.

* * *

Fifteen minutes later, Livy hurried down the front steps of her Camden Town walk-up, headed for the tube. Her fingers fumbled with the last buttons on her black mackintosh as drizzle dotted her slouch hat. She looked up just in time to avoid hitting her landlord, Mr. Langham, who blocked her path to the street. His three-piece pinstripe concealed much of his corpulence, but despite the suit, Langham cut an imposing figure.

"Miss Nash, just who I was hoping to see," he said, his nasal voice entirely at odds with his girth. "I'm hoping you might have something for me."

"I do, yes," she said. It was a lie. "I'm late, though. For the palace."

"The palace, of course. Hobnobbing with the royals, are we? Well, I won't keep you long, Miss Nash. Consider this your third notice regarding your rent, which has been in arrears for the better part of two months."

"I know, and I will have it for you by the end of the week. But I—"

"—can't keep His Majesty waiting, to be sure," Langham said, sneering. "I'll see you on Friday then. Or in a week's time, I'll be round with prospective tenants." He pivoted, allowing Livy access to the road. She offered apologies and scurried past.

God, how late would she be now? These days she was behind in everything. Late for work. Late with the rent. She'd always been bad with money. But lately, with rationing and Black Market Billy raising his rates on the Polish vodka she craved, her purse was considerably lighter. But none of that mattered today. She had to be on time today.

Breaking into a trot, Livy looked down and noticed a brown soup stain at the hem of the crepe dress. She figured she looked a complete wreck. Her hair always resembled a rat's nest, but today the rest of her matched. *Who gives a toss?* No one would be looking at her today anyway. The day belonged to all the honorees, Peter among them. They'd eye his widow and their little boy. John would be five now, Livy reckoned. The rest of the invitees would be ogling the king.

Revelers packed the train into central London, everyone smiling fit to pop. Why not? The London Victory Celebrations would be commemorated by a parade down the Strand led by His Majesty, George VI.

The clatter of the train rattled tenfold inside Livy's vodka-soaked brain. No one in her car noticed it, though. They'd fought for this day and looked as though they planned to enjoy it. All the men had pulled out their old uniforms. Some had put on enough weight in a year that they bulged out of belts and fitted tunics. A few still had that shell-shocked gaze, their eyes fixed blankly ahead as if they expected air-raid sirens to go off any moment. Some hugged their children, spouses, or girl-friends as if to make up for lost time. But most of them just looked relieved to be on the other side of it.

She envied them and their ability to just enjoy the day. For her, the war hadn't been something to be endured; it had given her purpose and meaning. Qualities her life now decidedly lacked.

If Peter had been here, things might be different. He would have loved a victory parade. Just like all these other happy folks on the train, he'd bask in every moment with family and ex-comrades-in-arms. He lit up any room with that big smile on his V-shaped face. They could have enjoyed this day together.

The first time Livy had met Peter Scobee, she'd just fallen out of a plane in a field in France. The beauty of that moonlit flight across the English Channel three years ago had calmed her jangling nerves. It had been a one-way flight behind enemy lines in a two-seat Lysander, painted black to make it less of a target for German anti-aircraft. Below her the torn and battered coastline of France somehow looked serene in the blue moon glow.

The landing was not so peaceful.

The pilot, who had to guide the Lysander with only a map and compass, put the plane down hard in a small clearing barely a hundred yards long on barren farmland just south of Paris. The front wheels bounced and jerked the nose of the aircraft up as the pilot struggled to get the small aircraft down. Four people, all dressed in black, ran alongside the plane as it skipped through the clearing, but the Lysander whipped past the reception committee, skidding to a stop just before a bank of trees at the end of the field.

"Get out. Quick," the pilot barked over his shoulder. "Too much noise on the landing. Might've alerted the Boche."

Livy stood, trying to reach her pack under the cramped seat. The torque of the plane caused her to lose her balance, sending her arse-over-elbow to the hard French terrain below. She managed to keep her head up, but the force of the fall knocked the wind from her as she landed hard on her back.

By this time, the reception committee had caught up with the plane, and a tall man wrapped in a tattered farmer's jacket offered her his hand.

Livy, embarrassed by the indignity of her landing, sloughed him off and got up on her own despite the unwieldy weight of her pack. She righted herself and looked up at him, his smile crooked, hair looking as if a comb had never touched it, right hand extended.

"Thank you very much, but I can do for myself just fine," she said, getting her wind back.

The tall man chortled. "Did you bring the hotpot, Lanky girl?"

Livy hated it when southerners scoffed at her Lancashire accent, which became stronger under moments of duress, such as falling out of a plane behind enemy lines in France. The more her face reddened, the louder he'd laughed. She'd hated Peter Scobee that day.

Now, turning away from the interior of the train car and the expressions of the happy and numb, Livy reminded herself that Peter deserved to be here among the lucky ones who'd made it home.

The train began to slow. She glanced at her watch. The ceremony began in twenty-five minutes. What time, she wondered, would it be over?

Livy hurried out of the Charing Cross station heading for Trafalgar Square and the Mall. There she fell in with a small crowd of the well dressed who had to be making their way to the palace as well. She wouldn't be the only one keeping the king waiting.

"Olivia. Is that you?"

Livy turned to see a muted-pink hat flouncing its way through a pack of the gentry, headed toward her. A moment later, Livy could see the head wearing it.

Patricia O'Toole's long face broke into a grin of recognition as she came up alongside Livy. Being the wife of Geoffrey, the publisher of the newspaper with London's second-lowest circulation, gave Patricia a certain status, at least in her own eyes. Despite the far-too-springlike-for-this-somber-occasion hat she wore, her frock would have been high-end at any of the finer ladies' shops in the West End. Livy reckoned the woman must spend a fair share of her husband's salary keeping up with their Kensington neighbors, even in the face of nationwide rationing.

Patricia also wrote the column for women that Livy proofread for the paper. But the boss's wife rarely made an appearance among the newsroom worker bees. The first time the two had met was at last year's Christmas party, which in the spirit of austerity featured stale biscuits, tea, and not one ounce of booze. Though they'd chatted only a few minutes about the column, Patricia had sussed out the new girl. Livy knew she took stock of all the fillies in her husband's stable, just to make sure they didn't measure up when it came to breeding and stature.

Livy turned and acknowledged Patricia with a forced smile. Her head thumped away, rattling with each step. Before another night of imbibing, she'd have to beg Black Market Billy for some aspirin.

"Ah, Mrs. O'Toole. Out for the parade?"

"Oh heavens no, dear. On my way to the palace, actually," the woman said, as if it were a visit to the chemist's.

"So am I," Livy said, "actually." The word came out more like "ehhhhhk-chew–ulleee," mimicking Patricia's affected, hoity-toity vowels.

If the slight registered, Patricia gave no sign. She was far too busy looking oh-so-shocked that one of the staff—Livy— would be trawling among the elite.

"Is that so? For the George Cross presentations?"

"That's right."

"Well, wonderful, dear," Patricia said, obviously containing her shock. "Geoffrey served with Colonel Dunbar. They still play tennis every Tuesday. But really I'd no idea at all. You mean you served?"

"First Aid Nursing Yeomanry."

"A FANY, then?" Patricia's lips turned down, as if suppressing a snicker.

Livy had been called a "fanny" before, but never by a woman.

A group of fair-haired Royal Air Force types brushed past them, going in the opposite direction. Patricia gave the RAF boys her warmest smile.

"All our lovely boys. Still can't help but feel for the families of the ones who never came back. Peter Scobee for one. Heard so much about him. Colonel Dunbar was singing his praises at dinner just the other night. I'm sure his wife must be so proud. Even though he was a spy."

"That what Geoffrey says?"

Patricia cut her eyes at Livy's impertinence, seemingly waiting for an apology. Livy kept walking.

"So where is Mr. O'Toole?" she asked instead.

"Probably already there, hobnobbing with Dunbar and the other fellows about how they miss the war. I told him if he wanted his wife to look presentable, he'd have to wait. It takes us girls a bit longer to look beautiful, doesn't it, dear?"

Us girls? Patricia might pass for forty-five on a good day, Livy thought.

Ahead, the crowd thickened and Livy could make out the gold trim of the gates of Buckingham Palace about a quarter mile ahead. The enclosure surrounding the sturdy gray building gave the palace its only exterior touch of elegance. The Blitz had left much of London looking as though a giant fist had crushed it. The palace itself had been bombed multiple times over the course of the war, sustaining only slight damage. In doing all this, the Luftwaffe had managed to strengthen the wartime bond between the royal family and the people.

As she drew closer, Livy noticed the Union Jack flying over the palace instead of the George Cross. Chosen on this day, no doubt, to show the united power of the empire.

"One day, we really must sit down and have a long chat, you and I," Patricia said, affecting a smile Livy felt sure she reserved for special occasions. "I simply must hear all about your experience with the FANYs. Perfect material for 'The Ladies' Front,' don't you think? The women behind the heroes. Oooooh, I like that. Oh, and dear"—she lowered her voice to sound conspiratorial—"you smell like a brewery." Patricia fluttered away, disappearing into the throng of men in uniform.

Ahead, the ornate gates stood open, and a group of about fifty people, all military accompanied by their spouses, walked in after passing a long-faced bloke who looked like every troll in every children's book ever written. He discreetly held a guest list at his side, which he peeked at as each approached.

It wasn't only her Lancashire upbringing that made Livy feel like a complete outsider at a "do" such as this. For most people in the kingdom, an invite to Buckingham Palace would have been the perfect reason to splurge on a new frock, tell all their friends, and then boast about it for months, even years, after. She'd received the official palace invitation weeks ago. No reason at all to assume she would be anything but welcomed by the stuffy guardian at the gate. But still she felt like a fraud. As though someone in the crowd would suddenly stop, turn around, and point at her, shouting, "That woman is an impostor!"

Just get through it, Livy told herself, as she edged closer to the gate.

She made her final approach, hands in the pockets of her mackintosh, eyes front looking, not at Long Face but directly at the gray structure ahead, which symbolized the British monarchy.

"Olivia Nash," she said. Her tongue felt unwieldy in her mouth.

"I beg your pardon."

Livy concentrated. "My name's Olivia Nash."

"I do beg your pardon, miss, but you'll have to step outside the gates. This is a private ceremony."

Her breath quickened. "I—I served with him—with Lieutenant Commander Scobee," she said slowly.

"Be that as it may, young lady, your name is not on my list. I shall have to ask you to step this way, if you don't mind. Thank you, Admiral. My lady. Good morning to you."

Livy waited until two more oldsters had cleared the gate and then snatched the embossed guest list right out of Long Face's gloved hands.

"Miss, really—"

Livy scanned the names. She turned the creamy vellum over, reread the list.

She couldn't find her name anywhere.

"Livy."

She wanted to vomit. Right here, right now. Humiliated in front of the Patricia O'Tooles of the world. A gate crasher at a party she didn't even want to attend. Long Face grabbed the list back, and Livy found herself leaning against the gates of the palace, her downcast eyes fixed on the silver buckle of a man's left shoe.

"Livy. Come with me."

Livy hardly registered the hand at her elbow as she was hurried past Long Face, away from the latecomers and across the street. Her eyes never left the ground. The anger that had caused her to rip the list out of that old bastard's hand left her as quickly as it had come. Now, she felt nothing.

Above her, Queen Victoria sat on the throne, all pale and stern in flowing robes, her scepter ready to brain any interlopers to the royal grounds. Towering over even the Queen, the bronze figure of Winged Victory looked out over London.

Right, the Victoria Memorial.

"Get hold of yourself. Lean on the memorial if you have to."

She knew the voice that sounded in her ear, although more than a year had passed since she'd last heard it.

Colonel Henry Dunbar let go of her elbow. He'd put on weight in the past year. Must have been all that port the old boys at Six guzzled. His hair seemed thinner on top and had grayed at the temples. The wrinkles around his eyes ran deep and down his cheekbones to his unsmiling mouth. Only the stiff black mustache appeared as hearty as it had been when he was overseeing the Firm.

"Now look, I tried to get hold of you yesterday. I even sent someone round to your flat, but you weren't home. I can't have you here at this ceremony today."

"Why am I not on that list?" she demanded, her voice rough.

"I'm sorry, Livy, but today is too important. Clara is receiving the George Cross in Peter's memory. We can't have distractions."

Livy looked over Dunbar's old uniform. She'd never seen him in full dress before. Which of those medals had he gotten for sending men and women to die in France, she wondered.

"I have a right to be here today, Colonel."

"It's not a question of what's right." He moved so close to her Livy wondered for a moment if he might kiss her. "You need to pull yourself together, Livy. The Firm has been off the books for more than a year now. The war is over. You've got to find some way to leave all this behind."

"Thank you for the lecture, *Daddy*, but I'm a grown-up now and I make my own decisions, and I'm here to pay respects to my—"

Tears pushed at her eyes as she tried to find the right words. Damn it, she would not cry in front of this patronizing tosser. What had she been about to say, anyway? Friend? That didn't cover it, really. The relationship she'd had with Peter defied description. Friend, of course. But what about commanding officer, comrade, confidant? Lover?

"I can't have you like this inside when Clara receives that medal, don't you see? Today is a celebration. It's not about you. It's about king and country. It's about loyalty. Loyalty to what we fought for."

Maybe it was the vodka, or the pain in her gut, or the memory of her and Peter in that German prison—along with Dunbar's old-hat rhetoric—that finally broke down the little decorum she could maintain. She grabbed Dunbar's well-pressed lapels and shoved him away with sudden ferocity. The colonel fell on the grassy lawn around the monument. The tall peaked cap toppled from his head.

"Don't you bloody well talk to me about loyalty." Livy spat the words at him.

Lying on the ground, Dunbar held his hands up, prepared for an attack.

Livy stopped. Her lungs heaved, her breath pulsing in loud gasps. Just like battle. She'd felt the same sudden urge during the war in times of crisis. Dunbar looked ready to defend himself. How she must look to him, Livy could only imagine.

She stepped back. On the ground between them lay a folded piece of paper. Dunbar had dropped the palace's official order of program for today's medal ceremony.

Livy picked up the paper, slid it inside her coat, and walked away.

* * *

An hour later Livy sat at a corner table in an almost empty pub off Piccadilly, sipping a vodka and tonic. It couldn't be any later than eleven. Not a proper lunchtime for another hour, and she was—to use the Lancashire phrase—pissed as a newt.

The faint sounds of the Victory Parade on a route down the Strand found their way through the open door of the pub and to Livy's back table. The barman, a small man with a clean apron and a face like a rat, peered outside as if he could actually see the parade. The only other customer that morning was a sunken-faced man in a Tommy uniform from the Great War, who sat near the door slowly eating chips.

"Looks like rain, it does," the barman said for at least the third time in the last half hour. "Rain right on the king's parade. Hitler's revenge."

Livy took another sip of her drink and reread the George Cross citation.

The KING has been graciously pleased to approve the posthumous award of the GEORGE CROSS to Lieutenant Commander Peter Lawrence Scobee, Special Operations Executive. Lt. Cmdr Scobee parachuted behind enemy lines in France in 1943 and, for almost two years, organized and assisted resistance movements in occupied France.

In July 1944 Lt. Cmdr. Scobee and members of his staff were taken to a Gestapo prison near Paris. He was executed in the prison on 10 August 1944 after being interred for more than three weeks. The GEORGE CROSS is presented to Lt. Cmdr. Scobee for his sacrifice and loyalty in the face of torture and extreme duress at the hands of the enemy in occupied France.

Livy folded the paper. "Members of his staff." No need for a mere *member of the staff* to attend the ceremony this morning. Might be distracting.

The light from the open door to the pub suddenly dimmed. A man stood silhouetted in the doorway. His head turned toward the old man in uniform and then snapped in Livy's direction.

"Looks like rain, it does," the barman said, as if by introduction.

The man sauntered to the bar and grinned at the landlord. The light behind him dimmed his profiled features, but Livy could tell his single-breasted suit was tailored. He didn't have a hat, and despite the barman's grim predictions about the weather, the man had chosen to not wear a coat that morning.

"Scotch and soda," the new patron said. His vowels had the lazy drawl of the educated gentry, although his voice seemed like one used to giving orders. "With Haig and Haig, if you have it."

The man turned from the bar and looked around the pub as if searching for a table. He placed a cigarette with three gold bands around the filter into his mouth and lit it with a gold lighter he pulled from another pocket.

Now this one certainly looked like the type who ought to be celebrating on the Strand as the king, the princesses, and Monty waved to the masses. Livy guessed the patron was just shy of forty, so the right age to have served. He looked reasonably fit, although she noticed signs of aging, such as gray at the temples of his dark, wavy hair and crow's feet that deepened when he drew in the smoke from his cigarette.

The barman brought his drink over, and the man eyed the honey-brown concoction as he dropped a few coins on the bar.

"Rain right on the king's head," the barman muttered, and pocketed the change.

The man's arrival had pulled Livy out into the open. She wanted privacy. She wanted to sit and drink in this dark corner all day if she felt like it. She didn't want some bloke giving her the eye or telling her, "A lady shouldn't be alone in a pub in the middle of the day."

The man in the suit sipped his drink and moved in her direction. What the hell? Wasn't this bugger smart enough to see this wasn't the time for flirting? No, they never saw it that way. Not one of them.

Slowly, she let her eyes drift up from her drink to meet his. He had a broken nose and a wide mouth with a big grin. Handsome. Complete trouble.

"Do you mind if I join you?"

"I'm busy."

"I can see," he said, looking at her drink. Then his eyes went down to her legs. Livy wondered if she'd wobble when she stood up to hit this cheeky Casanova.

"You're Olivia Nash, aren't you?" he asked, eyes returning to her face.

And he knows my name? "As I said—I'm busy."

"Yes, well, let me get to the point then." He reached inside his coat and placed a simple, white business card on the table in front of her. "I'm the foreign manager of the Kemsley News Group, which includes *The Sunday Times*, among others. You're with Geoffrey O'Toole over at the *Evening Press and Journal*, aren't you?"

Livy eyed her watch. The stranger ignored the hint.

"If you're content working for a third-rate paper, then please forgive my intrusion. But if you're a smart girl, then I'd like to discuss something a little different for you. With your foreign background, you'd be ideal for our line of work. Any chance you could run round to my office Monday? I'm just up on the Gray's Inn Road. Do you know it?"

Livy's mind raced through all the possible angles. A man walks into a pub, finds a lone woman drinking and manufactures a job that just happens to be in her line of work, all in an attempt to seduce her? But what else could it be? Newspaper work? No one even remotely familiar with her proofreading job would ever consider offering her a promotion. Much less track her down in a pub and dangle foreign correspondent for *The Sunday Times* in front of her sloshed nose.

This might rank as one of the most elaborate flirtations in history. Or it might be something else entirely.

"Gray's Inn Road?"

"That's right. We have a modest office there." The man swirled the ice in his glass lazily. Calm as you please.

Not a policeman either, she reckoned. Far too sophisticated. *Like he owns the world, this one.* Had her landlord sicced someone on her? No, toughs who collected rent didn't pronounce their vowels like the Patricia O'Tooles of the world.

"I know the area," she said, finally. Nothing about this felt right to her, but that's precisely what made it intriguing.

"Excellent. Shall we say around two, then?"

Livy took another drink. "If I can get away from work."

"I'm sure you can manufacture some excuse. Oh, and I'd suggest you clean up a bit before tomorrow. You're about to step up in the world, Miss Nash." The man downed the last sip of his drink and then turned to go.

"You there," Livy called to his back. The stranger turned. "How'd you find me?"

His wide mouth dropped down a bit as if he was disappointed she'd had to ask. "I'm a journalist. We ask questions."

Then he stepped out into the street, and the pub returned to its dark silence.

An interview for a new job, just like that? She wasn't a writer, and if this bloke knew enough to find her in this pub, then he obviously knew that as well. Whoever he was.

She looked down at what he'd handed her. The simple printing matched the unadorned card. It read:

Kemsley News Group.
Mercury Service.
"Get it first, but get it right."
Foreign Manager, Ian Fleming.

Chapter Two

Careless women never appeal to a real gentleman. Don't talk while dancing. When a man is dancing, he wants to dance.

Livy put down her pencil and rubbed her eyes. She was sick to death of editing this idiotic column. Her headache had returned as well, even though she'd not had a drink since the pub two days ago. With a couple of months' rent due in a few days, she'd have to cut back on the black-market booze. To soothe herself, Livy felt the thick embossed card given her by the stranger in the pub through the pocket of her skirt. Foreign work? Stepping up in the world? She didn't believe it and didn't trust him. Even though she wanted to.

Her desk sat in the middle of the second of three very straight rows in the newsroom of the London *Evening Press and Journal* (the P&J to those lucky enough to work there). The uniform lines were sandwiched between two walls with one window on either side. Bathrooms and a small lunchroom faced Livy, with the administrative offices situated behind so the publisher and editors could watch over her and the other worker bees.

The P&J resided in a soot-gray three-story building that had housed a butcher shop a few years before the war. The butcher and family had lived on the second floor, which now served as the present location of the not-so-bustling newsroom. The butcher went to war and the family moved to the country, so in '39, the P&J took up residence. But on hot days like today, Livy, whose desk was situated near a gap in the wooden floorboards, swore she could still smell rotted meat, even though it had been seven years since the butcher had owned the shop.

Another explanation for the stink might be the column Livy found herself proofreading. Tomorrow evening's edition would carry a particularly gripping "Ladies' Front" column with more advice for single women.

Never look bored in the company of a man, even if you are, the column advised. *Don't sit in awkward positions, and remember, if you must chew gum, do it with your mouth closed.*

As was often the case when the trite verbiage of "The Ladies' Front" became too much to bear, Livy swiveled her head toward the large window on her left that looked almost directly into the facade of a white office building. Nothing distinguished the block except an archway on the ground floor that led to a small courtyard, but its likeness to another building always took Livy back to 1943 just before her war began.

She'd been a motorcar driver at Squires Gate Airport in Blackpool, ferrying Vickers Wellington flyboys to their bombers morning and night. Then the letter came. The blank envelope opened to reveal a tersely worded statement:

Olivia Nash has been recommended for special service by her FANY commanding officer.

So, on a crisp fall morning, she took the train to London wearing her tweed suit, which was a little warm for the time of year but the only one she had. In her hand she held a white card with an address in Orchard Court near Baker Street.

The building Livy found seemed far too innocuous to be attached to the War Office. In fact, it looked like any other office building, except for the distinctive archway. A doorman met her as she entered and asked, in French, if she spoke English. He then led her to the second floor, where she met a tall, wispy sort of officer named Buckmaster.

"Right, Miss Nash, welcome. Let me just take you down the hall to our Miss Atkins," Buckmaster said.

The woman waiting for Livy in the austere office at the end of the corridor looked to be about thirty-five but had the forthright stare and bearing of someone much older. Miss Atkins sat behind a plain wooden desk and calmly lit a cigarette before saying a word. A single closed manila folder lay on the desk.

"Three years at Squires Gate in the motor pool, I see?" Miss Atkins spoke with crisp consonants and round vowels.

"I'm a FANY. That's my job."

Miss Atkins smiled at the quip, then opened the folder on her desk. "English father, French mother." She blinked. "I see your mother was killed in an air raid at Liverpool." She lifted her head and met Livy's gaze.

Maybe it was the way she addressed her mother's death. Without any sense of false sympathy. Maybe it was the way her expression softened just slightly. Whatever it was, Miss Atkins had changed the air in the room. She acknowledged Livy's grief, and the two women sat with it for a long moment.

Then she said, "Your mother was a Parisian, I believe. Her city—her country—is overrun by the Boche. We here at the Firm are sending young men and women like yourself to help those who are fighting behind the lines. Now, you speak French like a native. You're young, smart, and from what I hear more than capable. Your commanding officer at Squires Gate wrote that you subdued a German POW awaiting transfer?"

"He thought I'd be easy, that he could get past me."

"It says here you knocked him unconscious."

"I might've done."

"No doubt. The thing is, Miss Nash, that anger you seem to be holding on to can either serve you or destroy you. So, I can recommend today that you be sent to Scotland for training, but first I need to know if you're willing to take what drives you and use it. Do you understand me? I suppose that what I'm saying is I sense you would like to do more for your country than just being an RAF chauffeur?"

Livy's laughter surprised even herself. She couldn't remember the last time she'd felt this light, this excited. She still didn't know exactly what this "special service" might be, but now she'd willingly follow wherever Miss Atkins led her.

"If you're asking if I want to get off my arse and fight this war," Livy said, "then the answer is, where do I sign?"

Miss Atkins didn't flinch. She took a long drag on her cigarette, put it out in a glass ashtray, and opened the manila folder.

"Well, then, you sign right here." She pushed a sheet of paper across the desk. At the top it read, OFFICIAL SECRETS ACT.

Much later, after all the training, Livy and the others returned to the building at Orchard Park, which she now knew was headquarters of Section F (France) of the SOE (Special Operations Executive). Again she met with Miss Atkins in the plain office on the second floor. Smoking one cigarette after another, Miss Atkins complimented Livy's firing-range scores.

"Sergeant McHugh rated you the highest among all recruits in clandestine training," she said. "Even higher than the men. On the other hand, I'm not sure you'd make much of a paratrooper."

Miss Atkins then told her she would be flown into France at the next full moon to become the fourth member of the MANDOLIN circuit.

"MANDOLIN is the Firm's primary network outside Paris," Miss Atkins said. "Your commanding officer is already in place along with three members of the resistance. You'll be the circuit's new courier. You'll deliver messages to our other circuits, as needed. Your organizer, Lieutenant Commander Scobee, is one of our best people in France. You'll be in good hands. Still, this is dangerous work, Olivia. No point in softening it. If you're caught, you'll either end up in a Gestapo prison or shot on sight."

* * *

"Ya all right, Livy?"

The question jolted Livy out of her daze. The voice, which came from her immediate right, belonged to Myrtle Dickinson, a sweet girl from Burnley who had taken to Livy from the day she started work. Livy felt thankful for Myrtle's Lancashire solidarity among the stuffy P&J proofreaders. Most of the other women on staff had husbands and kids in London, and little tolerance for an errant comma. Since both Livy and Myrtle had the misfortune of having been born north of Wigan, naturally the pair had been pegged as bumpkins incapable of tying their shoes, much less understanding the nuances of the King's English.

"Can't seem to get through this latest column, Myrtle. Want to give it a read?"

Myrtle nodded like a smitten puppy, her cat-eye glasses bobbing on her nose. She loved "The Ladies' Front" so much that Livy couldn't bring herself to tell Myrtle it was complete rubbish.

"The Ladies' Front" had been the brainchild of the man in the corner office, Geoffrey O'Toole, publisher and founder of the P&J. The column had begun during the war, or so Livy had learned during her orientation, to help boost the morale of women holding down the fort at home while their men were away in France, North Africa, or Burma. The column had helped make the paper's modest reputation. Then again, reputation implied status, and the only status the P&J had among the other London newspapers was its lack of pages and its editorial devotion to "what makes Britain great." A thorough read of "The Ladies' Front" seemed to suggest that Britain's greatness could be maintained only if women kept their mouths closed.

Myrtle perused the column as if reading Sanskrit, but Livy's brief respite from the drudgeries of life at the P&J was short-lived. The familiar smell of hair tonic preceded the arrival of newsroom lothario Jeremy Huggins.

"Did you pop down to the parade Saturday?"

Jeremy threw a leg over the edge of Livy's desk and lit a Chesterfield. He had thick dark hair held in place by his signature tonic, a dimple on his right cheek, and clear green eyes. He blew out smoke, unbuttoned his jacket, and leaned toward her.

"Busy, Jeremy."

"That's too bad. You missed me in my uniform. Me and some of the lads from my squadron were riding in a Morris. Waving flags, blowing kisses at all the pretty girls. You should have been there. I might've blown one to you."

Livy endured this type of flirting from Jeremy almost daily. True, he was handsome enough, but his insufferable ego made her forget about his looks.

"I'm afraid I was wasting my time elsewhere," Livy said, wishing she hadn't loaned Myrtle the column so Jeremy might take the hint that she faced an imminent deadline.

"That's one thing I miss about the war, the lads all together," he went on. "We were facing the Luftwaffe, but there's something about the danger that brings you closer. We're all still best mates, you know."

He also routinely inflated his role in the war, referring to his combat heroics every chance he got although he'd served only in the Auxiliary Air Force deploying barrage balloons during the Blitz. While that had contributed considerably to the war effort, Jeremy always made himself sound like David Niven shooting Messerschmitts out of the sky.

"Friends in foxholes. Heard that one before, Jeremy."

"Well, I mean, how could you understand? I know you did your little bit and all, darling, but it's different, you know, when the next one coming could have your name on it."

Livy shoved her chair back so suddenly that the unflappable correspondent Mr. Huggins leapt off her desk almost at attention. "Excuse me, Jeremy," she said, almost hissing. "Need to powder my nose." She inched past him and, just for his benefit, said, "Don't call me darling again."

Livy stomped up the row of desks toward the washrooms at the front of the office. Behind her back she heard a few whispers, a snort or two, and the *clack-clack* of typewriters as the writers returned to their work and the proofreaders returned to marking corrections.

She told herself this anger would eventually go away, that she only snapped like this because of the headaches, the alcohol, and because she hadn't slept a full night in almost a month. It didn't go away. It didn't change her behavior either, but that's what she kept telling herself.

She hated this place. Right now, she hated almost every place.

Livy pushed open the door of the ladies WC and looked around to make sure she was alone. A glance at the cracked face of her mother's old watch told her she barely had time to get to the Gray's Inn Road and the two o'clock appointment with—what was his name? Fleming? What would be her excuse to leave work early this time? Was it even worth it? She flicked on the faucet, splashed a bit of water in her face, and then covered it with a hand cloth on the sink. She caught her breath in this long moment of escape and wished it never had to end. But it always did.

"Livy?"

She looked up.

Myrtle stood framed in the doorway, looking her most anxious. "He wants to see you. Mr. O'Toole. Right away."

*　*　*

"Miss Nash, you know my wife, of course."

Livy eased into the stiff black leather chair across from Geoffrey O'Toole. Patricia sat beside him, claws sharpened to a point after a fresh manicure.

Livy said, "Yes, we bumped into each other Saturday."

The boss had money, and it showed in his clothes and the furnishing of his office. The newsroom of his paper might be a drab affair, but his corner of the building, where he entertained clients and interviewed the few newsmakers who deigned to talk to him, had a look befitting a minister or even the publisher of a real newspaper. A corner window dominated the office, surrounded by walls of thick dark wood. O'Toole's desk felt more like a battleship than office furniture, with its sleek surface and reinforced edges. Photos of O'Toole, his dark hair slicked back and tiny glasses perched on his nose, shaking hands with a number of minor dignitaries, hung in ornate wooden frames at strategic points all along the walls.

"Nash? That's Irish, isn't it?"

"I believe it is, sir." He asked the same question every time they met.

"But you're not Irish, are you?"

"No, I grew up in Blackpool." Another peek at her watch. She'd have to hurry now to make that two o'clock.

"Oh, that's right. The Illuminations. Yes, Mrs. O'Toole and I love the seaside." He shared a glance with his wife, who didn't look at all like she loved the seaside. "I hope you don't mind I asked my wife to sit down with us?"

"No. Perfectly fine," Livy said. Then it hit her. The glare from Patricia. The sudden summons. Saturday before the palace, before the pub.

"You smell like a brewery," she'd told Livy.

"The Ladies' Front" had been Mrs. O'Toole's baby since her husband first introduced the column. It had made her a sort of celebrity in some circles. Truly, if the *Press and Journal* had a star, it was Patricia O'Toole, and she wouldn't be happy with a lush proofing her words.

Livy's stomach dive-bombed.

"Shall I get my girl to fix you a cup of tea?" O'Toole asked.

"Um, no thank you."

"I trust you found today's column to be relatively clean," Patricia said.

"I read it several times, yes," Livy replied.

For a moment, the O'Tooles looked at Livy, the same vacant smile stamped on both their faces. Bloody hell, was she getting the sack?

"Well, Olivia, I don't have to tell you how important Mrs. O'Toole's . . . and your work is to the success of the P&J. 'The Ladies' Front' continues to be one of the most popular columns with our readers. It's more than just words on a page for many people, Livy. It's a—a . . ."

"A code of conduct," Patricia added.

"Yes, yes, quite right. Some of these girls pay very close attention to what Mrs. O'Toole has to say. I wouldn't be at all surprised if it doesn't help them make it through the day. It is a bit surprising then, Olivia, that you, who proofread the column, seem to be rather out of sorts lately," O'Toole continued. He pushed his glasses up on his nose and leaned forward to open the single brown folder on his desk. He read over it while Patricia glared at Livy like a lion who had missed supper.

Livy's palms felt clammy. This was it.

"According to your file, you've been late to work three times in the past month and have been late back from lunch on four occasions over the same period. And Saturday before the ceremony, Mrs. O'Toole here said you had the—um—smell of spirits about you."

"She did. Yes. I'm afraid she did," Patricia chimed in.

Livy tried to remember how much money she had left. How long would it be before Langham kicked her out?

O'Toole sighed a disapproving breath. "My dear girl, I want the very best for my employees here, and in return I ask that they meet the world-class standards of the P&J. Do you understand? Miss Nash?"

"Yes—yes. Sorry."

Patricia leaned forward in her chair. "Olivia, I don't presume to know what sort of dilemmas you may be facing when you leave the office every afternoon, but I do know that practically every problem faced by women your age, and older, can be solved by the practical advice and counsel found in the column you yourself proofread every week. Perhaps if you had paid a little closer attention to the content of the piece and did a little less nitpicking over the occasional missed comma or—"

Livy wanted to tell them the column was insulting and ludicrous and beneath her. That she belonged elsewhere doing important work and not sitting here being judged by two people whose only claim to respectability derived from their money and class.

"Olivia?"

"Yes. I understand."

Livy knew any sort of pushback from her would result in a much longer lecture on the virtues of living according to Patricia O'Toole's unforgiving principles, but at this point she didn't give a toss. They'd sack her just the same.

What time could it be? Surely past two. Too late for her two-o'clock appointment now.

* * *

Once Geoffrey O'Toole finally got around to the "your services were no longer required" bit, Livy had shuffled out of his big office and made for Jeremy's desk. She couldn't bear facing sweet Myrtle. There might even be tears, and right now she needed a drink more than anything.

What Jeremy Huggins lacked in charm, he more than made up for in procurement of quality booze. It took only a modest amount of eye-batting and pouting to convince Jeremy to sneak down the second-floor fire escape with her and his bottle of Gordon's. The clouds of the day before had dissipated, so they stole away to a small bench behind a pub next door. Jeremy led the way, which made Livy wonder how many other girls he'd led astray from the P&J. Not that she cared. She found him vile, so Livy felt no qualms about using Jeremy for his gin. Fending off his advances for the next hour or so required nothing more than the occasional glare. In exchange, she enjoyed the best drink she'd had since the war.

The last real liquor she could remember—not the watered-down, often bitter swill she'd had to settle for during rationing—had been supplied to her by a Frenchman named Luc. He'd been one of five in her SOE circuit in France. Most nights the group took refuge in the storeroom of an abandoned café to avoid Gestapo patrols. It had taken a while for Livy to warm to Peter Scobee, the commander, but she'd immediately taken to the others. Andrè had been a farmer until his wife was killed in an air raid. His sister, Michelle, and Luc, an older man who'd worked as a mechanic until his garage had been taken over to service German staff cars, completed the small network code-named MANDOLIN.

The French members of the circuit didn't know Peter's and Livy's real names. They were always Marcel and Annette Desjardins, a brother and sister from Paris whose family home had been taken over at the beginning of the German occupation. André, Michelle, and Luc knew not to ask questions. They did their jobs.

Michelle, who was a few years older, soon became something of a big sister to Livy. Despite her small frame and waifish figure, Michelle served as the group's cook. She scraped together their meager rations and created lavish meals for the five, and usually ate more than anyone else. Her older brother seemed a typical Parisian. André smoked too much, which stained his teeth and bristly blond mustache a dark brown.

Luc, the ex-mechanic, could get almost anything. He supplied drinkable wine and broke the tension with some of the dirtiest jokes Livy had ever heard. *Why doesn't Eva Braun swallow when she gives Hitler a blow job? She doesn't like sour Kraut.* The dirtier the joke, the more Luc's big grin and wolfish eyes stood out even at night.

As Jeremy poured her third glass of gin and began another story of his wartime exploits, Livy considered how low she had sunk. Sitting on a lonely bench in the middle of the day enduring the come-ons of a third-rate Casanova might not be an all-time low, but it ran a close second. She set her glass down between cracks on the ancient bench, and her fingers brushed the thick business card in the pocket of her skirt. Fleming. What time now? Almost half four. Gin and self-pity had stolen the afternoon.

She didn't have a job. She didn't have Peter. And soon enough she might not have a place to live. Fleming and an appointment for which she was two and a half hours late was all she had at this point.

Livy put up her hand, stopping Jeremy midstory. His perpetual smile sagged.

"Do you have a quid for a taxi?"

Chapter Three

~

Thirty-five minutes later Livy left her properly soused companion sitting in a cab with a promise to return as she took the stairs to the second floor of the building on the Gray's Inn Road. Three hours late now. Livy doubted Fleming would still be there, and if he was, she reckoned he'd no longer be interested. But she had to try.

She pulled the business card from her skirt and stepped off the landing. The hallway before her felt narrow and secluded. One door stood at the very end of the corridor. Livy hesitated before stepping out onto the polished hardwood floors. Something in that first stride felt portentous to her. The hallway looked long and ominous, as if the walls on either side were closing in with each step. Then again, maybe that was just the gin talking.

She stopped at the door at the end of the hall. MERCURY SERVICE had been stenciled on the opaque glass. There was a slight glow on the other side. Maybe he was still there. Livy let out a breath, straightened her skirt, and reached for the doorknob.

It opened before she touched it.

A blonde woman in a business skirt and a blouse that looked expensive even to Livy's less-than-qualified eyes was in the middle of putting on her coat. She flashed a perfect smile and then pivoted to the man behind her.

"Your two o'clock is here, sir."

Livy recognized the man behind the blonde. Ian Fleming leaned on a broad clean desk, a cut-glass tumbler filled with something dark brown in his hand. He glanced down at the face of his watch.

"Just one second, Pen," Fleming said to the blonde. He reached forward and retrieved a travel brochure from a stack of papers she had under her arm. The front of the colorful trifold advert featured bronzed men and women sunning on a golden beach and wading into the ocean wearing snorkels and flippers. The legend at the top read JAMAICA.

"I need something to keep me company after you've gone," he said.

A cold look passed over the blonde's crisp Nordic features, but only for an instant. "Shall I freshen your drink before I leave, sir?" she asked.

"Thank you, but no, my dear. Good night."

She gave Livy another look and then hurried past, her heels clicking on the hardwoods as she retreated down the narrow hallway.

Fleming dropped the Jamaica brochure on the desk behind him and downed the last of his drink. Livy didn't know whether she should step into the office or apologize for wasting his time and flee. Her mouth felt dry. She felt wobbly from head to toe. This wasn't another newspaper job. It was something more, and it frightened her as much as it drew her. So she just stood there.

"You might want to close the door—should you decide to come in," Fleming said, and retreated behind the big desk through another door.

She stepped through the entrance. Briefly she remembered Jeremy waiting in the cab. Then he vanished from her mind.

This looked like no newspaper office Livy had ever seen. No newsroom. No bustle of activity. The compact outer office had thick, wood-paneled walls. The secretary's desk was the only substantial piece of furniture in the room. A new Royal Arrow typewriter and a black telephone sat in the center of the desk. Otherwise it was completely free of clutter. A large print of Turner's *The Battle of Trafalgar* hung behind the desk. Two leather armchairs sat at an angle out front. The look felt sleek, modern, and expensive.

Livy pushed on toward Fleming's open office door. She noted its thick oak and the rubber seal that ran around the frame. Not the type of door an editor would ever need. Livy wondered what this man might be saying or doing in his office that he didn't want overheard. She stood in the arch and took in the room.

The inner office didn't seem much bigger than the outer, perhaps about twelve feet square. A small picture window dominated the far wall with a view of the neighboring brownstones that stretched as far as she could see. In contrast with his secretary's workspace, the surface of Fleming's old-fashioned oak desk was buried under newspapers, some dog-eared and opened. A cannonball paperweight kept several carefully stacked piles of papers together. Alongside rested a pair of reading spectacles as well as a pack of Chesterfields and another pack of cigarettes in a white box with three gold bands.

These small details, however, paled compared to the wall-length map of the world that hung directly behind Fleming's desk. The chart stretched from Alaska and North America on the left to Siberia and the South China Sea on the far right. Tiny lights embedded into the map itself glowed like an elongated Christmas tree from one corner of the world to the next. Most of the lights seemed concentrated in North and South America, Europe, and Africa, but the occasional single light flickered in Czechoslovakia or Peking. Moscow even had its own small bulb. Livy guessed there to be at least ninety to a hundred lights total.

Fleming didn't stand when she entered the room. He carefully placed one of the cigarettes with the gold bands in a holder and lit it with a heavy gold lighter. Then he gave her a head-to-toes appraisal, like you might size up a secondhand automobile with a few too many miles.

"I was detained—at work," Livy said.

"Quite, quite," he said, languidly shifting his eyes back to her face. Then, smiling, he said, "Do sit down."

Leaving the door open, Livy took a seat in the plush leather chair across from this more-than-mysterious man. He wore another navy suit with a white cotton shirt, but this time with a spotted bow tie. Fleming looked pressed and crisp even though it was the end of the workday. He reminded her of so many officer types she'd met in the war. The privileged men at MI6 who'd turned their patrician noses down at the "amateurs" of the Firm. But this one seemed to be wooing her, and not for the usual reasons a man courted a woman. Still, if it proved to be the latter, Livy would leave him with a broken limb.

"Cigarette?" he said, studying her with those lazy blue eyes that seemed to obscure the gears turning in his head.

"I don't smoke."

Fleming's wide mouth turned down as if the answer was unexpected. "Drink, then?" He half gestured to a credenza to the right of his desk stocked with several bottles, various cut-glass cocktail tumblers, and a leather ice bucket with wet tongs lying on a tray next to it. "Vodka, wasn't it?"

Livy's right hand tensed. She didn't want a drink. She wanted to know what the hell this was about.

"No thanks," she said.

"I admire your restraint. Smoking tends to make me want a drink and drinking makes me want another cigarette. Cyclical, I'm afraid." He slid open the credenza and removed a half-filled bottle of bourbon and another of branch water. Deftly he mixed the two and returned to his chair. "Detained at work, you said?"

"That's right."

Fleming took a sip of his drink and gripped the cigarette holder between his teeth. "You don't trust me, do you?"

Livy almost snorted. "Look, you're an impressive man. Nice office. That map. The lot. But things haven't exactly been going my way of late, and if you're on the pull, then this is not going to end the way you want. So I'd suggest you say what was on your mind and then we can both be on our way."

Fleming's mouth curled into a predatory grin. "Your working-class candor is not without its charm, Miss Nash, but I assure you I'm not in the habit of chatting up drunk girls in pubs."

"Right then, so you find me in the middle of London and invite me to interview to be a foreign correspondent for *The*

Times? Is that it? Like you said, I'm a proofreader for a third-rate paper. Not even that now. I was sacked today. Or perhaps you already knew that."

"Can't say that I did. Why did they let you go?"

Livy huffed. "As you said, it's a third-rate paper."

Fleming stood and walked to the door. Livy tensed and wondered if the interview, if it had ever been that, was about to conclude. Instead Fleming closed the thick door. As he did, the rubber around the frame seemed to seal the entrance with a soft suction sound.

Closing the door now. All nice and alone. Livy's patience was gone. Her heart banged against her chest. She wanted to scream. Instead she gripped the sides of her chair and held on.

"You're unusually blunt for a woman of your age," he said, returning to his desk. "So, let me return the favor. I did ask you here today to talk about a job, as a matter of fact. As I said yesterday, your foreign experience during the war will serve you well should I decide to use you. In other words, I didn't traipse across London yesterday because I think you're the next Somerset Maugham."

"Sorry?"

"I don't give a damn if you can write."

"This is a foreign news service, isn't it? You—wait, is this another proofreading job for the boys on your big map back there?"

"Miss Nash, I am interested in you because you were an agent with the Special Operations Executive. I am interested in you because I'm told you were one of the Firm's best. You came home. Many of the girls we dropped into France ended up being captured."

"Many of the boys too," Livy said.

"Be that as it may, I am interested in you because of your wartime reputation," Fleming said, parrying her rebuff with a compliment. "I've heard stories about you. Your exploits during the war. Tell me, is it really true that you walked right into a Gestapo headquarters and demanded they release a prisoner?"

"It was a long time ago." She remembered every detail, but she'd not tell Fleming that. "A very long time ago."

"A mutual friend of ours even told me the Germans had a name for you. Spitfire, wasn't it?" Fleming's wide mouth curled into a grin worthy of the Cheshire Cat.

Luc had been the one who told her about the nickname. He'd found it funny as well. Livy hated it at first. Like being called *shrew*. But RAF Spitfires had helped win the Battle of Britain, and if the Germans had a nickname for her, then that meant she'd gotten under their skin.

"You're very well informed, but I still don't have a clue what it is you want from me," Livy said with a little more venom than she intended.

"Olivia, when you came back from France, our intelligence services wouldn't give you the time of day despite your qualifications. Since the war you've been doing work that seems, frankly, beneath you and has caused you to become something of a bitter wastrel with a taste for bad vodka. So, if we can find the Olivia Nash who fought for her country, then I just may want to add another light to this rather ostentatious map behind me." Fleming crossed his long legs and clinched his cigarette holder between his lips. "In short, I'm asking you to spy for your country again."

Livy heard the words but still didn't trust him. "I thought . . . this was a news service."

"Oh, it is. Very much so."

"A news service with spies?"

Fleming nodded, as if this was the most natural thing in the world. "Some of my correspondents report the news, while others work at the behest of His Majesty's Secret Service."

This is more bloody like it, Livy thought.

Fleming smiled and opened a drawer in his desk. Then he slid a single sheet of thick paper across to her. Livy recognized the seal and the form itself. It felt like a lifetime had passed since the first time she saw the Official Secrets Act.

"And what exactly do you want me to do, Mr. Fleming?"

"Now, in order to answer that question, you'll need to sign on the dotted line there," Fleming said, offering her a black pen with gold stripes. "Then all shall be revealed."

Livy pretended to read over the familiar document as Fleming waited. Did she really want this again? A life of secrets? But wasn't that better than what she had now—no life at all? Her war had ended in more pain than she'd ever known, and it had all begun with signing this very same piece of paper. Livy's mind raced, remembering the end of the war, her war.

The Gestapo prison near Paris. The firing squad. The explosion that shattered the courtyard where Peter and the others had stood, waiting to die. Yet she had lived.

That day the old Livy had gone through fire and come out the other end. She didn't feel pity for her new self. No, Livy understood her quite well. Pity is what she felt for the older, naïve version. That Livy—the one before the courtyard—had so much to learn about the world and evil.

She had realized then there would be no going back to her old self. The girl from Blackpool who relied on others to see her through tough times was gone. Whenever she drank, which was every night now, Livy felt pain in her jaw in the exact spot where that German bitch in the prison had hit her. That pain, as well as others too painful to relive, reminded her of who she was now.

The line at the bottom of the Official Secret Acts awaited her signature. What choice did she have? Who'd want to hire a proofreader fired from the likes of the *Press and Journal*? No job meant no flat, and where would she go once Langham kicked her out? She'd have to throw herself on the mercy of her mum's niece in Liverpool. And do what? Marry some bloke. Have a few kids. Beans and toast every night and the occasional pint on Saturdays.

Fleming smoked, waiting.

"I signed this once before, you know."

"Only covered wartime, alas," Fleming said. "If you'd prefer to not sign, then we're finished here and you can get back to whatever plans you might have for the evening."

Plans? Livy considered her life since the war. Wasting time with drink and relationships that ended after a week or two. Ticking off the minutes at the P&J. And after today she didn't even have that.

No choice but this.

Livy signed quickly and pushed the fancy pen back across the desk, wondering where this might lead. She hadn't known what she was getting herself into the first time she'd signed either.

"That was the smartest decision you've made all day," Fleming said, pocketing the pen. He left the form on his desk, perhaps so Livy could ruminate on the contract she'd just made with His Majesty's government.

Fleming blew a cloud of smoke across the room. "What do you know about Nazi spy networks?"

"I know enough," Livy fired back. "Look, this job, there's a salary, isn't there?"

Fleming blinked. "Of course. Miss Baker can handle the paperwork for that tomorrow."

"Good. That's good. Go on, then."

"Thank you." Fleming stubbed out his cigarette. "Now, during the war the Germans had spies all over Europe, of course, but one of their networks was far bigger and more effective than any we have ever seen. Not unlike the Soviet Red Orchestra network back in the thirties, this one was vast, efficient, and damned well devastating to more than one of our operations. It's a miracle one of its agents didn't learn about the invasion before the sixth of June." Fleming paused, refitting another cigarette into the holder. His gold lighter flashed and he drew in smoke.

"That's history, though," Livy said, still wondering how any of this might relate to her.

"The war is over, but the agents of this particular network—remain—in—place." Fleming drew out each word, like a primary-school marm. "For the past year we've been rounding up German rocket scientists to try to keep them out of Joe Stalin's clutches. Controlling a network this vast would give us eyes and ears throughout Europe. Think what that would mean for the next war."

"If there is one," Livy said.

Fleming chortled. "The next war began before the last even ended. It was always going to be West against East. We just had to settle Hitler first. The network, however, apparently survived. And the reason was loyalty. We had German double—even triple—agents working for us throughout the war, but not one member of this network turned. Until now.

"A few weeks ago, one of our patrols in Vienna picked up a Frenchman selling weapons on the black market. His flat was in the Russian sector, but when we threatened to turn him over to the Reds, he suddenly started telling the most remarkable story about being an agent in this infamous Nazi spy ring. The man was terrified and demanded protection before giving us any information. What he told us made it clear that the network and its agents are still very much operational."

Fleming leaned back in his chair, cigarette between his teeth, grinning.

"But most important of all, he identified the leader of the network for us. Turns out this chap began as a traveling magician. Mephisto was his stage name. So, we've taken to calling the network after him. Apparently, he had quite the reputation in France and Germany before the war. Mephisto, as well as an accomplice or two, would pick up information from an agent at each stop of the tour and then funnel what was useful to the German High Command," Fleming said, pulling a thick gray file from atop a stack of newspapers on his desk.

"This Mephisto used several aliases, I'm told, and was quite successful at erasing his past. But based on what we've learned from the agent who turned, Mephisto is a French national. His real name is Edward Valentine."

Fleming pushed a small publicity photo across the desk toward Livy. The picture showed a tall man dressed in tails, wearing a turban. The man stood in a shadow so that only his eyes—all bugged out and Houdini-like—could be seen. He held a fanned deck of cards in front of him. Every card was the ace of spades.

"That's Valentine," Fleming said, watching her. "But we believe you knew him by a different name during the war. Luc."

Livy picked up the publicity photo and studied it. The cards masked most of his face, but she'd looked into those mischievous eyes so many times. Luc. Her nerves jangled.

"He's alive, then?"

Fleming nodded.

"I was there—at Fresnes when a mortar struck. He should have been killed. I don't understand. Are you sure?"

"Our informant's story checks out. Completely."

Luc—the traitor—alive. Livy felt a tremor run through her body as she remembered the last time they'd met. Somehow he'd avoided the shell in the courtyard that day. Not only that, but he was alive and the head of this vast spy ring.

Fleming said, "I take it you do know this Valentine?"

"I knew him as Luc, as you said. We were in the same circuit for the Firm. I trusted him then. Even liked the bastard."

Livy tried to sound nonchalant, but now the memories of Luc and the war felt more vivid than ever. She remembered how bitterly cold that day in January '44 had felt when Michelle arrived before dawn at the abandoned café where they always met with bad news. Her brother, André, had not come home. He'd gone to Chaville, a town southwest of Paris, to secure a part for the wireless from an electronic shop there and hadn't come back. Peter reassured Michelle that they'd find him, but Livy knew he was worried. When people went missing, they stayed gone.

Luc volunteered to take her to Chaville. He drove her the twenty miles south. He made jokes like always to calm her down. They both knew how much was at stake. If André had been tortured and talked to the Gestapo, their whole circuit could be rounded up before nightfall. Luc drove through the town slowly. They stopped at a market. Livy pretended to be the captured man's wife, angry that her rakish husband hadn't come home. The vendors laughed; some shrugged at the scorned wife's distress. No one admitted to having seen the wandering husband.

The last place Luc stopped was the town hall, which had been taken over by the Germans. "If the buggers have him, he'll be in there," Luc said as he let the motor idle outside the three-story gray building. Two Gestapo guards stood outside the front doors, smoking, their MP42 submachine guns hanging from their shoulders.

"I'm going in," she said. "I'll be out with him in ten minutes. If I'm not, then go," she said. Luc kissed her on the cheek.

Livy opened the car door and hurried toward the front. She had no idea what to do, and that thrilled her. Just play the mistress, the character, and get André. She charged right at the smoking guards, showed them her Annette Desjardins ID, and was taken inside.

At the front desk she pled her case to a sleepy-looking, bald Gestapo captain who probably hadn't seen action since 1940. Livy said she knew her good-for-nothing lover André had been mistakenly taken into custody after visiting her in Chaville to say he would not leave his wife back in Paris. Simultaneously crying and yelling, Livy told the captain she wanted to see the *fils de salope* and spit in his lying face.

The sleepy captain had no idea how to deal with a woman scorned, so he scanned his ledger and ordered one of the young guards back to the cells. Livy paced and cried and kicked the furniture as she waited, praying that her gamble would work. She knew the risk. If they didn't have André, they'd suss her out. In the space of half an hour she could be back in the same cell. Then, the questions, the torture. They wouldn't stop until she had given them everything.

The man the guard escorted out had bruises on the right side of his face. His eye was almost swollen shut and his upper lip looked about three times normal size. Despite the toll of the beatings, she could see it was clearly André.

Livy reacted, in character, to André's wounds. She stifled a gasp and gently touched his bruised face. Then she slapped him on the untouched side, letting loose a rant of some of the raunchiest French swearing she could muster. It was quite a performance.

The guard said something quietly to the bald captain. He turned to Livy. "This man was picked up for being on the street after curfew," he said in perfect French. "He's the one you are looking for?"

"Yes, this is the pig," Livy hissed.

The captain dismissed them both with a wave of his hand, and the young guard took the screaming woman and her beaten lover out the front door.

Her rescue of André made Livy's reputation among her circuit and others. It also elevated her to a level alongside Peter.

Before Livy had been his subordinate, but now she felt like his partner, and he treated her as such.

That night Luc pulled her aside and said, "That was a masterpiece today, girl. The Boche don't have a chance against you."

Luc the traitor. Valentine. Mephisto. Whoever the hell he was, he owed her two years of her life. All Livy wanted was the chance to be in the same room with him. To look him in the face and to hurt him as badly as she'd been hurt.

Livy tossed the Mephisto photo back onto Fleming's desk. "So you want the Mephisto network. Is that it? And I'm to be a part of—what? Retrieving it?"

"Something like that."

"Meaning?"

"The next step, Olivia, is that we begin the process of seeing if you're ready for this work."

"I just fought a war. I'm ready. Now."

"Your feistiness would be an asset in certain circumstances," Fleming said, his wide mouth curled into a half grin. "But for what I have in mind, it might also get you killed. Not to mention what it would do to the operation. No, this job requires subtlety. A quality you decidedly lack. So, I've no intention of shipping you off to Moscow tomorrow to eavesdrop on Joe Stalin just yet."

"Fine, then," she said. "Let's get started."

"You don't sit back and wait for things, do you? I daresay there isn't a submissive bone in your firm little body."

Again, that predatory grin. The more pleased with himself Fleming seemed, the more Livy wanted to give him what for. She caught herself grinding her teeth, which she turned into a forced smile. Some men just made you feel like a show pony. Another time, another man, she'd have walked out. This time she held her tongue on the assumption there might be a point to this particular leer.

"So that's why you want me to work for you—because I knew him?"

"Yes. And you were a damned fine agent for the Firm. But there is another reason. You see, you've been requested."

"Requested?"

"A young woman approached one of our people in Paris. She says the Mephisto list is up for sale. They want to negotiate. But only with Olivia Nash. The girl called Spitfire."

Chapter Four

～

Livy had eaten breakfast and bathed by seven the next morning. She then put ground acorns in a pot, poured hot water over them, and pretended it tasted like coffee. By the time she got to the second cup, she could almost imagine it had a kick like the real thing.

She'd barely slept the night before. Her mind continued to process the previous day. Sacked at the P&J. Then Fleming. Luc alive. Mephisto. Her presence requested in Paris.

"But not just yet," Fleming had told her at the end of their chat. "The world has changed. We're not fighting a war out in the open. Now the war is in the shadows, and being in the shadows requires a certain amount of . . . delicacy." His posh accent teemed with the languid vowels of the aristocracy.

"And I'm not delicate?"

"Oh dear God, not in the slightest."

Then he leaned around his desk as if to look at her legs, but Livy soon realized the true source of his interest was her dress.

"I imagine this sort of frock's de rigueur for ladies on the *Press and Journal* copy desk?"

Livy crossed her arms over her chest.

"Yes, well, we have our work cut out for us then," he said, sighing, and reached into his jacket. Fleming placed a thick business card on the table and slid it over to her with his fingertips.

A street address in Kensington had been typed in the center of the card in a simple font.

"Be at this address at eleven AM tomorrow morning. Do not be late. There is a bakery at the corner of the street. I forget the name. Bring raspberry scones. Make sure they're fresh."

"That's it? I don't even know who to ask for."

"Just follow orders, darling Olivia. That's all you have to do for now." As she rose to leave his office, Fleming studied her. "By the way, ask her what sort of dresses she thinks might flatter your figure."

Now Livy had two more hours to kill this morning before she needed to set out to Kensington. What to wear? God, she hated fussing over clothes. Never one to give much thought to what she wore, Livy favored plain, serviceable skirts, dresses, and jumpers so she didn't need to think what skirt went with what blouse. Having no idea what she might be in for this morning, she chose a simple pleated skirt, a cream blouse, and a light navy jumper. It felt a bit big, so she shoved the arms up to her elbows.

Livy hadn't cleaned the place in weeks, so she used some of her nervous energy to pick up clothes. She found a half-eaten piece of toast under her bed. Just like her mother, she thought. Never really interested in keeping a house. Too much to do outside.

With that in mind, she set off for the address a full hour and a half before the scheduled appointment.

The walk to southwest London took Livy past the stark reminders of the war Fleming had asked her to leave behind. Five years after the height of the Blitz and whole buildings remained crushed, rubble just cleared off the sidewalk. It looked as if a giant fist had randomly smashed this block and the one after but left the next intact.

Women pushed prams with other mums, chattering away about rationing, while men worked in the street or hurried back to work. The crumbled buildings had become part of the landscape and, like a row of flats or shops, were ignored. A young couple sat on a bench in front of what had once been a church but now looked like a demolition sight. They shared a bag of chips and kissed after the last one.

And just like that her mind went to Peter. She could still feel the surge of passion they had shared that one night in the abandoned café. The night before they'd been captured.

Peter and Livy had spent the weeks after the invasion with the maquisards in Vercors, a mountainous region in southeast France. The other members of their circuit had remained in Paris to relay information to the advancing Allies. Peter Scobee made his reputation fighting alongside the armed resistance fighters in Vercors. But as the Nazis pushed back, Livy and Peter fled north. Hunted, like the rest of the scattered fighters.

After five long days, sleeping wherever they could, they finally made it back to the abandoned café near Paris where they'd spent so many nights with the others. Livy missed Michelle especially and hoped they could reunite with the others too.

Dirty and beyond exhausted, Peter and Livy collapsed into their makeshift beds in the storeroom. A leak in the roof above where Livy slept had left her pile of blankets and rags soaked. She'd slept on rocky ground and in brambles, but the mildew stench was too much.

Peter offered her his dry ad hoc bed. That's how it started. Simply. He offered to take hers. She wouldn't let him. They'd have to share.

Livy felt the desire inside her building. God, she'd felt it for weeks. The connection with Peter had been strong since she'd brought André back from the German prison in Chaville. The minute-by-minute living-and-breathing danger of Vercors had forged an even deeper bond. At least for her.

Livy knew Peter was married with a young son back home. He'd made no secret of how much he missed them. She'd seen their pictures, for God's sake. But home—England—seemed like an alternate universe compared to the surreal relentless day-to-day of war.

She told herself—before he kissed her the first time—that this was just an escape. A way to forget it all for one night. But it didn't stop there. How could it? They tore into each other like starving people devouring a full-course meal. Livy, who had never been accused of being shy and retiring once in her life, pushed Peter down and took off his trousers as if they were on fire. Then she took him inside her and pushed and pushed until the relief came so quickly that they both began to laugh.

Despite their exhaustion, they continued to find energy for each other and the next time lasted much longer. Their bodies were in sync in the same way their minds and hearts had been in the field.

When they finally slept, it was in each other's arms, which surprised Livy. A night of shagging was one thing, but she hadn't expected the tenderness and vulnerability she felt from this man. So they lay together and tried to sleep, mere hours before the dawn. Hours before the war and their lives might end.

"Miss?"

A shiver went through Livy as she turned to see a constable on her right. The kissing couple across the street had gone.

"You look a bit lost, miss."

Livy held up the card Fleming had given her. "I think I know where I'm headed. Thank you, Constable."

The policeman smiled and walked past her. She put a hand to her mouth. Steadying herself against a phone box, she took a long deep breath. She'd crossed over into the better part of London and couldn't afford another daydream episode.

The Blitz had not spared the posh homes of Kensington, although Livy noted that reparation seemed much further along here. Ah well, she thought, the rich get what they want when they want it.

She followed the High Street to an address just off the Earls Court Road. From the bustle of the main thoroughfare, Livy found herself on a narrow street dense with homes considerably smaller than the showplaces of Kensington. Nevertheless, these compact Georgian houses retained a certain old-world glamour despite the occasional peel of paint.

Livy found the address and then went back to the bakery on the corner, where she dutifully purchased the required pastries and headed back to her destination.

At precisely 10:57 AM she rapped on a bright-red door and waited. A minute later she knocked again, this time a bit more insistently. She waited. A minute later the door cracked open about six inches.

"What?" The voice belonged to a woman, although the light was so dim on the other side Livy couldn't discern her features, only a silhouette.

"It's—it's eleven. I'm on time." Livy didn't know what else to say.

"It can't be eleven."

"Yes. Eleven. I—I brought the scones," Livy said, as if they might be some sort of entrance code.

The woman inside sighed dramatically. "Fine." The door slammed.

Every bone in Livy's body screamed, *Get out of here and tell Fleming to get stuffed,* but a voice at the back of her brain kept her there. A voice that—quite loudly—said, *Be patient. You need a job and you can always drink later.* Livy didn't like the voice, but she heeded its advice.

Then the door opened, wider this time. A woman stood on the other side, looking as if she had just stepped out of a Noël Coward play. She must have been in her midforties, Livy guessed, but with the transparent sexuality of someone much younger. She held a cigarette holder at the end of one long gloved hand as if the effort was beyond tedious.

The whole pose suggested casual contempt.

"You're early," the woman said in a husky, trained voice that bore none of the sleepiness it had held minutes ago.

"I just wanted to be on time."

"Being on time, darling, is *not* being early and catching your hostess unawares. Now . . . do come in."

The woman stepped aside and appraised Livy from head to foot as she passed. Her mouth curled down as she finished the survey.

"Are those clothes from your personal wardrobe, or is that some sort of—costume?" she said, tossing back thick golden hair that spilled out of an ornate turban. One hand held closed the expensive dressing gown she wore over a silk slip.

"These are mine." Livy's bolt-and-run impulse grew stronger by the second.

"Where *does* he find them?" the woman said to herself as she grabbed the scones from Livy and disappeared into the kitchen, taking a long pull at her cigarette.

Livy stood in the middle of a compact drawing room where two well-kept Queen Anne chairs sat on either side of a tea table in front of a covered hearth. This area of the room was immaculate. The other side of the room, which consisted of a stiff sofa and accompanying table, was buried under a pile of newspapers, open books, and even a few dirty glasses. It looked as if a typhoon had hit one side of the room.

The woman came back into the room, carrying a tray with everything ready for light tea, including quite posh-looking cups and a matching pot.

Having dispensed with her cigarette, the woman placed the tray on the table and gestured for Livy to sit. Smiling without a trace of irony, the woman placed a cup and saucer in front of Livy. Next, she used silver tongs to pick up one of the scones and gently put it on a small plate for her guest.

It seemed as if she'd gone into the other room as an arrogant diva and come out as the perfect English hostess. Livy assumed the former was her real self.

"Clotted cream or jam, darling?"

"Jam. If you please."

"The tea's Earl Grey. I hope you don't mind. It's the only tea as far as I'm concerned. Milk?"

"Sure. Milk's fine."

"You have a name, I assume?"

"Livy."

"A surname?"

"It's Nash. Livy—"

"Miss Nash, then. My name is Sherbourne. Emma Sherbourne. You no doubt have heard of me."

Livy had no intention of playing along. "Can't say I have."

Emma Sherbourne's lips pursed slightly and her gaze hardened. "I am an actress of some repute. Although I've not had the opportunity to play . . . your part of the country, I do love the vowels of Lancashire. So . . . colorful. You said milk, yes?"

"Yes," Livy said, lifting her cup to the milk.

"Miss Nash, it is customary to pour the tea before adding milk."

"Tea, please—Miss Sherbourne." She'd had just about enough of this tea party nonsense.

"It's *Missus*, darling." She poured the tea and fairly flounced over to the other chair. Then, with effortless precision, she prepared her own tea and scone, adding extra cream and jam. She then took one small bite of the scone, chewing it slowly. When she finished, she dabbed the corners of her mouth with the lace napkin and placed it on her lap.

"Miss Nash, no one in polite society extends the pinkie when holding a teacup. Thumb and forefinger will do nicely. The proper place for your napkin is your lap, and if you insist on blowing on the tea before taking one of your very loud sips, then I shall have to wear earmuffs."

Livy slammed her cup down, luckily on the saucer. "Look, luv, what is all this? I'm told to show up with scones at this flat of yours, which most of it looks like it hasn't been cleaned in a year, and you sit there in your fancy dressing gown and tell me how to take tea? That's not what I signed up for."

Mrs. Sherbourne grinned and took a very elegant sip of her Earl Grey. "Do you know Shakespeare, Miss Nash?"

"I know his plays."

"Then you must know *The Taming of the Shrew*? No? Personally I find it distasteful, but my job, like Petruchio's in the play, is to tame you. The shrew. Or perhaps you prefer spitfire."

Livy resisted the urge to throw the tea in her face and storm out.

"I prefer to be treated like an adult."

"I'm sure you do, dear, but the way this works is I give the orders and you follow them. So, you brought the scones. Well done. But you were early. Tsk-tsk. Now, in an attempt to tame you, I am teaching you to take tea like a proper lady. Is that quite clear, Miss Nash? So—put your napkin in your lap and sip your tea quietly. There's a good girl."

Livy hated her. But she did exactly what she said.

* * *

The raspberry scones routine continued the next two days, with Livy arriving at Mrs. Sherbourne's door precisely at eleven. Each time, the Great Actress, as Livy affectionately thought of her, met her at the door with a broom, dustpan, and several large crates. Despite the cleaning implements, Sherbourne still wore her turban, dressing gown, and those long bloody gloves.

She shoved her head under the pillow, but the sound didn't go away. It only muffled it.

Bam-bam-bam!

Livy sat up in bed and registered the midmorning light. The rhythmic banging had returned, but now she knew its source. The ache in her head originated at the door to her flat. She shuffled out of bed quickly to stop the horrible noise. Livy opened the door a crack and allowed her wobbly body to slump against the wall.

Mrs. Sherbourne stood on the other side of the door.

"Miss Nash, you seem to have forgotten our rendezvous this morning."

Livy's head took over the throbbing as the light from the walk-up seared into her brain. So, like a good soldier, she retreated, flopping on the bed and covering the head she deeply wished she didn't have.

* * *

Sometime later she woke up again to the smell of coffee. Actual coffee. The kind of coffee she had not tasted since Peter had found a bag of old beans in a cupboard at the café where they lived. The cup sat on her bedside table next to a full glass of water.

"Drink them both. The water first." Mrs. Sherbourne sat in the lone chair, at the foot of the bed.

Livy lifted herself enough to take a long swallow of water. "How'd you know where I live?"

Mrs. Sherbourne grinned and her eyes fairly twinkled. "Really, Miss Nash, a child could answer that question. Drink your water."

Then she took light tea on her own, even treating herself to a second scone, while Livy cleaned the filthy half of the sitting room.

"Make sure all the theater books are in the same crate, darling. There's a good girl," she purred.

On the third day, once Livy had finished sweeping, tidying, and washing and drying the stained glasses, Mrs. Sherbourne invited her back to the sitting room and offered her what was left of the day's tea. She'd been kind enough to replace the second scone with a piece of wheat toast, although the jam jar was now empty.

"You did so well with your tea today, Miss Nash. It's almost a pity you still have to dust the room. But I'm expecting guests and can't very well have a mess, can I?"

Livy'd had enough. Was this Fleming's idea of a joke? Making her clean and tidy for this over-the-hill thespian? She'd left one demeaning job where she'd kowtowed to people who didn't deserve her respect only to end up in another. Livy snatched up the feather duster and would have smashed every lamp in the place had she not remembered that she'd put aside just enough money for another of Black Market Billy's bottles of that delectable piss otherwise known as Polish vodka.

And he delivered.

For Livy, the rest of the night was something of a blur.

* * *

The next morning, her head throbbed a bit more insistently that normal. Usually it ached at the back of her skull. This hangover had more hammerlike qualities: *bam-bam-bam.* Then quiet. Then—*bam-bam-bam.*

After another sip, the vodka taste disappeared and Livy began to crave the coffee. "Fine. So—thanks for the libation. Now, if you don't mind—"

"I do mind. I'm not going anywhere, darling."

"Look, Mrs. Sherbourne, you may be old enough to be my mum, but you're not. It's my flat. Now clear out."

But the Great Actress sat in her chair and folded her gloved hands across her lap, as if she had all the time in the world.

Livy fumed, put down the unfinished water, and sipped the coffee. God, it tasted good. It actually had flavor, rich and dark.

"Finish the water."

"This is my flat and if there is any taming to do, *I'll* do it. So when my head stops wobbling about, I'll find you a few bob for the coffee and then I'll thank you to piss off."

"We will have to work on your charming personality, won't we?"

"Look, I've had three days of cleaning your flat and taking tea, and I'm fed up. This is not what I signed up for. You want to train me for proper fieldwork? Train me, then. But I'm not your lapdog. And don't give me that rot about taking orders. I've taken orders, luv, from far better than the likes of you."

Livy pulled herself out of bed. Even though her head felt like the apex of a seesaw, she managed to reach her purse in the bathroom.

"Olivia, darling, I don't think I've ever told you that I was a guest at Ravensbrück at the very end of the war."

Livy froze. She'd heard stories. Michelle, the other girl in her SOE circuit, had told her that Ravensbrück was the camp where German doctors experimented on women.

"I didn't know," she said, her voice barely a whisper.

The grin still had not left Mrs. Sherbourne's face. "It's not something one shares over tea, is it?"

She placed the tip of the glove on her left hand between her teeth and began to carefully remove it. By the slow pace, Livy guessed it had some sort of packing material in each finger. The hand beneath the glove was warped and distorted, her pinkie and ring fingers missing above the knuckle. The intact fingers resembled twigs more than anything. The back of her hand and the palm looked as though they had been crushed. Only her left thumb appeared untouched.

If Mrs. Sherbourne felt ashamed of the hand, she didn't show it. She carefully placed it on her knee for Livy to get a good look.

"I was fortunate, actually," she said. "They didn't capture me until near the end, so my stay at the camp was short-lived. They had quite a few of us from the Firm, you know. I was the oldest, so they looked to me for—what would you call it?— strength, perhaps. We knew we didn't have long. This was '45, mind you, so we knew the Nazis wanted to tidy things up before the Russians or the Americans arrived. And Ravensbrück wasn't a prison anyway."

"I held their hands before they took them away," Mrs. Sherbourne said, her normally melodious voice sounding quiet and mechanical. "Gemma went first and then Cecily, and the others. I always thought I'd be next, but for some reason they left me alive. Maybe they just liked to watch me when one of our girls was taken away. It hurt. Badly. Even more than losing these," she said, nodding at her broken hand.

"Still, I was fortunate, wasn't I? I'm sitting here now, having a nice little chat with another one who *survived*," she said, pronouncing the last word as if it could have been a curse.

"There aren't many theaters that will have me like this," Mrs. Sherbourne said, pulling her glove back on. "Perhaps there are some in your neck of the woods, but I haven't quite stooped to that level just yet."

Livy didn't know what to say. She moved back to the edge of her bed, her gaze shifting to Mrs. Sherbourne's battered hand. Livy could imagine just how it happened. The hammer to the fingers. The questions. No answers. Again the hammer. The unending pain. Over and over.

"You were at Fresnes, weren't you?" Mrs. Sherbourne said.

The name of the prison—the place where Livy's heart had been shattered—sent a tremor through her body. Mrs. Sherbourne's eyes held hers, and there was a kind of sadness in them that Livy had never seen before. Livy'd misjudged this woman but good. She knew now they were part of a select group who carried deep scars from a past they were duty-bound to keep hidden. They were comrades.

Quietly, Livy cleared her throat and told Mrs. Sherbourne everything.

Chapter Five

ᔕ

Fresnes, 1944

Livy and Peter were picked up on the road to Paris.

Peter's heroics at Vercors had made him one of the Gestapo's most-wanted men in France. Some of the maquisards they'd fought alongside told them they'd heard German soldiers asking about the agent known as Bulldog. If they knew Peter's code name, Livy knew the journey would be even more of a risk. She'd told Peter as much, but as usual, he seemed determined to test his apparent invincibility.

After their night together in the café, Peter took Livy to a nearby farmhouse where Luc had hidden a gray Citroën. The car had never been used in a mission, but Livy knew that didn't matter. Luc, who had remained in Paris, changed a flat tire for them and checked the engine. The Frenchman worked quickly even though the heat of the day caused him to sweat through his linen shirt.

As he worked, Livy and Peter argued. She thought the trip north was reckless. The Gestapo would have multiple checkpoints. She suggested they stay in hiding in Paris until the

Allied Forces arrived. Peter just smiled and told her not to worry.

She'd always trusted Peter. After their night together, truth be told, she loved him in a way she didn't quite understand. Livy looked up to him like an older brother and admired his bravery and calm, but the war had brought them together and made her rely on him in a way that was more like real love. They hadn't spoken about last night. Once they woke up, they'd gotten to work.

Now she just felt stupid. Love? After one night on a pile of old towels and rags? How many married men and women had sought solace in a moment of physical intimacy while the bombs fell and the machine guns rattled outside?

The frustrating thing about Peter was how impregnable he seemed. He'd smile that crooked grin, and somehow Livy felt that all would be well. He took her hands and reminded her of all the sentries they'd bluffed their way past. This would be no different.

"I've got you with me," he said. "The Gestapo may be looking for me, but you're the one they need to worry about."

He meant it, she knew. They had successfully navigated countless German checkpoints with their papers and their nearly flawless French. And when that didn't seem to be enough, Livy resorted to a little flirting with the young Gestapo guards. Their eyes lit up like firecrackers when they saw a French girl, and if one of them happened to be pretty enough and spoke a bit of German, well then, she could get just about anything she wanted.

But the gnawing feeling in Livy's stomach worsened as they bounced along the road to Paris in the battered gray Citroën.

The Germans knew their days were numbered and they wanted to take their pound of flesh while they still could.

They drove in silence, Peter at the wheel. The wind from the open window whipped his thick dark hair as he kept his eyes on the road ahead.

Peter didn't so much as flinch when he saw the big black car up ahead and the field gray uniforms that suddenly snapped to attention when they caught sight of the car rumbling down the back road. Then a hand came up, indicating *stop*.

Livy wanted him to run them down, just keep driving right through the bastards. But he didn't. Peter slowed down as he approached the roadblock and said, "Don't worry."

* * *

Their papers identified them as Marcel and Annette Desjardins, brother and sister. The registration of the vehicle was current, but still they were stopped and held by the road for nearly four hours before the order came to move them north. Once they reached Fresnes, their papers and all their belongings were taken and burned in an incinerator. Livy knew that meant they would be treated as spies. Someone had betrayed them.

Back in the SOE training camp, instructors had told Livy and the other recruits about Hitler's "Commando Order," which sought to get around those pesky Geneva Convention laws about treatment of prisoners. The order could not have been clearer. Allied commandos, saboteurs, and spies found behind enemy lines did not have to be treated as prisoners of war but could be shot on sight. If they didn't shoot you on sight, they'd take you back and torture you until they decided to shoot you. The Gestapo could also choose to turn prisoners over to the SD, the intelligence wing of the SS, for interrogation.

At Fresnes, the Germans put them in different cells almost immediately. They'd talked about this at training as well: what to do if you were captured, how to endure torture, what you could and could not tell them. The first day Livy sat in her cell and the words of her instructors ran through her mind like a ticker tape. She focused on what to do, what to say, and forced her mind not to go down the path of *what if* or *what next*.

She expected the worst.

What she got instead was the velvet-glove treatment.

They sent a woman to bring her lunch the very first day. She looked to be around Livy's age, with a kind smile. She didn't wear a uniform, just a simple dress with her hair pulled back. Three times a day she brought Livy her meals on plates with real silverware laid out nicely on a tray, not just shoved in under the door and left on the cold concrete floor.

That went on for three days. Then the meals became erratic. She'd get breakfast, but no lunch. The portions became smaller. Finally, they stopped coming altogether.

The first day without food she saw no one. She didn't even hear anyone out in the hallway. It felt as if she'd been forgotten. For a few hours, she wondered if perhaps the prison had been liberated and somehow she had been left behind.

The next morning, before dawn, the door to her cell opened and a large SD officer in full uniform brought her an apple. He looked like a grown-up Hansel from the fairy tale, Livy thought. All bulky and shoved into a Nazi uniform. He sat down in the cell's only chair and introduced himself as *Hauptsturmführer* Faber. He smiled and told her they would be getting to know each other quite well over the next few days, and that he hoped they would become close friends "despite their differences." Livy devoured the apple in a few bites. Faber, who Livy guessed weighed near sixteen stone, delicately ate strudel from a china plate and sipped tea while they spoke. For a big man, his manners seemed impeccable.

Hauptsturmführer Faber's attempts to throw Livy off her training failed. She said nothing. When asked for her name, she always said Annette Desjardins. She then asked about her brother Marcel. When Faber probed her cover story, she gave him small details. As she had learned at SOE camp, the best legend was one that had elements of truth from the agent's own life.

"Where are your parents?" he asked.

"Gone."

"How do you mean—gone?"

"My mother died in an air raid. My father got sick. Cancer."

The questioning went on for two days, and then Faber became impatient. The first day he ordered the quiet German woman to take off Livy's clothes while he stood in the doorway and watched. She sat naked in the cold cell for a full day without food.

The next day the woman brought back her jumper and knickers. Two Gestapo guards accompanied her and they watched, leering, as Livy dressed. Then they held her in a chair while the German woman, who had brought her food the first few days, slapped her face until her mouth bled down the front of her clothes.

This continued for another two days. At mealtimes the woman would come in with her two Gestapo thugs, and she would beat Livy until she bled.

On the morning of the eleventh day, Faber returned with his tea set and strudel, and offered a fresh apple to Livy. She ripped it from his hand and ate quickly. The German smiled.

"You see, we don't want to treat you so badly. Young girl like yourself. Do you know your face is bruised now, hmm? So maybe you just talk to me, answer a few very simple questions, and I will tell my girl to bring you breakfast. She can bring you eggs and bacon and jam right now. And all your clothes. I know you must be cold. I'm shivering in here, and I have this uniform and belly to keep me warm. You are so small. So very small. So, let me help you. We'll even start with something simple. Who is Bulldog?"

Livy felt the last bite of apple stick in her throat, but she didn't respond. She followed the ticker in her head, and shrugged.

Faber smiled. "You see, we know your code names, and we know that Bulldog is here. We are certain. But I don't think it is you. No. Bulldog is a man. So, tell me, did they name this man after Churchill? Hmm. How important he must be, then. No, it's not a woman, we know that. A woman would not be so important to the British, I think."

Each time Livy shrugged and answered, *"Je ne sais pas."*

Faber continued, probing here, trying to find a flaw in her story there, but Livy just shrugged and answered the same.

Finally the big man grew weary and left. Livy knew the German woman and her two thugs would be back soon. That's the way it would work. The punishment might even be worse this time after her reticence, but that didn't matter.

All that mattered was that somehow, Faber had learned Peter's code name and knew Bulldog was now at Fresnes.

Livy realized they'd not only been betrayed, but by someone very close enough to them.

The pattern of Faber—the soft touch—and then the woman and her thugs—the fist—continued for the next two days. But Livy never broke. But now, the prison seemed even bleaker. She had always believed Peter would find a way out of Fresnes for them. Perhaps the Allied force would liberate the prison before anything happened to them.

But as Faber persisted in questioning her about Bulldog, it became increasingly real to Livy that she and Peter might die here. As that thought took root in her mind during the endless hours of sitting, she clung tighter to the feelings she had for Peter. She loved him. No other word came close to expressing what she felt, what kept her going. Sitting in her bare concrete cell, her face swollen from the beatings, she thought about him night and day. He supplanted the ticker of the instructor's commands she'd tried to keep in her head.

She remembered the day she'd practically crashed into France, falling out of the plane like some idiot girl, and there he was, laughing at her.

The more her face reddened, the louder Peter had laughed. She'd hated him then. Now the memory of that day, and all the subsequent days, kept her alive. The feel of the wind in her hair, a smudge she remembered on Peter's chin (jam from a sandwich he'd had in the truck while they waited for her at the drop site), and the tone of his voice when he mocked her accent all replaced Faber's questions and the German woman's goddamn fists.

Then the visits stopped. For the next two days Livy sat in her cell alone. At noon on both days, a guard—one she hadn't seen before—came with something that looked like boiled cabbage on a plate, placed it on the floor inside the cell, and left without a word.

Livy worked through all the possibilities. They'd given her the silent treatment before. This didn't make sense. This wasn't the logical progression if they still held hope of getting information out of her. No, this change meant something.

The thought hit her the first night and she panicked, but she told herself to hang on and reassess tomorrow. When morning came and the next day brought the exact same routine, she began to accept it. They must know now Peter was Bulldog.

She ignored the pain of the bruises on her face and the hunger. Livy knew what would happen to Peter and to her as well. God, had he confessed? Had he been pushed so far that he talked? No, Peter wouldn't tell them a thing. He'd take his cyanide pill before breaking.

No, please God, don't let that have happened. Don't take him. I have to see him once more, she thought. Livy wanted to be near Peter right now more than anything in the world. To tell him what he'd meant to her, not just that night, but all along.

The anguish of those thoughts left her gasping. She pushed them away and tried to think what would happen next. She thought through what they would do to her. Now she would be expendable. They'd shoot her and throw her in an unmarked grave.

Surprisingly, these thoughts didn't upset her. They served as a distraction from the truly terrifying image of what they might do to Peter. Or what they might already have done. So she watched her death in her mind, wondering how the bullet might feel and how quickly it would be over. Would it be like a curtain falling? A film reel breaking in the middle of a picture? What they did with her afterward wouldn't matter. The pain and the fear would end, just the way it had for her mother.

* * *

They came for her on the third day. The German woman gave her the skirt they'd taken from her and a pair of black lace-up shoes that seemed to be at least two sizes too big. The two thugs escorted Livy down a corridor of cells and then a steep circular stairwell. Livy slipped once. The woman shouted at her to stand up. "Walk or I will shoot you now, English bitch!"

At the bottom, one of the thugs opened a heavy metal door, and sunlight streamed into the dark staircase. Livy almost fell again. The sunlight stung her eyes, causing her to bend over at the waist.

"Blindfold her, you idiot," the German woman yelled, and one of the thugs pulled her up while the other tied a kerchief tight around her eyes. Then she felt a push in the small of her back and heard the crunch of stones under her shoes. Up ahead she heard other voices speaking German and commands being given. The sounds of boots crunching on gravel, and also—was it?—the sound of birds twittering. They sounded so ridiculously normal she wanted to laugh.

Her shoes stubbed into something hard. Brick or concrete. A voice commanded her to pick up her feet. Livy had little time to register much else as one of the thugs shoved her against a wall and roughly maneuvered her shoulders so that she faced out into what must have been a courtyard. She felt a shoulder against her left arm and smelled what had to be other prisoners. The odor was at once overpowering and noxious and at the same time one of the most comforting things Livy had ever sensed. She brightened in the company of her fellow prisoners.

Could Peter be there? If so, then they would be shot together. That had to be the reason for all this. But why blindfolds? What exactly did the Germans want to hide from prisoners about to be executed?

Then she heard another door open and a shuffle of gravel as soldiers came to attention with the new arrival. No, wait, two people had walked into the courtyard.

"This is all of them." She recognized Faber's unaccented, polished High German.

She felt the tension of those beside her. No one moved and they didn't speak, but the heat of their anxiety was palpable. They could be shot at any moment and never see it coming.

The person who had come out with Faber moved around the courtyard and stopped several feet to Livy's left. She heard a sigh, and then a man's voice said in French, "Now, now. Say nothing."

He moved down the row of prisoners and stopped directly in front of her. Livy felt a scream rising inside as the man stood before her. What the hell was the bastard doing? *Do something! Anything!*

Then she felt fingers, soft manicured fingers, at her temples as the man slid down the blindfold.

She blinked several times before his face came into focus, and even then she didn't trust her eyes.

Luc stood before her. The mechanic who'd been part of their circuit. The man who'd entertained the five of them with his bawdy jokes. But this didn't look like the Luc she knew.

Now he wore a tailored double-breasted suit with a blue silk tie and white shirt made of soft cotton. A brown fedora was tilted to one side of his head so that the brim almost covered his right eye.

"*Bonjour*, Annette." It sounded like Luc's voice, but this made no sense. She stood in a courtyard in a bricked-off area that must have once been a small garden but was now just dirt.

"Get away from her!"

Livy looked to her left. Everyone around her remained blindfolded except a tall man with thick dark hair at the end of the row. Despite being handcuffed, Peter Scobee looked on the verge of choking the life out of the man who stood before Livy.

The outburst prompted Faber to pull his black Walther from its holster and aim at Peter's head.

The moment felt surreal to Livy. Breath wheezed from her chest. Then the man she knew as Luc produced a deck of playing cards. He shuffled them with dexterity and cut the deck using only one hand. With a smile, he offered the cards to Livy.

"Please, choose a card," he said in French, his voice much softer and more lyrical than Luc's laconic grunts.

Livy didn't have air for words, so he repeated his request.

"Please, pick one."

Livy lashed out, grabbed one card out of the deck, and held it at her side.

"You must look at it. Please."

She looked at this man—Luc—and then at Peter. He stared straight ahead, unable to watch this bizarre magic show.

Livy lifted the card, the four of hearts.

"Now just slide it back into the middle of the deck, please."

She did, and then this man—he was no longer familiar to her—shuffled the deck several times, cut it rapidly with one hand, and held the pack still.

He stared at Livy and his wolfish eyes gleamed. "Now, Annette, if you can pick your card out of this deck, then I shall tell *Hauptsturmführer* Faber not to kill your brother Marcel— or Bulldog, as we know him," he said with a wink at Faber.

Livy turned to see if Peter might, in some way, be able to help. But his eyes remained fixed on something in the other direction.

"Go on," Luc said, holding the deck out to her. "You have a one-in-fifty-two chance, but you might get lucky."

Faber laughed and looked at his watch.

Something changed inside Livy at that moment. The game was up. She knew they would shoot Peter and her, and probably all the others as well. Livy also knew that if she had the chance, she would kill them. She would kill them all.

She reached out to the deck. Her fingers tripped along the edges of the cards. For some reason, she chose the one on top. If this proved to be nothing more than a cruel trick, then it made sense that her card would be easy to find. She grabbed the card and turned it over.

"What a pity," the man who wasn't Luc said.

Livy held the ace of spades. With a slow flourish, the traitor turned the deck over so she could see that every single card in the deck was an ace of spades.

"The cards weren't in your favor, were they?" He put the deck in his inside jacket pocket and nodded at Peter.

"As I said, there is your Bulldog, *Hauptsturmführer*. You have your orders."

Faber lifted his pistol again.

"Wait," Luc said. He held his hand out toward Faber. The German looked confused at first but then smiled and placed the Walther in the traitor's hand. Livy felt as if a giant held her chest in its grip. She prayed Luc would shoot her. But he didn't.

He pointed the gun at Peter, hesitated for just a moment, and then fired. The gun's crack echoed around the brick walls of the enclosed courtyard.

Peter's chest collapsed. The force of the shot punched him in the midsection and he fell to his knees, his hands still cuffed behind his back.

The next few moments blurred together. Livy ran toward Peter's body, but hands pulled her away almost instantly. The man who had been Luc and one of the guards held her by the shoulders. Faber barked something in German as Livy fought to get to Peter. Then another set of hands had her around the waist and dragged her back toward the door to the stairwell that led to the cells.

She began to scream, "No!" louder and louder as Faber and Valentine watched her impassively. The other prisoners, who had also been blindfolded, had been forced to stand against the courtyard wall by the other soldiers. Livy felt her hair being pulled now, and she spun round to see her torturer, the German woman. A guard wrenched the stairwell door open.

He must have heard it first, because Livy saw the guard lower his gun and look up. The German woman shoved Livy into the stairwell, unwittingly saving her life. One of the guards came in with her, but Livy stood the farthest away from the courtyard when the blast happened. She barely registered the accelerating whistle of the shell a second or two before a wave picked her up and tossed her against the steel railing of the stairs. Then, nothing.

* * *

She woke up thinking this was a dream. The pain in her wrists, elbows, and legs cut through the fog in her brain. The back of her head throbbed away, but that was from hunger, the prison, yes, and—she remembered—Peter.

Livy got to her knees slowly as a wave of nausea swept through her. She leaned against the first metal stair and waited for the room to stop spinning. When it did, she saw she was far from alone. One of the German guards who had helped drag her inside lay facedown, his midsection resting on the doorway so that his legs were still outside. He didn't move. He seemed dead.

Just inside the doorway, the German woman lay on her back, her arms and legs splayed at awkward angles. She had a large bleeding gash across her nose, probably the result of flying debris. Livy watched her chest as it slowly rose and fell. The woman had been lucky.

Carefully, Livy made her way across the floor, now covered in pieces of brick and uniform and small bits of tree branch. She stepped up to the body of the guard and squinted into the sunlight. His right leg had been blown off above the knee, and blood from the stump formed a pool that seeped into the courtyard.

Livy recognized the gray uniforms of the SD guards, and even some of the blindfolds still intact around the heads of prisoners. They lay flat inside the brick enclosure, heads down. A couple stirred slowly, seemingly uninjured. Another prisoner sagged against the courtyard wall, screaming. His arm taken at the elbow. Everything was a clutter of limbs and blood. No sign of either the traitor or the big German, Faber. The courtyard was all such a horrible mess, who could tell anything? It smelled like the back of a butcher's shop.

Still, Livy looked past it all and tried to find Peter. Damn it, what had he even been wearing? She couldn't remember.

Someone moaned behind her.

Livy turned. The German woman was getting up. Her fingers flexed and her neck lolled about as if she was trying to clear the darkness from her head.

Livy didn't hesitate. She leaned down to the dead German soldier and unclasped the holster on his belt. Five feet away the woman continued to stir, trying to rise to her knees.

With one clean jerk, Livy ripped the small Mauser from the dead soldier's belt. She aimed at the woman as she rose to her knees.

Livy waited for her torturer's eyes to focus and recognize what was about to happen. The German woman only blinked and sneered.

"*Mort aux Boches*," Livy said. She emptied the Mauser.

Chapter Six

〰

Mrs. Sherbourne listened patiently until Livy stopped speaking. "And then?"

"I just stopped. Sat on the steps. Shock, I suppose. Next thing I know American soldiers were carrying me to a medic tent. Turns out they're the ones who fired the shell."

The two women sat across from each other. Silent. Livy could feel her breath—rising and falling—and nothing else.

Finally, Mrs. Sherbourne prodded her battered fingers back into the special glove. It looked painful, but the grin never left her face.

"I'm sorry for what happened to you, darling Olivia. Now that we know one another a bit better, I can say, sincerely, that I hope we can continue our work. One thing you must know about dear Ian is that despite his caddish behavior, he is loyal to a fault. He would not have sent you to me if he did not believe you have potential. If he decides you can get the job done, he will stand by you. As will I. No matter what sort of hell you have been through. But if you cannot do the work, Ian will dispense with you like yesterday's paper. You'll learn that if you are lucky enough to stay on with him.

"Darling Olivia, London is not a prison cell, and there is still a life out there for you should you choose to live it."

As she stood, Mrs. Sherbourne assumed her air of superiority and quality breeding. She must have been a corking good actress.

"Miss Nash, I will expect you at precisely eleven tomorrow morning. Should you fail to keep our appointment, I will tell Commander Fleming that you are unsuitable for work with the Kemsley News Group. Do I make myself clear?"

Livy nodded.

The Great Actress pivoted, stepped over Livy's dirty knickers, and flung open the door. She stopped in the doorway, paused for effect, and looked over her shoulder.

"And don't forget the scones."

* * *

After that, Livy arrived promptly each morning with two fresh scones wrapped in brown paper. The time she spent with Mrs. Sherbourne had evolved. The taming had ended. The new phase had commenced.

They took tea first, with Livy following strict English protocol. Then Mrs. Sherbourne delved into what must have been a prodigious wardrobe, because, apart from the dressing gown and turban, Livy never saw her in the same dress twice. Then the day's adventure began.

The first day they went to a boarded storefront near Piccadilly, which housed a man Mrs. Sherbourne referred to as "the finest dressmaker in the world." The man, who stood almost a foot shorter than Livy but weighed probably twice as much as her, took almost two hours taking measurements of every inch of her body. If a man had poked and prodded her this much back home, she'd have clouted him. But the short, round dressmaker kept it strictly professional.

The next day began, as always, with light tea and then a trip out to the country. Mrs. Sherbourne told Livy to dress for physical training. The drive out of the city brought back memories of the energy she had felt after being whisked off to SOE training three years earlier.

Soon after that first meeting with the frosty Miss Atkins at Station F headquarters in Baker Street, Livy and several other recruits were sent to the highlands of Scotland for five weeks of commando training. Never having been much of a student growing up, Livy immediately took to the get-your-hands-dirty approach at this school for saboteurs. She learned to build bombs and how to find the most effective places to plant them. The men—and the half dozen other women—spent nearly a week on small arms training. They also practiced what their instructor called "the silent kill." Livy didn't flinch as the big Scottish sergeant major showed her exactly where a man would be most vulnerable to a hard and fast slash of her hand. She knew a few grabby lads growing up she'd have liked to use that one on.

Later, at another "finishing school," Livy and the others underwent parachute training. Packing the chute, double- and triple-checking it, then the night jumps. Livy broke out in a cold sweat every day for the first week. She'd always hated heights and used to close her eyes when her dad walked the tight wire at the Tower Circus in Blackpool. She wouldn't have survived without another recruit—a French girl living in Devon—who talked her through it. Margot, who had a wicked sense of humor and spoke English with a thick Marseille accent, advised her not to fight the fall.

"Like Errol Flynn when he fights all those pirates in the pictures," Margot said, "You have to laugh in the face of danger."

Now gazing out the window of Mrs. Sherbourne's two-seater Ford Anglia, Livy wondered what had happened to Margot. How had her war ended? Livy shook the thoughts away. She felt ready to stop sitting around and finally train again.

They spent two days on a firing range with gruff red-headed Major Taylor, who reacquainted Livy with the Fairbairn-Sykes fighting knife and the Webley revolver she'd trained with at the SOE camp in Scotland.

After that, a woman Mrs. Sherbourne referred to only as Gwendolyn met them at a dance studio off Leicester Square to give Livy a refresher course in close combat. Although she had the sleek figure of a ballerina, Gwendolyn's hands felt like they were made of rocks as she put Livy through her paces.

The instructor took her through a refresher course of the SOE drills, beginning with blows with the side of the hand. Livy practiced on department-store mannequins as Gwendolyn reminded her of the proper technique for boxing punches and the potentially lethal jab to the chin with a flat open hand. The following days were spent on body holds and releases. Those nights, Livy returned to her flat to discover new bruises on her forearms and thighs.

At the end of the week, Mrs. Sherbourne took Livy back to the shop of the world's smallest dressmaker, who already had mock-ups of four outfits for Livy. Two were formal gowns, and the other two were fitted suits like you might see worn by the

Duchess of Such and Such when she attended matches at the All England Club.

Through it all, Livy minded her manners. She didn't snarl at the new clothes, she didn't blow on her tea, and she followed orders like she was back in France.

As the days progressed, Mrs. Sherbourne never again mentioned the war, Ravensbrück, or what Livy had told her.

Once Livy asked if there was a Mr. Sherbourne.

"Yes. There *was*," she said without elaborating.

Mrs. Sherbourne kept the specifics of her marriage as well as her experiences in the war in a hidden place. Somehow, this bonded the two women more than anything else. Livy too had a secret place where she kept private things. That's where she kept Peter.

*   *   *

"Now, we must start to get a bit more serious about our time together," Mrs. Sherbourne said as she and Livy strolled up Shaftesbury Avenue toward Piccadilly Circus. Friday afternoon marked the end of two weeks with Mrs. Sherbourne. The day brought out everyone and the sidewalks teemed with people, while cars trudged past double-decker buses on the street.

Mrs. Sherbourne lingered a moment at a jewelers' shop window before taking Livy's arm and turning the corner. Ahead of them, a large advert for Craven cigarettes dominated one side of the street, while flashing signs for Brylcreem and Jacob's Cream Crackers lit up the other.

"Good, because it's been a laugh so far," Livy said, smirking.

That morning one of the suits made for her by the designer had arrived, and Mrs. Sherbourne had insisted she wear it on their jaunt. The dress felt like silk, although Mrs. Sherbourne said it would be impossible for even the designer to find such material during rationing. Still, it felt so light and breathable, and fit her perfectly. Livy had never worn anything like it. The lavender dress came with a slightly darker fitted jacket with padded shoulders. A black slouching hat with a subtle purple feather—if such a thing was possible—on the side finished the outfit.

Mrs. Sherbourne practically ordered Livy to wear lipstick, even in the middle of the day. "You can't wear plimsolls with Chanel, darling. Now pucker up." Livy found the metaphor a trifle insulting but puckered up anyway.

The whole getup made Livy feel like a spotlight was following her down the street. Every other man seemed to smile at them or tip his hat. Mrs. Sherbourne, however, treated it like a command performance, with the entire male population of London as her audience.

"During the war, the villains all wore jackboots and monocles," Mrs. Sherbourne began, "but things are different now. No one knows who the villains are. Yet."

She pulled Livy into the recessed window of a tobacco shop and turned her facing the street.

"Do you see them all, darling? All running from one place to the next, spending what little pence they have on tea or the cinema. Still so blissfully happy that the last war is over," she said, grinning like a cat on a steady diet of canary.

"Last war. Mr. Fleming's fond of that phrase as well," Livy said.

"There's a new one on the way, darling. And unlike the last one where the Gestapo was kind enough to wear those tailored gray uniforms, this war will be fought in plainclothes. You see, that's the trick. Finding out who's on your side and who's on theirs. They could be walking past us now. They could be inside the shop. They could be one of us."

"I know how that feels," Livy said, remembering the look on the face of the man she'd known as Luc when he offered her that trick deck of cards. If she spotted him walking up Shaftesbury right now, she'd choke him to death in the street. If only Fleming would give her the chance.

"Yes, I'm sure you do," Mrs. Sherbourne said, her eyes suddenly searching and sad. "But I have a feeling this new war might teach us a whole new meaning of the word *betrayal*."

Later that afternoon they retreated to Mrs. Sherbourne's flat.

"This is our last day together, darling," she said, sitting on the edge of her favorite Queen Anne chair. "Now don't pout. That means our work here is done for now, and you are required elsewhere. But there is one final course to your education. Tonight at the French Embassy there's a soiree, and you are cordially invited."

Mrs. Sherbourne handed Livy a thick cream card with raised letters. The invitation to the *Ambassade de France* had been extended to Mademoiselle Suzanne Bélanger.

"You're going to play a character tonight. Suzanne Bélanger, a member of the French *Résistance* who fought with the maquis at Vercors. That is the reason they are letting you in the door. Don't worry. You won't have to make a speech. However, once you get inside, things get a bit more complicated."

"You don't say."

"Suzanne, *s'il vous plaît*."

"I speak French, Marie Antoinette. Now, go on."

"The party will be attended by other survivors of the occupation, a few English military types, and the standard embassy party circuit. You know, the wealthy with a taste for French champagne. But there will also be a surprise guest."

"Hermann Göring?"

Mrs. Sherbourne's grin fell. "I trust you'll keep that Lancashire sass under wraps tonight. You enter the party as Mademoiselle Bélanger and you leave the party as the same. It's a simple assignment. Maintain your cover at all cost. Like falling off a log for you, darling.

"Oh, and you'll be receiving microfilm from an operative at the party. Only trouble is, we've no idea who it is." Mrs. Sherbourne smiled.

Livy did not.

"Is your tea a bit warm, darling?"

Chapter Seven

Livy spent the rest of the day frantically going through French language books, leaflets, and yellowed menus she'd kept in a large suitcase under her bed. The case, covered in dust, hadn't been touched in over a year. Thankfully, Livy found her language skills a bit less rusty now that Mrs. Sherbourne had put her through her paces the last two weeks. Still, speaking French again put her right back in the war side by side with Peter.

Dusting off her French was worrisome enough, but the dress she was supposed to wear put her in a right dither. Mrs. Sherbourne had had the diminutive dressmaker create one gown to be less showy. Still, the dress gave her fits. *Simple and elegant* had been Mrs. Sherbourne's admonition to the designer. The black dress had wide shoulders and a high waist with sleeves that showed a hint of skin. The feathered hat made for the dress even had a black veil that came down to her nose.

She took a moment and looked at herself in the mirror. *Not half bad. Maybe the little designer is all he was cracked up to be.* Gazing at herself from top to bottom, with a spin-around to look at her bum, Livy had to admit she looked downright lush.

* * *

Livy's heart began to race the second she got into the cab that would take her to Knightsbridge near the Albert Gate, home to the French Embassy. She felt the typical nerves one might feel after a long hiatus from fieldwork, but this was more than butterflies. Something about this assignment felt wrong. Mrs. Sherbourne had provided her with few details. "The contact will find you," she'd been told. No code phrase. No recognition signal. The only information she had was that the contact was an emissary from the Mephisto network and that the microfilm was a token of legitimacy. Her first assignment for Fleming and she was bloody well going in blind.

The driver pulled into a queue of limousines and black taxis depositing dignitaries outside the gray five-story building. Livy tipped the driver extravagantly as she got out, nearly catching a heel on the curb as she joined the other well-dressed partygoers.

She tried to keep her breath under control as she moved toward the entrance. Alongside her strolled women in expensive gowns and men who wore tuxedos like a second skin. Up ahead a man with steel-gray hair, wearing the dress uniform and kepi of the French Army, bowed and groveled at each guest after receiving their vellum invitation, which he discreetly checked against a guest list in his right hand.

The memory of her recent excursion to Buckingham Palace caused Livy's heart to march double-time. However, the Frog gatekeeper took one look at her invite, stole a barely discernible glance at his own list, and broke out in a broad smile.

"*Bienvenue*, Mademoiselle Bélanger."

Livy responded in kind, as the pounding in her chest normalized, and strolled into the embassy like she owned the place.

A line of staff formed a kind of human walkway from the front entrance through the main hallway to a large room on the right. They all wore black tie, cutaway coats, and a tasteful tricolor French flag pinned to their lapels. *Très élégante.*

The hallway itself reflected the haphazard state of French government in the year since liberation. General de Gaulle's portrait hung alongside the current head of the provisional government, Félix Gouin, even though de Gaulle had resigned to start his own political party.

Despite the challenges of building a postwar government, the French could still throw a party. The room itself gleamed under the sparkle of a chandelier with what looked like more than a hundred lights reflecting off the gold-engraved cornice. The large picture windows that faced the street were draped with plush blue curtains. A small platform, swathed in red fabric, stood at the other end of the room, which housed a quartet quietly playing "La Mer."

Rationing might be the reality outside this room, but inside the bustling assemblage drank, laughed, and took the time to assess each new arrival.

One of these folks had a present for Suzanne Bélanger.

At that moment, a tray of champagne flutes whizzed past Livy balanced on the palm of another black-tied servant. Livy snatched the bubbly just to give her something to do with her gloved hands. The champagne smelled de-lovely, but Livy thought better of taking a first sip. She had to be sharp, charming, on guard, and, of course, French.

She took a breath and surveyed the crowd. Even in her oh-so-elegant black dress with the sparkly studs, Livy felt like a cow standing in the middle of Buckingham Palace.

Mrs. Sherbourne was right. This wasn't like the war. Messy hair and a dirty face made you look like you belonged there. Here, she felt sure half the guests could see right through her. This lot knew instinctively who didn't belong. They sussed you out quick. That's how they got to be where they were, by keeping the undesirables in their place.

The anxiety of that particular thought caused Livy to tilt the flute to her lips and take an ale-sized swallow. She was about to wipe her mouth with her cuff and call for Pierre to bring another when a figure just behind her spoke with a trace of Glasgow.

"Sometimes you wonder if all these people ever do is attend parties."

Livy held off another gulp and turned to her left. The man who spoke stood several inches taller than Livy and was considerably older. With his steel-gray wavy hair, Livy guessed him to be just past fifty. He wore a somewhat baggy double-breasted tuxedo, which draped his lanky frame. The suit might have made him look like a well-dressed scarecrow if not for the boyish twinkle in his eyes and his puckish smile.

"Someone must, I sooo-pose," Livy answered, laying on the French dialect a bit thick.

The man looked at bit surprised; then his smile quickly recovered. "Perhaps you are one of the guests of honor tonight?"

"Well—um—it's embarrassing a bit. I don't know," she said, playing the shy, out-of-her-element French girl.

"My apologies, mademoiselle. I did not mean to make light of the occasion. My name is Grant Duncan," he said, rolling the *r* in his first name. "I'm a journalist. On his night off. Not that a journalist ever stops working."

Livy smiled and offered her hand. "Suzanne Bélanger."

"*Enchanté*, mademoiselle." Duncan took her hand, bowing slightly. "Yes, people can't seem to get enough of this sort of thing. Honoring the heroes of the war. The deserving heroes, I should say. Although I fear occasions such as this help them see the war as far less complicated than it actually was."

"*Vous avez raison*," Livy said, trying to sound casual. She wondered if this prolonged chat might be a signal. A Scot at the French Embassy seemed an unlikely contact, but she had to be prepared. For now, she'd keep him talking. "But you must take time to celebrate, yes?"

"Of course. We all must try to convince ourselves that the conflict is over and that peace is everlasting."

"And it also gives us a perfect reason to drink the French government's champagne."

Duncan laughed and inclined his head toward her. "Well put. Tonight there are only heroes. And champagne." They turned to each other and clinked glasses. Livy held her breath, thinking now would be the obvious moment for him to pass her the microfilm.

Instead he turned to go.

"I've taken far too much of your time, mademoiselle. Forgive the intrusion. Perhaps we shall talk again later."

"I should like that," Livy said.

Duncan gave her another slight bow and then took off into the crowd.

Contact or no, Livy liked the Scot's candor, and having an actual conversation speaking English with a French accent took a bit of the edge off her mounting anxiety. So she moved further into the crowd, still in search of her contact—whoever the hell that might turn out to be.

So Suzanne Bélanger floated into the crowd, smiling and nodding. She chatted with a man who claimed to be a direct descendant of Napoleon and whose breath smelled like stale onions. She met two women who had fought the Nazi offensive at Vercors. One of whom Livy felt certain she remembered.

Finally, the French ambassador, a balding man with round glasses and a tepid mustache, said a few words about honoring the "heroic *partisans*" without whom France would not be free today. He failed to mention the specific help they'd received from Britain and the Yanks, but why quibble? It was a night for celebration, drinking, and then, of course, dancing.

The ambassador surrendered the microphone to a jazz quartet who, much to Livy's delight, began with a jaunty "La Marseillaise" followed by a peppy version of "Belleville" that would have made Django Reinhardt reasonably proud.

No sooner had the quartet begun to swing than someone behind her cleared his throat. Livy turned to face the sort of man who wore evening dress in a way that would make Clark Gable look like a slouch. He had dark hair, the kind of smile you like to see sitting across from you at a nice restaurant, and several rows of medals covering his well-developed chest.

"Mademoiselle Bélanger, what a surprise to see you here," he said in a French accent that seemed all too real.

"And you too, Monsieur—?"

He didn't reply. *No names.*

Instead the handsome French stranger offered her his hand. "I would be quite pleased if you'd do me the favor of a dance."

Feeling relatively sure this man had to be the contact, Livy decided to play along. "Of course. But I must warn you, I have two left feet."

He took her hand and feigned a grin. "Then I'll be sure to step on both of them."

Whoever this stranger was, he had the air of a diplomat. They spun across the floor mostly avoiding the other couples. Despite his self-deprecating comment, he fairly glided them around the room through the other couples as the hot quartet picked up the tempo.

Dancing with a handsome Gallic spy? Not a bad way to spend an evening.

"You are a gifted dancer, monsieur," Livy said, purring the French vowels in his ear.

For a moment their bodies were so close she could almost place his rather delicious scent. He smiled and tilted his head toward hers. For a second Livy thought he might kiss her.

Instead he bared his teeth and said, "I think we can dispense with the niceties, mademoiselle." As he spoke, he spun her away and then pulled her back into him.

Livy felt his lips graze her ear.

"I speak on behalf of a friend from Paris," he whispered.

Livy's heart pounded. She tried to look like a woman having a good time at a party, not a spy straining to hear her contact.

"She sends you a token of her trust and asks to meet you in two nights at the Théâtre du Grand-Guignol."

The band ended "Belleville" with a flourish, and the assembled responded with polite applause. The stranger took Livy's hand and plastered on a fake smile.

"It has been a pleasure, mademoiselle," he said, kissing her glove gently. As his hand let go of hers, Livy felt the stranger press something small into the center of her palm.

She gave him a smile before abruptly turning the other way. As she did she glanced into her glove to see a black canister about the width of a half crown. She knew enough tradecraft to recognize microfilm.

Like any good leading lady at the end of a scene, Livy made for the exit. Suzanne Bélanger would pop out to the privy and bid everyone *au revoir*.

Livy dropped the microfilm container in her clutch and stopped long enough to gawk at a portrait of Napoleon's great-great-great-whatever. She gave the place a cursory look for the tall and Scottish Mr. Duncan but didn't see him. Oh well, time for a hasty retreat, a taxi home, and a hop into her warm bed.

With all the guests inside, the hallway had cleared of the line of servants, so Livy scurried to the front of the embassy without fanfare. The doorman signaled a cab for her. Just like that, two cars turned the corner and made their way toward the embassy drive. A sleek new Packard, by the look of it, with a long black nose and four doors led the way. Ye olde reliable black London taxi brought up the rear.

Livy had stepped down on the curb toward the taxi when she felt something behind her. A man stood behind her right shoulder. His breath, which reeked of some sort of foreign tobacco, arrived before he did.

Livy didn't fancy a shared ride with Bad Breath, so she turned to allow him access to the back door. He grabbed her arm hard. She turned, instinct taking over, ready to wrench her elbow out of his grasp; then Livy felt hard metal pressing into her side.

"Please, mademoiselle, we take this car," he said in a thick accent Livy couldn't immediately place. "Is better this way."

Chapter Eight

The man stepped away from Livy to open the door of the Packard. In his right hand he held a small black automatic with a rather mean-looking silencer attached. He kept his back to the doorman at the embassy to keep the gun hidden.

Livy took her first look at the man. He wore a dark suit over a shirt whose collar badly needed ironing. His brown fedora dipped below his eye line, so Livy only caught a glimpse of a repeatedly broken nose like a boxer's and a mouth with a fat upper lip draped by a big drooping mustache.

She considered calling out to the doorman, but that might mean Bad Breath would shoot her immediately, hop in the Packard, and be gone.

Sensing her hesitation, he stepped toward her. "Mademoiselle, please, we must hurry," he said, pointing the muzzle of the silencer at her chest.

Livy stepped down into the car and scooted across the leather seat to the other side. Bad Breath joined her, and the Packard eased away from the curb. She couldn't see the driver's face, just broad shoulders and a hat jammed down on a square head. The lights of the taxi just behind illuminated the big car's interior.

"I believe you have something I want." Bad Breath pushed back his hat, and Livy caught a glimpse of more of his face in the light from the cab. He had strong blue eyes under heavy lids. Despite the Stalin-like mustache, he was young. No more than twenty-five, she guessed. He reeked of some of the most pungent cigarette tobacco Livy had ever had the misfortune to smell.

He held his left hand toward her, the gun unwavering, pointing at her heart.

Livy felt his anxiety and intent. She was at this man's mercy, and most men with guns didn't have a lot of that.

"Please, give me what you received tonight," he said, "and I will let you go."

"I did not re-ceeve eeny-thing," Livy said, keeping up the French.

Bad Breath didn't hesitate. He whipped the gun across Livy's face, striking the side of her face hard with the barrel of the automatic.

Livy grabbed her cheek and felt blood on her fingers from a cut, probably around her temple. Now she was awake. Jolted out of the complacency of the elegant evening—the clothes, the champagne, the dancing—Livy felt no panic. Instead she became more aware of the leathery smell of the car's interior and the way the light from the rear car cast shadows across Bad Breath's face. Every sense seemed keener. She felt fully awake in a way she hadn't since the war.

Still, her face hurt plenty.

Bad Breath went on. "We are professionals, mademoiselle. Please, do not insult me. Give me what you received tonight."

Livy weighed her options. If this was the cinema, God knew Errol Flynn would throttle three men with one blow and then escape with the microfilm into the night as gunfire erupted all around him. But in real life, any sudden move from her and she might end up dead.

Bad Breath apparently didn't like the delay, so he wrenched Livy's hand from her face and replaced it with the muzzle of his gun.

"I will not ask again," he said.

Livy believed him. That dead look in his eyes scared her.

Nothing she could use as a weapon. Her clutch purse would have the stopping power of a feather. She could try punching him with her free hand, but that might get her a bullet in the brain, and then he could just take the microfilm and shove her out in the street somewhere.

She knew his type. The Nazis had them a dime a dozen. She didn't have long.

And then, in that split second, Livy noted how calm she felt. Had she missed this? Missed the adrenaline surge she now felt, the racing of her heart, the life-and-death of it, all in a single moment?

"Mademoiselle, now," he said. The silencer pressed into her forehead, and she knew, in that moment where everything slowed down for her, that she had no choice.

"Fine, luv," she said, dropping the accent. "You're the man with the gun." He released her arm and lowered the weapon slightly. Livy unsnapped the clutch and, after a moment of searching, held the small canister in her glove.

Bad Breath took it greedily and muttered something to the driver in a language Livy didn't understand. Not once did he take his eyes or the gun off her. A real professional, this one, she thought.

The big Packard slowed to a stop, and he dropped the canister in his coat pocket.

"We are not far from the embassy. I'm sure you will find a ride soon. *Au revoir*," he said with a hint of irony, keeping the muzzle of the silencer trained on Livy.

She turned, popped the latch on the door, and stepped out into the street. Before she had the chance to look back, the Packard's door had already closed, and the car peeled off into the night.

Livy stepped out of the road onto the curb. She put a hand to her face. It stung. The side of her jaw was probably bruised, and when she pulled her fingers away, she saw blood from the cut. She'd taken the worse of this one, no doubt. And she'd lost the microfilm.

Truth was, she'd failed her first real assignment. Earlier, she'd wondered if Mrs. Sherbourne had staged the entire evening. A little theater to see how the new girl handled the posh side of the secret world, complete with music, dancing, a handsome French contact, and top-secret microfilm. *The plot may be riddled with cliché, but nevertheless a crowd pleaser.*

That didn't hold water now. The man in the car, the man who had the microfilm now, couldn't have been an actor. Livy knew he'd been seconds from putting a bullet into her head and taking what he needed.

Despite all that, she was relaxed. She felt like running after the car and tracking the bastard down right now. Gone was the self-pity and shame that had been her constant companion. This was her lot in life.

Fine. Round one to Bad Breath. She'd retreat to her corner, regroup, and be ready for more.

Chapter Nine

~

The morning after the French Embassy party, Livy sat in the outer office of Kemsley News patiently waiting for an audience with Fleming. She wore one of her new outfits, a particularly spiffy utility suit with a vaguely nautical look. She hoped her ensemble might distract from the big white bandage taped to her right temple to cover the gash caused by Bad Breath's pistol.

Livy felt quite different on this, her second, trip to Fleming's office. The first time she'd blundered in, slightly soused and several hours late. Now she sat in the outer office after taking one for the team.

The young blonde woman, who introduced herself to Livy as Miss Baker, sat at her desk typing a long correspondence on letterhead with an air of mannered nonchalance. When she finished, Miss Baker carefully folded the typed letter and sealed it into a thick vellum envelope. Then the routine began again.

She'd met Livy at the door with a polite smile. Told her Mr. Fleming was in a meeting and would be with her shortly. She never mentioned the obvious bandage on Livy's temple or so much as glanced at it. Livy wondered if some of Fleming's other "reporters" showed up in a similar condition.

"Don't you ever get tired of it?" Livy asked.

"Tired of what?" Miss Baker's voice fit her like the narrow skirt she wore. She sounded smart, educated, and smooth.

"All that typing. Back at the P&J, they have rows of girls typing all day. Like machines. Just hammering away at those keys. After a few months they start to lose it a bit."

Miss Baker pivoted in her chair and took a cigarette holder from the top drawer of her desk. She made the act of placing the cigarette and lighting it seem as elegant as a tango.

"I suppose," she said, letting the smoke exhale out of the side of her small, red lips, "that would depend on what one is typing."

Livy nodded, glancing toward Fleming's office before realizing Miss Baker was still looking at her.

"You'll want to watch out for that one."

Livy tilted her head toward the closed door and said, "What? Him?"

"Of course. Don't tell me he hasn't made a pass at you yet." The blonde spoke quickly, her voice hushed.

"No, I'm just here for the work."

"Aren't we all?"

Livy was still trying to figure out what Miss Baker meant as the blonde took a pull on her cigarette holder.

Finally, she said, "Have family from up your way. Preston. Know it?"

"Best bookshop in Lancashire's there," Livy said. "Used to beg me da to visit. Football club's rubbish, but you can't have it all."

Miss Baker's icy demeanor transformed into a dazzling white smile. She held out her right hand. "I'm Pen."

"Olivia, but my friends call me Livy."

"So, I'll call you—Olivia, then?"

"Too right," Livy said, grinning, taking Pen's hand.

As if a whistle had sounded to end the moment, Pen spun away from Livy and inserted a clean sheet of foolscap into the typewriter. Her carefully manicured nails attacked the first keys. The seal on the inner office door opened with a smooth *whoosh* and Fleming walked out with another man.

Livy sized him up almost instantly as an American, before even hearing his voice. He had a certain quality in the way he walked. It was a bit bouncy. Most of the American men she knew had that sort of buoyancy to them, like they were warming up for a baseball game or something.

"Well, I certainly hope you'll keep me in mind, Mr. Fleming," he said. Long vowels. Hard *r*'s. Definitely a Yank.

"Oh, to be sure," Fleming said, with more than a trace of weariness.

"Good to meet you, sir," the American said, nodding at Pen and then picking up his fedora from the coatrack. Just before he left, his eyes darted over to Livy for an instant. Well-dressed and spit-polished, the Yank smiled at Livy. Not the glamorous Miss Penelope Baker, but Livy.

Good-looking. Nice suit. A face made for the cinema. Livy caught herself returning the smile when she heard her own name.

"Olivia," Fleming said. "Pen, make sure we aren't disturbed."

"Of course," she replied, with a sideways look at Livy.

Inside the office, the door sealed shut. Fleming took a seat at his desk. The lights across Europe, North America, and Asia glowed on the map behind him.

"I hear the French throw a nice party," he said, taking a sip of coffee from a plain black mug.

"It was quite the do."

"Too much champagne, perhaps?" Fleming said, indicating Livy's bandage.

"I did have a bit of difficulty with my ride home."

Fleming considered this and lit a cigarette. "And the microfilm?"

Livy's mouth felt dry. "I had it. But a man with a gun wanted it, too."

Fleming blew out smoke, his wide mouth curling down. "I assume you put up some sort of resistance?"

"Well, I didn't cut meself shaving," she said, touching her cheek.

"What was he like, this man?" Fleming anxiously tapped his middle finger on the cluttered desk. "You got a good look, I suppose."

"Foreign. Big mustache. Smoked foul-smelling cigarettes. Broken nose. Not an amateur."

"Nationality?"

"I'd say Eastern Europe. Maybe Russian."

"And now he has the microfilm?"

"As I said, he had the gun."

"Quite, quite." Fleming mashed out his cigarette, leaned back in his chair, and gave Livy a look like that made her feel like a misbehaving child. "Nevertheless, an inauspicious beginning."

Livy had no intention of accepting the rebuke without pleading her case. "I went to that party blind. No clue who the contact was and no idea what the microfilm might even be. Maybe if I'd known, the ending might've been different."

Fleming looked ready to end it all right now. "My dear Miss Nash, I had to find out if I could trust you. Quite out of the blue, our people receive a message requesting you—of all people—to negotiate the sale of the Mephisto list. Not only was I testing the veracity of the other side, but I also wanted to see whose side you were on. The Mephisto list will have many suitors. I sent you in blind, as you say, precisely because we do not know each other and I couldn't trust that you wouldn't disappear with that microfilm."

She knew he was right. In the war, agents had rarely known every piece of the puzzle in case of capture and subsequent torture. Livy wondered if she might have to crawl back to the P&J and hope for Mr. O'Toole's mercy. *Not just yet.*

"He gave me a message, though," she said. "The contact."

Fleming spread his hands as if to say, *And?*

"He said the microfilm was a demonstration of the contact's trust, and we're to meet her tomorrow at a theater in Paris. The Grand Guignol."

"And the chap who gave you that cut didn't overhear?"

"No, that was private."

Fleming spun around in his chair and stared at the map of the world. Livy wondered if he was looking at the dimmed bulb over Paris.

"Well, then, at this point we may have no other choice," he said.

Livy wondered if she should respond. She chose silence. Finally, after what seemed minutes, Fleming turned to face her again. His mouth a straight line.

"Despite your bungling of last night, you are still the person they asked for. You have a better chance than anyone of getting that microfilm back and bringing us Valentine. That is, if you have the stomach to continue."

Bungling? Livy wanted to dispute that particular claim. But she held back and said, "I give as good as I get, Mr. Fleming."

"We shall see about that, won't we?"

The bastard gave no quarter. But at least Livy didn't have to grovel at O'Toole's heel just yet.

"I've had two weeks of Mrs. Sherbourne and her drama school, and I think it's high time you tell me exactly what it is you want me to do—and while we're at it, what exactly was on that film?"

Fleming lit another cigarette, studying her as he did. Then he said, "Would you care for a drink?"

"I'd like a double. But I think I'd prefer a clear head right now," she said, sitting back in the leather armchair.

"Let me take your last question first," Fleming said. "The microfilm, this apparent symbol of trust, contained the names of half the agents in the Mephisto network."

Livy sighed. No wonder Fleming was treating her like a stupid little girl.

"I imagine the fellow who gave you that bruise was with the state security arm of the Soviet MGB."

"How could they have known?"

Fleming gave her a small, painful grin. "They're spies, dear. It's what they do."

Not for the first time in this office, Livy felt far out of her element.

Fleming went on. "I told you earlier about the one informant we had in Mephisto. A fellow from Nice, who we picked up in Vienna, of all places. We were keeping him in protective custody in a small jail near Marseille. This morning he was found dead in his cell. His throat had been cut and his tongue cut out. We suspect the guard was bribed, but the other prisoners in the same small jail aren't talking."

"Can't say I blame them."

Fleming pushed a file across his desk toward her. "This is what the poor chap had to say while he still could."

Excerpts from Interrogation of Claude D regarding MEPHISTO network. Conducted 26–4–46. Vienna, AU. Some passages have been edited for clarity and content.

I was working on the docks in Nice back then, in '38. Offloading the ships that came in. It was hard work, you know? Long hours. The pay was no good, but you take what you can get. You know, a lot of ships come in at the docks. Who knows who might be stowed away on one?

I think maybe that's why they wanted me. I could tell them what was coming in, going out.

But it started when me and some of my friends took a trip to Paris. It was the Easter holiday, and—well—we were all young then and none of us married, and we didn't really care for church, so we went to Paris. For Easter.

It was four of us, but my friend Charles and I were closest. You have to understand, Charles liked women very much, you know. He was from Paris and he knew so many girls there, and he promised we would all have a girl that Easter weekend.

He said, "There will be even more to pick from, because all the priests are working." Charles said some very funny things then.

He said, "We are all going to *Chez Moune* in the Pigalle. You have never been anywhere like this, Claude," he said. "It's only for girls. Girls who like other girls. You won't believe it."

Our other two friends, Jean and Hugo, they were not interested. Andre always talked too much. He said, "Why do I want to see freaks?" Idiot.

Anyway, we went to *Chez Moune* that night. See, it was only for *gouine* **(TRANSLATION FROM THE FRENCH—"LESBIAN"),** you know, but Charles knew one of the men who ran the club and he let us in. And he was right. You wouldn't believe it. Like a dream, you know. **(EDITED)**

So there was one girl that I met there. Nathalie. And she liked girls but she liked men, too. So Nathalie and I started talking while Charles was in the *chambre rouge*. I didn't know who she was then, or that she was a spy. I talked to her because she was so beautiful. Perfect. She had blue eyes that looked right through you, and her mouth . . . she would sip her drink and the wetness on her lips would drive me wild, you know.

So I didn't help them because of Germany or Hitler. It wasn't that. I didn't care about that. It was money. Yes? Just money. And her. Nathalie. And her eyes and that mouth. You see, she had this girlfriend there, and the *chambre rouge* was off-limits . . . for some. But not for us, you know. **(EDITED)**

Yes, yes, but Nathalie told me about him. The magician. One of Hitler's favorites, she said. You see, Hitler liked all of this black magic, witchy stuff, you know. Weird *things. He thought there were dark powers on Earth. Powers people didn't understand. So, this magician was good enough to play in Berlin, and that's where Hitler saw him.*

Nathalie said all I'd have to do was get information and pass it along to the magician or one of his people. Or her. Yes, she said that. But I never saw her again. Not after that one night.

Ca pute! (TRANSLATION FROM THE FRENCH—"THAT WHORE.")

Nathalie told me to go back to work on the docks and to watch the newspaper for when Mephisto, the magician, would play a show in Nice. That's when they would give me the signal and get me started.

So I waited, and maybe three or four months later I saw the advert for the magician. He was playing at a club in the city. So I bought a ticket for the show, which cost me almost fifty francs. So I went, watched the show, and then after I met one of his people. A fat man. Bald. He had been in the show, too. I don't remember his name, but he spoke French.

So this fat man gave me a thick envelope and told me I had to give it to another man before he boarded a certain ship. I think the ship was called the St. Anne or something. I said, why can't you give it to him yourself? The fat man laughed at me. "Delivery boys deliver," he said. "The man who gets this envelope and I are in management." He told me if I did this job without a mistake, then I would be given more jobs. Jobs that paid well. They needed eyes on the ships and the docks. So I said fine, I'd be his errand boy this time, but how would I know this man? He says, "Don't worry, he'll find you."

Hmmph. Of course. He said if I did this one simple thing, the man would have something for me. And that I could make lots of money this way.

So I made sure to get a shift the night this boat pulled out. Maybe an hour before it was scheduled to leave, I went down to the gangplank and waited. They were casting off the first lines when a man finally approached me. He wore a long coat and a big hat pulled way down on his face, but I could tell it was him. Mephisto. The magician.

So I give him the envelope, and he opened it in front of me. It was filled with money, Reichsmarks. He counted it all. Took his time. Maybe he didn't trust me, I don't know. Finally, he smiled and said, "You've done well."

Then he pulls something out of his coat pocket. One of those push-button knives, you know. He didn't point it at me or anything, he just held it.

He said, "You could be a great help to me. Working here in the dockyards. I'll bet you see and hear so many things."

Then he gives me another envelope. "Go ahead. Look inside," he said. And it was filled with francs. Not as much money as the thick one I gave him, but enough.

"If you tell me, or my associates, what you see and hear when you're down here, then there will be much more of that. But if you tell other people, then maybe I'll visit you again." And the whole time he's saying this, the knife is in his hand.

"Do you understand me?" he said.

I nodded, and he left.

That's the way it worked, you see. I reported to them what I saw. If someone moved weapons or materials or explosives to another country, I would let them know. I kept notes.

Usually I talked to his associate, the fat one. I never learned any names.

So, his magic show came to Nice every few months. We were occupied by the Italians there, but all over Vichy and the occupied zone near Paris, Mephisto still played the circuit. I don't know, but maybe that's how they did it. Maybe he had people like me everywhere he played, and in each city he gathered information.

I don't know, though, because I never met anyone else who worked for him.

But I did. All through the war.

Then after the invasion in '44, it practically stopped. I saw Fatty maybe twice after that. Just him. I'd see him standing at the dock, smoking or something, and when I had a break we'd talk. Same thing. I'd tell him what was happening, and he'd give me an envelope full of francs.

I never went back to Paris. And I never saw Nathalie again. Maybe she was the reason I did it, you know? Her . . . and the money too.

Livy closed the file. "So who's the fat man?"

"No idea. As poor Claude says there, they used no names."

Fleming pushed aside a pile of newspapers and unfolded a small map of Western Europe on his desk, facing Livy. "The red dots represent cities where Mephisto's magic show played more than four times from 1938 to the end of the war. Blue dots represent less than four."

The map looked like a child had been let loose with red and blue pens. The dots covered most of Britain, France, Germany, Spain, Italy, and every country west of the Soviet Bloc.

"That must be more than a hundred agents," she said.

"One hundred twenty-two."

Livy thought about Luc the mechanic. All this time she'd seen him as a dirty little bastard who had sold Peter and his unit out to the Germans for money. If Fleming was right, then Luc's betrayal went much deeper.

"It's clear from Claude's story that the agents don't know one another. If this is true, then they are still out there. In place. Waiting."

Livy's mouth suddenly felt very dry. "And the microfilm?"

Fleming nodded. "The microfilm, and the message you received, came from someone at the top of the network. Someone who wants out. She's our best chance of getting the complete list."

"Who is she?"

"The woman who recruited Claude." Fleming pulled a brown folder from a stack at his elbow. A white paper band sealed the folder from top to bottom. With a slight flourish, he produced a sterling silver knife from his desk and deftly sliced the band. Inside Livy saw two sheets of foolscap and a small black-and-white photo. Fleming held the small picture, studying it with a grin as cigarette smoke curled around his face. "Nathalie Billerant. I see why Claude was so taken with her. Quite beautiful. But then, they often are." Fleming placed the photo in front of Livy.

Beautiful? More like a film star, Livy thought. *Garbo meets Vivien Leigh.*

Fleming put his cigarette holder in a marble ashtray and walked around to the front of his desk. "I'm taking a risk on you, Olivia. Please, don't make me regret it."

"I won't."

"Fine, then. We'll have to move quickly on this. You'll be going to Paris as a correspondent for *The Times* doing a story on the Grand Guignol theater. Mrs. Sherbourne will contact you later with press credentials. She'll also arrange your plane to Paris. You're going to meet this Nathalie Billerant and see what she's got to say. We can offer her money, if that's what she wants, or asylum in England. But we want the entire list. Clearly, we're not the only ones who see its value."

Fleming moved to the credenza behind his desk, setting aside two cut-glass tumblers. He looked at Livy, who shook her head.

"I do have one more question," Livy said. "Why do we want people who worked for the Nazis? Shouldn't we be arresting them instead of recruiting them?"

Fleming poured his drink, flashing a rare sincere smile.

"I do like your spirit," he said. "No doubt there are plenty of anti-Bolsheviks in the Mephisto network who'd love to join the fight against communism. But there are probably just as many, if not more, who will work for whoever has the most money. The intelligence agency that controls that network controls Europe. It's as simple as that."

"And what about the magician?" Livy asked. "Luc, or Valentine, or whatever he's calling himself."

"As odious as Valentine is to you, we want him on our side. The network is one thing, but having its master working for us would be quite the coup. But I have to rely on your best judgment, girl. If you recruit Valentine, I need to know he'll cooperate."

"You want me to offer this bastard a job?"

"You're the only person we have who has actually met him. You have history with him, albeit an unfortunate one."

More like the War of the bloody Roses.

"If you believe personal feelings will interfere with you carrying out this assignment, then I shall simply have to let these people know Olivia Nash is not available," Fleming said.

Being asked to go to Paris and negotiate with Edward Valentine made Livy want to retch. But the look on Fleming's face told her he had no qualms about doing precisely what he'd just threatened. An image of Valentine being feted in London after another agent brought him back flashed through her mind. No, she'd not have that. She'd do what Fleming asked. But at some point she'd be alone with Luc the traitor, and by God, she'd have her say.

Besides, she needed a job. This job. She'd felt something last night. Even when the gun had been held to her head, she'd felt alive. In those moments the dark weight of Fresnes and the slaughter in the courtyard, all the pain that pushed her to fall asleep almost every night with a glass of vodka in her hand, faded. She had something to prove to Fleming as well as herself.

"I'll get the job done, sir," she said.

"Excellent," Fleming said, lighting another cigarette. "The perpetual cycle: smoking and drinking. It shall likely kill me one day."

Livy stood to go.

"Olivia—do you have a gun?"

She stopped. "From the war, yes."

"Good. If we can't recruit Valentine and acquire the list, then you must make certain no one else can either."

Chapter Ten

❧

Livy left Fleming's office, shaking as she walked down the Gray's Inn Road toward the Underground. Every tall man she passed reminded her of Luc. His bawdy jokes played like a newsreel in her mind, followed by the sound of that braying laugh of his. Was he already in her head? She stopped. Looked around for her tube stop. She stood on a corner in front of a Chinese takeaway she'd never seen before.

By the time Livy had backtracked and found the entrance to the Underground, she'd managed to calm down a bit. She forced herself to pay attention to her surroundings and refocus. Her nerves still tingled, though, and when her stomach began to cramp, she realized she'd not eaten last night. Trying to scrimp on the little money she'd put aside working at the P&J, she'd neglected the shopping for a week. The cupboards at home were bare.

She was starving. A pub occupied the next corner, as they almost always did in London. The Lamb needed a fresh coat of paint on its red awning above the brick facade, and the windows looked like they hadn't been given a wash since the pictures started talking, but still, food was to be had inside. The exterior looked dodgy, but what the hell. Livy's stomach might grumble about the Lamb's cuisine later, but right now her appetite didn't care.

She'd nearly reached the front stoop when a familiar figure pushed open the pub's green door and bounced into the street. He held the door for her without making eye contact, but she recognized the jawline, the fedora, and the jaunty American posture.

Livy tried to pass quickly into the dark, smoky confines of the Lamb, but his voice stopped her. "Wait a minute."

She hesitated.

"Where do I know you? Don't tell me." The American studied her face for a moment and then snapped his fingers. "Oh yeah, you were up in the Kemsley office. Waiting for Fleming. How could I forget? The bandage."

Livy blanched and touched her cheek. Few things annoyed her more than her own self-consciousness—and those who gave her reason to feel it.

The American shook his head and sighed. "That was rude. I'm sorry. Truly. My head is somewhere else. I'm Tom, Tom Vance. My apologies, Miss—?"

"No problem," she said, hoping to sound final. A big man in tweed smelling of smoke and lager bulldozed between Livy and the Yank and out onto the sidewalk.

Tom Vance placed two fingers on Livy's elbow as she pivoted away. "If I may, you're not planning on eating in there, are you?" Those vowels. A southern American, she thought.

"The thought had crossed my mind."

The American stepped away from the door and nodded for Livy to follow. She gave him a look. Probably about thirty-five years old; looked to be from money by the cut of his jib. Nice shoes too. Dark, wavy hair. Her stomach gurgled, so she took one step back onto the sidewalk.

"Maybe the shepherd's pie in there is having a bad day, but I think you might be taking your life into your own hands," he said.

She didn't so much as smile, but Livy had to admit the Yank was funny. Buoyant and funny.

"So, what do you suggest?"

"Well, I was just thinking to myself that I haven't even tried the food in my own hotel, and I leave tomorrow. I can't vouch for it, but I have a pretty good feeling the main course won't still be alive."

"Your hotel. I see." She knew where this might be going. Still she asked, "And where's that?"

"The Dorchester."

Livy let the door of the pub close behind her. The sodding Dorchester. *Well, well.* The idea of having a meal at the best hotel in London with an undeniably handsome American had its appeal. He wasn't trying to get her to his room. Yet. And, after all, she was starving. Couldn't say yes immediately, though.

"So, you're in the newspaper business, Mr. Vance?"

"I'm with the UP." Livy didn't respond, so he added, "*United Press.*"

She pursed her lips. "I believe I may have heard of them."

Smiling at her sarcasm, he said, "Now, that doesn't seem fair. You didn't tell me your name, or who you're with. You have the advantage."

"Yes, it appears I do. So the UP put their correspondents up at the Dorchester? Or are you just special, Mr. Vance?"

That smile again. Would have put Cary Grant's to shame. Almost. "Only one way to find out, ma'am."

All banter aside, Livy needed food. She stepped to the curb and put her hand up for a taxi. Then she pivoted back to Tom. "I prefer *Livy* to *ma'am*, if you don't mind."

* * *

The world outside might be suffering under rationing, but the Dorchester was having none of it. The décor in The Grill, as it was elegantly called, might make anyone forget that the British people—and most of Europe—were collectively tightening their belts. The room was long and seemed roomier due to the mirrored walls and coffered ceilings. The bar, which occupied the wall across from the main dining room, was all copper and wood. Every table was filled, but the lights and the glimmer from the surrounding glass gave the restaurant an intimate elegance.

Livy had insisted on finding the ladies' room in the lobby after the ride over. She'd be damned if she was going to have a late lunch at the Dorchester with a great bandage on her face. Never one who could be bothered to take the time and lather herself with makeup, she nevertheless felt relieved to find a stick of cream rouge in her purse, which she applied to her normal cheek as well as the one with the splash of purple. The effect was colorful.

Tom Vance proved grand company. Literate and funny with a self-deprecating charm, he came across as a southern William Powell. She couldn't complain about the food either. Livy ordered roasted chicken with carrots and Westcombe cheddar. Someone in the kitchen had lovingly prepared the main course so that the fowl was moist and flavorful. Honestly, she'd been hungry enough to have the questionable shepherd's pie at the Lamb, so her only challenge at the Dorchester was not to gobble the whole plate down in one bite.

She passed on wine. Didn't really see the point in it. If you're going to drink, she felt, then why not drink? Her body craved alcohol, though. She needed something to take the edge off the residual stress from last night's soiree at the embassy and her impending flight to Paris and a possible reunion with Luc. But she knew one drink would lead to another, and she had to have a clear head if she wanted to keep this job.

So she felt grateful for the food, but especially the repartee with the handsome Yank across from her. As they chatted over dinner, Livy's mind wandered back to the last time she'd been with a man. Only one since Peter. A Russian military officer she'd met in a pub. How long ago now? God, months. That had been a different time. Fueled by the very worst of her drinking bouts, the affair lasted only a couple of months. Would she sleep with Tom? Honestly, she had trouble focusing on the conversation. Her mind kept going back to what lay ahead. But still, she'd heard Wellington bomber pilots say having a go the night before helped their aim. 'Course that was rubbish.

But still—

"Someone was a bit hungry," Vance said, looking across the crisply ironed tablecloth at Livy's clean plate.

She put down her knife and fork. Mrs. Sherbourne would have been so proud. She even lifted her teacup like a royal. As she brought the Earl Grey to her lips, she leaned across the table and said, "Am I supposed to believe you and I just *happened* to meet outside that pub, Mr. Vance?"

He touched his linen napkin to the corners of his mouth. "If it had been my intention to follow you, Livy, I believe I might've taken a far less circuitous route."

"Bit of a coincidence though, don't you think?"

"Happens all the time. We were in the same neighborhood, after all."

Livy mentally added *less-than-convincing liar* to her internal list of Tom's attributes. But why would he want to meet her again after seeing her in Fleming's office? She took it as a fait accompli that any gentleman given the choice would be far more taken by Pen Baker's icy blonde sex appeal than by some northern girl with a rat's nest of a hairdo and bandage on her right cheek.

Still, she found herself sitting across from said gentleman at the Dorchester. As her Grandma Nash used to say, "The Lord works in mysterious ways, but everyone else is just takin' the piss." If Tom Vance was having one over on her, then it was a damned expensive joke.

"Besides," he added, "my mama used to tell me that things always happen for a reason."

"Did she now? And what's the reason for our meeting, then?"

"I don't know. Maybe I should ask my mama."

"Oh, is she staying at the hotel as well?"

Vance raised his glass to acknowledge the quip. "Actually, I'm all alone in the big city. Trying to stay out of trouble and to remember always look right before crossing the street."

Livy still didn't buy that their meeting was accidental, but Tom's charm seemed more authentic than calculated. She found him good company, and like people back home, conversation came naturally to him. Here they were, two people alone in London whose accents immediately identified them as outsiders. For the first time in days, Livy felt somewhat relaxed. Something about the way he listened to her and how easily he smiled drew her in. They laughed and flirted while avoiding talking shop altogether. She'd been mortified he'd suss her out as nothing but a copy editor with him being a successful correspondent for the *United Press*. Or so he said.

Livy declined dessert. The check came. Outside, Tom insisted on hailing a cab for her and paying for the short ride across London to Camden Town. The sun had come out and London in late June looked and felt as good as any place ever had. A flawless blue sky hovered over the capital, with a trace of a breeze keeping the denizens of Mayfair at a respectably cool temperature. Livy felt downright buoyant as she stood next to Tom outside the hotel waiting for the doorman, a tall Yorkshireman who wanted to sound like the Duke of Kent, to flag down a cab.

She'd been mildly insulted Tom hadn't invented some excuse to get her to his room. Would she have gone? Inviting him back to her messy flat in Camden Town was completely out of the question. Still, he smelled, looked, and sounded to her as scrumptious as the roast chicken she'd just devoured.

And she could tell his interest in her, for whatever reason, was genuine. She put her arm through his, feeling the smooth fabric of his jacket.

"I suppose I should thank you for dinner, even though you clearly ambushed me at that pub," she said.

He looked down at her. Lips first and then up. "Is this your counteroffensive?"

Livy rolled her eyes and put her right hand on the front of his jacket to turn his body in to hers. He inclined his head toward her mouth. She stopped him.

"Your doorman seems a bit nosy," she said, whispering.

They both glanced over. The Dorchester doorman stood by a black London cab, hand on the rear door, staring.

Tom smiled. "Not very discreet, is he?"

Livy took off his fedora and slapped it to his chest. "If you're going to wear a hat like that, you may as well put it to good use," she said.

Vance's grin cracked his wide face open, and he held the hat up, shielding their faces from the street side, as he leaned down for the first of several very long and slow kisses while the doorman waited. Patiently.

* * *

The taste of those kisses kept her smiling on the fifteen-minute ride to Camden Town. Had the cab not been waiting, she'd have found herself back in Tom's hotel room testing out the night-before theory espoused by those bomber pilots.

Opening the door to her flat, she felt no surprise in seeing a thick brown unmarked envelope lying on her bed. She opened it and let the contents spill out across the bedspread. That action alone banished the Dorchester and Tom Vance's smile to a remote outpost of her mind.

She studied the items one by one with a certain detachment. First a blue passport in her own name, a press card with KEMSLEY NEWS engraved at the top, then two other passports, including a French one for Suzanne Bélanger and a Swiss one for a Collette Deschaume. Finally, she found a BOAC ticket scheduled for departure from the new London airport at Heathrow.

Mrs. Sherbourne had thought of everything.

As night fell and the darkness crept across Livy's one-room flat, she poured the very last shot of the Polish vodka. Sitting in the chair across from her bed, she sipped the bitter alcohol and allowed herself to cry softly as she thought of the last time she'd seen Luc and Peter. Once she'd finished—the vodka now gone for good and her tears wiped away—Livy went to the small closet where her clothes hung and pulled out the biggest traveling bag she owned. She carefully folded her two new suits and packed in as many more clothes as she could fit.

She went once more to the closet, got down on her knees, and reached into the very back to retrieve a metal box. The top rusted and wheezed as she opened it. Inside—among letters, photographs, and other reminders of the war—lay a small pistol and silencer.

The Webley .32 semiautomatic had come as standard issue for many SOE agents in France. Livy's had scratches along the stubby barrel and grip. She unscrewed the black silencer, cleaned it, and then disassembled the gun and put it back together.

Three French words had been inscribed down the side of the silencer. MORT AUX BOCHES. *Death to the Hun.*

She pointed the gun at a lamp across the room and imagined Valentine there as helpless as she and Peter had been at Fresnes. The gun in her hand this time. Would she put revenge over the job? Fleming's orders had been explicit. Get the list *and* Valentine. Still, she wondered how it would feel to have him at her mercy and then watch him die. She knew she could do it. She'd shot the German woman—her torturer—after the blast at the prison. That, however, had been a matter of survival. This time would be different.

Livy pulled the trigger. The click sounded clean.

Chapter Eleven

~

The wing flaps of the big DC-3 turned down, and the hum of the propellers dropped to a minor key. Over the intercom the pilot announced, in both English and French, the final approach to Paris.

Livy considered how much different her arrival in the French capital would be this time. Three years ago she'd been dropped into a remote field in the country under cover of night, carrying—among other things—a cyanide capsule. This return trip would be far more civilized.

Glancing around at the other passengers on the flight, Livy saw several single men in suits who wore the haggard look of an official on business as well as a number of holiday travelers. Maybe they just wanted to escape rationing and the nagging specter of London's bomb-flattened cityscape. But would Paris be any different?

Escape—that's what she had in common with the others on the plane. Livy, who didn't like thinking about herself too much, knew this jump across the English Channel might well be lifting the curtain on a new act for her. A second act in which she intended to resolve some loose plot threads left dangling in the first.

Some of Livy's anxiety on the plane began to dissipate as she walked through the terminal at Le Bourget. The ticking clock in her head that usually led her to Black Market Billy for more Polish vodka now eased as she scanned the building for her contact.

The airport itself showed little of the bustle you'd expect from a major city like Paris. The walls and floors had the look of transition about them. Livy wondered if they'd been quickly painted over after liberation, but there hadn't been enough money in the coffers to make it gleam.

Livy passed under an archway with BIENVENUE À PARIS hurriedly stenciled over a peeling gray wall. On the other side of the arch, the airport opened into a bright lobby with large windows that concealed any imperfections in the decor. Several drivers stood there, wearing spotless gray-and-black uniforms and holding signs with the names of hotels such as Crillon and Le Grand.

At the end of the line stood a tall, dapper man holding a placard reading KEMSLEY. Livy sauntered up to him, smiling.

"Miss Nash? Welcome to Paris. I'm Dennis Allard, Kemsley's Paris bureau chief," the tall man said with an old-world bow of his head. "Not that there is much of a bureau to be chief of, at the moment."

Livy guessed him to be in his midforties. He had black hair gone gray on the side that he had swept back rather dramatically from two prominent widow's peaks. She thought he looked like Basil Rathbone as the Sheriff of Nottingham, except in better clothes.

Allard took her case and directed her toward the front of the main building.

"Right, I've got everything taken care of for you. I arranged your flat personally. Have you been to Paris before? Of course you have. Your French is excellent, I hear, so you'll get along nicely with the locals. If you need anything—anything at all—you must ring me at once. I'll pass along my number once you're settled. Right. I'll get my car. I know you've had a long and tiring journey, so just have a rest. You read French as well? Naturally. Here's *Le Monde*. It's de Gaulle's paper, but it has potential, I think. I won't be a moment." Allard dropped the paper in her lap, turned, and headed for the exit, his long legs striding twice the length of everyone else's.

The man had barely given her time to respond, as if nothing she might say could possibly interfere with the plans he'd already made. Everything about him said formal, polished, and absurdly efficient, yet he had a twinkle in his eyes when he smiled and seemed genuinely pleased to see her.

* * *

Forever impatient, Livy nevertheless did as she was told and found a seat where she could peruse the front page of *Le Monde*. A quick scan of the headlines told Livy all she needed to know about France's current politics. The socialists, the communists, and the Christian Democrats shared almost equal space alongside the former president and war hero de Gaulle. In a country where even the government was still officially provisional, telling the good guys from the bad might very well depend on the day.

As she turned the page, a familiar face near the baggage claim caught her gaze. The man stood waiting with a small group of passengers. He glanced in her direction and they locked eyes. Tom Vance was in Paris.

He did an unintentionally comedic double-take punctuated by a quick smile. As he turned and walked toward her, Livy had a chance to size him up. He wore a royal-blue pinstriped double-breasted suit with a white pocket square. Livy had to admit he looked pretty unruffled for a man who'd spent a couple of hours on a plane. But the familiar grin didn't change the fact that his presence here seemed more than a little dodgy.

"The Kemsley office, wasn't it?"

"Beginning to think I'm being followed, Mr. Vance," Livy said, ignoring the joke.

"I'm here for work. How about you? You're one of Fleming's scribblers, huh?" he said, sounding surprised.

"Indeed I am."

"Well, well." He stood bag in hand, an awkward moment as the life of the busy airport unfolded around them. "You know, we just might be here working on the exact same story," he said. "If so, we could help each other."

"And what makes you think we're here for the same reason?"

"I don't know. Funny that we keep bumping into each other, don't you think?"

"As your mum used to say—everything happens for a reason," Livy countered.

"I beg your pardon." A third voice had joined the conversation, and this one sounded straight out of drama school. Allard stood over Vance's left shoulder, the friendly-uncle demeanor now a pursed glower. "May we help you, sir?"

Vance turned, head down, hand out. Deferring to the older man like a good southern boy. "No, no, I was just reintroducing myself to Miss Nash here."

Livy suppressed a grin. Cheeky Yank.

Allard kept the stone-faced look going as Vance retreated.

"Well, I better collect my bag," he said, ruefully smiling at Livy. "Pleasure to see you again, ma'am." Then, to Allard, *"Au revoir,* Jeeves."

True to his word, Vance sauntered back to baggage claim. Allard, trying to master his bristling, turned his smile on again. "The car is just outside, if you're ready." Livy stood and joined him. "Do you actually know that man, Miss Nash?"

"Know him? Hmm, wouldn't say that, no."

"I shouldn't think any respectable woman would."

*   *   *

Allard turned on the English charm on the drive into Paris. Clouds kept the sun away as she caught her first glimpse of the French capital in two years. Allard kept up a sort of tour-director chatter as he turned the gray Renault away from the more rural environs of the airport toward the cluttered sky of the city.

Judging by the crowds at the airport and the smattering of obviously non-Parisians walking the streets, curiosity had driven people back to the great city. Maybe they wanted to see what the Nazis had done to it. Two years after the liberation, Livy was surprised to see the burned husk of a German tank still sitting off the side of the road. The remnants of the brutal occupation lingered for the casual voyeur. People always flocked to the scene of the crime, hoping to catch a glimpse of the corpse or find something left behind by the murderer.

Livy remembered the newsreel of Hitler visiting the Arc de Triomphe, and the tanks rumbling down the Champs-Élysées to begin the long occupation. The clouds over the city darkened as Allard turned off the main road, passing an old woman laboriously pedaling a battered bicycle. Allard downshifted, driving parallel to the Seine, chugging toward the Eiffel Tower.

Glancing into the rearview mirror, Livy noticed a black Peugeot she'd first seen as they left the airport. The car kept a respectable distance but had clearly been with them the entire way.

"You do know we're being followed?"

Allard's eyes never left the road. "Everyone follows everyone here. That car followed me to the airport. Deuxième Bureau by the looks of it."

So, French intelligence knew of her arrival. "And that doesn't bother you?"

"Not in the slightest. We are a legitimate news service. As far as the French are concerned, you may very well be a correspondent."

"Shouldn't we be talking to them? It is their country, after all."

"Miss Nash, no Allied intelligence agency worth its salt would share information with the Frogs right now. The Deuxième Bureau is riddled with Reds. Not to worry, though. I'll drop you off and then lead them on a driving tour of Montmartre. Eventually they'll get tired and leave me be."

Allard whipped the car onto a side street in front of a small block of flats on the Quai de Grenelle, just beyond two large hotels with what had to be breathtaking views of the river and the city's horizon. Allard hit the brakes a bit too hard and parked the car on the walkway in front of number fifty-seven. Now he became her personal bellhop, taking the bags from the boot and up to a small gray doorway with no sign of a knocker or bell.

A tiny woman, wearing a dressing gown with an ornate embroidered Chinese dragon, answered Allard's insistent rapping after a few minutes. The woman's wiry gray hair looked ready to break out of its tight black hairnet.

"*Oui?*" she said, cracking open the door as if they might be burglars.

She cursed under her breath upon seeing suitcases and two guests on her doorstep. The door slammed shut. Livy heard more cursing as the old woman removed the chain, and then the door reopened. Allard stepped inside with Livy's bags and was about to make an introduction when the old woman stopped him.

"*Non,*" she said, holding out a wrinkled hand with freshly painted purple nails.

"Ah, *oui. Pardonnez-moi.*" Allard plopped the bags down, found his wallet, and counted out several hundred francs, which the old woman promptly recounted and slipped into the pocket of her gown. She gave Allard a single key and jerked her head up the stairs.

"Madame Riveaux, Mademoiselle Nash of Kemsley News in London," Allard said.

Madame Riveaux gave Livy a withering glance, shook her head, opened the door behind her, and disappeared into her rooms.

"Electricity is still being rationed here. Hopefully the blackouts don't last too long. Never said this was the Ritz, but then you're not Rita Hayworth, are you?" Allard said as kindly as possible.

The room, which was one of two at the top of the staircase, could manage only a small bed, a small bath, and a small writing desk and chair.

"Wouldn't a visiting English reporter be staying at a hotel?" Livy asked.

"Indeed. That's why most of the hotels are full. The press is flocking back to Paris. But you're not alone. Who do you think is staying in the other rooms?"

Having stowed her bags and opened the curtains of the room's lone window to reveal a view of a brick wall, Allard turned to go. "I'll be back to pick you up around half seven. There are cafés and brasseries closer to the Tower. Right? And don't dress for the theater. The Grand Guignol isn't quite the Paris Opera."

He left her alone.

It might not be the Dorchester, Livy thought, but it was a damn sight more comfortable than the inside of a prison cell at Fresnes.

Chapter Twelve

～

Livy took Allard's advice and wandered away from the Seine toward the Rue St. Charles before settling in a brasserie on a side street. The streets felt at once familiar and new. Livy had grown up listening to her mother talk about this café or that bookshop in her beloved Paris. Because her initial exposure to the City of Light had come during the war, Livy had had very little time to savor the culture and cuisine. Still, the city felt a part of her in a way. Memories of her mother flooded through her mind as she caught snippets of the Parisian dialect and smelled the city's savory scents.

Yet even though she spoke French like a native, Livy had always felt like a British girl in France. That's exactly what she was. To the core.

The restaurant Livy settled on had been one of her favorite haunts during the war. The interior had been given a fresh coat of paint, but otherwise the chairs, the tables, and the bar looked just as they had during the dark days of the occupation. She hoped its ownership had also not changed.

Livy ordered tea first, although she longed for a glass of French wine to ease her nerves. She smiled to find bouillabaisse, a fish stew more often found in the south of France, on the menu. The dish came with small slices of crisp toast, but she decided to skip the garlicky rouille sauce.

Allard's dismissal of French intelligence as being inundated with communists gnawed at her. She knew people in Paris, and if he was right, she just might be able to use that to her advantage.

At the end of her meal, she asked her waiter, a round-faced boy who couldn't be more than seventeen, to give the proprietor a message. She said, "Tell him I'm a friend of André's and I have a message for him." Her French was beginning to feel more like second nature now.

The boy nodded and headed toward the kitchen. Livy hoped the wartime code phrase would provoke a response.

It did.

Minutes later a big man with dark hair and a belly that hung over his dirty apron stepped out of the kitchen. His eyes narrowed as he scanned the patrons. Then he saw her. He waited until he was seated on her right side to finally speak.

"Annette," he said quietly. Hearing her wartime alias sent a shiver through Livy's body. "I was certain you'd been killed."

"Sorry to disappoint, Paul."

Paul Cornet grabbed her hand and kissed it. His thick fingers felt rough and greasy. During the war he had been a liaison between SOE, the Resistance, and Free French Intelligence. Livy hoped some of those old connections remained.

"Here you are again, but I do not think you are a tourist, no?" His strong Marseille dialect was lyrical as ever.

"Clever as always. And the bouillabaisse is better than I remembered."

"But you have not touched the sauce, so stop flattering me and get to the point," he said, his smoky voice rumbling in his chest.

"You still have friends in the Deuxième Bureau?"

"Yes. I have—friends."

"I lost something to one of Stalin's boys, and I need to have a tête-à-tête. Do you think one of your friends might be able to arrange something?"

The big man shifted in his seat. "You ask too much of an old man, Annette."

"Just relay the message. That's all I ask."

Cornet looked around at the other patrons. Drinking, laughing. "Since I am able to run my place now without the Boche, maybe I owe you one. But only one," he said, emphasizing the last two words. "A few of them—Russians—come in here from time to time. We talk. One is older. Smart. I like him. He comes in with a younger one. A hothead. Him I don't like. He smells, too. So I'll see what I can do. But next time—you try the garlic sauce."

* * *

She found Allard waiting outside precisely at seven thirty. They drove back across the Seine into Paris's notorious red-light district known as Quartier Pigalle. While parts of the great city seemed vacant, even depressed, this particular area teemed with people, thanks largely to the number of Allied soldiers still roaming the streets. The neon of Pigalle gleamed in the night.

"Your contact is a Madame Martel. She has your ticket as well as press credentials for your interviews tomorrow," Allard said, whipping the Renault past a line of prostitutes who encircled three American GIs.

"And we're sure Miss Billerant no longer works at the theater?"

"That's my understanding. She left under some sort of cloud about a month ago. Until then she'd worked as a seamstress."

Allard pulled the car over at a corner, free of Parisian *femmes*, and killed the engine. "There are three short plays on the program tonight, running just under two and a quarter hours, so I'll meet you outside the theater at eleven."

The nursemaid act was wearing a bit thin on Livy. However, she didn't know her way around this part of the city, nor did she fancy being accosted tonight by Sergeant Smith from Kansas or whoever, so she nodded and got out of the Renault.

Livy turned off the Rue Chaptal and felt as if she'd stepped back in time fifty years. A few haggard prostitutes stood in doorways, their faces heavy with rouge and lipstick, voices husky from too many cigarettes, calling to male and female audience members en route to the theater's entrance. Gaslight illuminated the narrow alley that housed the Théâtre du Grand-Guignol. Strictly translated, it meant "Big Puppet Theater," but the Grand Guignol was far from a children's playhouse.

Allard had warned her that the theater's reputation was for producing plays that included the most violent aspects of society. Performances routinely depicted graphic murder, torture, and mutilation onstage, all enacted in a way that seemed so real the theater boasted that patrons often fled in the middle of the show in terror.

Livy, whose taste in theater ran more to the classics, walked down the cobblestone alleyway toward the entrance without the sense of dread that other patrons might have felt. She'd seen real horrors in the war. Her mind flashed back to Fresnes and the courtyard after the shell had hit. She remembered soldiers without legs, pieces and parts of bodies here and there.

Tonight, this was just a show.

The building itself could have been a small hotel or row of flats except for the poster on an easel out front with the title Un Crime des une Maison de Fous, accompanied by the lurid image of an eyeless young woman reaching out. Après Coups—Doing the Deed—was another title on the bill. Livy shook her head as she made her way to the front door.

Madame Martel stood next to the box office, scanning the arrivals. Livy guessed her to be about forty-five and more than a bit severe, as she wore a tailored black suit with her dark hair plastered against her head.

"Miss Nash, a pleasure to welcome you." She spoke English with very little trace of an accent. "To be frank, I am surprised a newspaper such as yours would find our theater interesting."

"We thought readers might want to know how the occupation impacted the city's famous nightlife," Livy said, more than pleased with this bit of improvisation.

"As you may know, the theater—like all of Paris—is struggling to regain what we once had. Your story means so much to our work here. Now, we have a box seat for you near the rear of the house, so you can observe the performance as well as the effect it has on the audience."

"Don't worry, madame. I don't scare easy."

Martel led Livy through a small lobby decorated with more blood-soaked posters advertising the theater's previous titles, then down a narrow staircase and into the theater itself. If there had not been a stage and curtains at one end of the space, Livy would have sworn she'd entered a small church. The walls curved upward toward rafters where two carved wooden angels looked down on the seating.

The theater felt small, claustrophobic even, which Livy assumed added to the sensations depicted onstage. Most of the audience sat close to the stage in orchestra-type seating, but a few sat in a small balcony just above. Martel led Livy to one of four private boxes under the balcony.

Martel handed her a program. "So, you watch the show, and then I can answer any questions you might have tomorrow. I hope you are quite comfortable, Miss Nash. Tonight's first play is one of our classics. *Crime in a Madhouse*. A favorite of our audiences. At least those who can make it to the end. So—enjoy the show," she said, with a slightly arched leer.

While the script didn't exactly rival the literary heights of Shakespeare, Livy could see why this particular two-act play of unpleasantness might engage an audience, though they seemed nonplussed by the carnage onstage. She watched as a young Frenchwoman named Louise begged to be released from an asylum only to have her eyes gouged out by a crazy old bird called One-Eye. The grand climax featured two other nutters burning One-Eye's face off on a hot plate and then popping off to take communion.

The gore didn't faze her. She scanned the audience, wondering which woman might be the one who'd reintroduce her to her old friend Luc. To Livy's right, a young couple held on to each other during the shocking finale, but once the lights were restored, they began to laugh. A few rows behind them three young men, who appeared to be university students, whispered, pointing to the exit. One even yawned.

Livy's gaze wandered to Madame Martel, who stood at the bottom of the stairs to the lobby, anxiously watching the audience's reaction.

The lights dimmed again, although the main drape remained closed. *"Mesdames et messieurs, je vous présente Le Grand Diablo!"*

The curtains ruffled, and a short, pudgy man in black tails strolled center into the glow of the footlights. Le Grand Diablo—an interesting linguistic combination—struck a bizarre figure. Completely bald with a mustache curled at the ends and one permanently arched eyebrow, Diablo looked to be the post-gore comic relief. No doubt behind the curtain, stagehands shifted the set for the next bloodbath.

Livy glanced down at the cracked face of her wristwatch and saw Madame Martel note the small gesture.

Onstage, Diablo began an uninspired performance of the interlocking rings. He showed the audience three seemingly solid metal circles and proceeded to pass them through one another effortlessly. After a few tepid claps, he went on to catch some coins out of the air, disappear cards, and—rather effectively—pull razor blades on a string from his mouth.

By now, the audience had warmed up a bit to Le Grand Diablo, so when he asked for a volunteer for his next trick, a few hands went up. Diablo immediately chose a U.S. serviceman sitting in the front row.

The young man, a corporal with a bony frame and freckles, swaggered up to the stage with that same sort of bounce Livy had noted on first meeting Tom Vance. *Maybe Yanks are born with it,* she thought. The corporal stood several inches taller than the magician, which Diablo played for effect, standing alongside the American on tiptoes at one point.

Finally, Diablo brought out a deck of cards and fanned them for the audience. The theater's intimacy aided him, as even Livy, at the back of the house, could see each card clearly.

"Now, peek a cart. Eee-neee cart," Diablo said in a parody of an English-speaking Frenchman, which drew laughs from the crowd as well as the lanky corporal. "Plees shew your cart to zee aww-deence."

The corporal flashed the eight of hearts. Diablo instructed him to place it back in the deck. The American did so, as the magician turned his head. "No peek-eeeng," he said.

Diablo performed a few fancy shuffles, then let the corporal cut the deck once. Then he fanned the cards and reached inside his cutaway coat. He pulled out what looked to be a .38 revolver.

"Now," Diablo said, smiling, "Find yawr kart or—*bang bang.*"

Livy's mouth went dry and she leaned toward the stage. The American, who had retreated a few steps when Diablo produced the gun, snickered nervously at the audience.

"You 'ave a one-in-feeftee-two shans," Diablo said, egging the audience on.

The corporal laughed, shrugged, and reached into the deck. Livy held her breath

"Eees zat yawr kart, monsieur?"

The American looked at the card, chuckled, and shook his head.

"Zen what ees eet?"

Livy knew what the card would be before the corporal turned it to the audience. It was the ace of spades.

Diablo then fanned the deck. Every single card had become an ace of spades.

"Eet ees not your luk-ee day, monsieur," Diablo said, grinning. He cocked the hammer on the revolver and fired. The sound of the shot reverberated throughout the tiny space, eclipsed only by the scream from the audience.

But when the noise died down and the smoke from the barrel dissipated, the audience saw the American serviceman bent over, his hands over his head. On the other side of the stage, Diablo's gun had a sign hanging from the barrel that read BANG!

Livy couldn't get her breath. A fist held her chest tight in its grip. She felt as if she'd gone right back to the prison just before the mortar fell and turned everything to jam.

The audience began to laugh, slowly at first, but as the image of the short, fat French magician with the cartoon gun aimed at the nervous skinny all-American corporal sunk in, the cackling grew louder.

Livy put a hand on her chest, closed her eyes, and gasped for air. Her head reeled from the escalating laughter and the smell of the gunpowder.

Madame Martel appeared beside her box. "Miss Nash, are you unwell?"

Livy stood up, excused herself, and rushed out of the box as the laughter morphed into applause for Diablo. She half stumbled through the lobby of the theater and out the front door. She bent over and tried not to throw up. As her stomach calmed, she leaned back against the stone facade of the entrance and felt her breath slowly coming back.

But the ever-present Madame Martel stood behind her. "Please, madame," Livy managed, "give me a minute."

"I'm afraid the mademoiselle ate something earlier that didn't agree with her," a man said.

"And you are?" Martel asked.

"Tom Vance, *United Press.*"

Chapter Thirteen

❦

Vance calmed Martel enough so she believed her theater's performance hadn't left a visiting English reporter violently ill. That gave Livy time to compose herself so she could at least breathe freely without fear of her legs crumbling underneath her.

Still, what she had just witnessed onstage couldn't have been coincidence. Nathalie, her contact, had worked at the Grand Guignol recently. Seeing that card trick was no more chance than Tom Vance showing up in Paris again.

Still, Livy wondered if her embarrassing exit had blown any chance of meeting the contact. How could she now, surrounded by the Yank and this fawning Frenchy?

With Martel successfully shooed back inside, Vance stepped down where Livy leaned against the building.

"You all right there, Miss Nash?"

"I'll be fine," she said, stepping away from him. Livy needed time to think.

"Now, I can see how the dismemberment might have made you queasy, but that magician? Unless, of course, you're offended by the excessively corny."

"You're missing the rest of the show, Mr. Vance."

"Aren't you sweet?" he said. "I just wanted to make sure you're hunky-dory." He pulled out a pack of Camels and offered her the pack.

"Don't smoke."

"Might help calm you down," he said. Livy shook her head. "Suit yourself." He lit himself one, drawing the smoke in deeply. "I have no choice in the matter. Sort of the family business."

Livy's head had stopped doing cartwheels, so she turned to face the nattily dressed Vance. "Thought you were a journalist."

"Well, I am. Just like you," he said, flashing that smile. "But the family money's in tobacco."

"Fascinating, but I do have an early meeting—" Livy turned to step off the sidewalk and stumbled on the cobblestones, catching herself before falling outright.

Vance lent her a hand, which Livy accepted and then quickly brushed off.

"Look, we keep running into each other. There's gotta be something to that. Why don't you let me buy you a little something to calm that weak stomach," he said. "I think there might be a café around here where the waiters keep their clothes on. Whattya say?"

*   *   *

Half an hour later Livy sat at a small table in a café a few blocks from the Pigalle. Vance babied her, ordering her a cup of tea and white toast with strawberry jam. He had an espresso and what appeared to be a ham sandwich. He ate with a certain relish that belied his expensive clothes and rich-boy affect.

"So, theater aficionado, are you, Mr. Vance?" Livy said between sips of the rather disappointing Earl Grey. Mrs. Sherbourne would have been appalled.

"I think we're acquainted well enough for you to call me Tom," he said, munching a razor-thin sandwich. "But I think we were there for the same reason."

"You're writing an article about the Grand Guignol? How patrons view it in light of the real horror of the war, concentration camps, et cetera, et cetera?"

Vance didn't miss a beat. "Well, of course," he said, sipping his coffee. "They don't make it here like they do at the Dorchester."

"That's an espresso," Livy countered. "Be happy it's not acorns."

"Oh, I am."

"So we happen to be in the same city again, working on the very same story. I wonder, where did you spend your war, *Mister* Vance? The tobacco fields, I suppose?"

Vance bristled slightly. "Oh, you know, I was here and there. You?"

"I sat at home and darned socks for the RAF."

Vance shook his head. "My guess is you were making life hard for the Germans in the wilds of France."

Livy drank tea.

"Didn't get enough of this during the war? Aren't you sick of it?"

"Oh, are we being honest with each other now?"

Vance shrugged. "You first."

"We all saw things we'd prefer to forget. Didn't you, when you were 'here and there'?"

Putting his espresso back in its small saucer, Vance shot his cuffs and straightened his tie. "Okay. Cards on the table. I was a Jedburgh. With some of your boys."

Livy had known one or two others in the Firm who'd joined Jedburgh teams. The operation paired American and British agents with a French Resistance fighter. The Jedburgh teams parachuted behind Nazi lines late in the war to prepare for the Allied invasion. Many of them had been shot down, captured, or executed in prison.

"No women allowed on the Jeds," Livy said.

"Well, it's no fun taking machine gun fire when you're dangling at the end of a parachute."

"I suppose not."

Truth was, Livy liked this man. Maybe it was that southern American accent, but he seemed so damned genuine. Still, his presence at the Grand Guignol made her question everything. Vance's meeting with Fleming. The Dorchester. That long kiss while the cab waited. Her feelings for him, if that's what she had, would have to wait. In this line of work, there were no such things as coincidences, and right now she trusted Tom Vance as far as she could throw the Eiffel Tower.

Livy dug a few coins out of her clutch purse and put them on the table. "I hope it won't offend your *Gone With the Wind* sense of chivalry if I pay for myself. I believe I owe you one anyway, and I really do have an early—"

"Livy, we want the exact same thing," Vance said, dropping the Rhett Butler act.

"Really now, me mum raised me right."

Vance ignored her parry. "I meant we are on the same side."

"Oh? What side would that be?"

He leaned toward her. His voice low. Tobacco and the pine scent in his cologne mixed in a very pleasurable way. "Livy, London was about something different. You know that. But now—well, this isn't a game."

"I was never any good at sport anyway," Livy said, standing. "Good night, Mr. Vance. I feel reasonably certain we'll see each other again."

* * *

Livy didn't mention Diablo's entr'acte or the second appearance of Tom Vance to Allard on the drive back. As far as the older man knew, she had gone to the theater for an evening of blood and guts in an attempt to contact Nathalie Billerant, and the contact hadn't shown. Still in the process of figuring out what both of the night's events meant, Livy felt it best to keep the full story to herself.

Allard dropped her off at Madame Riveaux's boarding-house a few minutes after eleven with a promise to return the next morning. She had a follow-up interview at the theater with select members of the Grand Guignol staff.

The search for Nathalie had better bear fruit tomorrow, Livy thought. Deep down she feared she'd blown the best chance to make contact, get the list, and arrange a meeting with Valentine.

Exhausted from the evening and from keeping up appearances with both Allard and Vance, Livy looked forward to a long bath and a longer nap in her tiny bed.

As she closed the main entrance behind her, the landlady's door popped open. Madame Riveaux, wearing the same Oriental dressing gown, stood in her doorway, holding a piece of paper between her thumb and index finger.

"For me?" Livy asked.

The Frenchwoman shook the paper at Livy as if ringing a bell.

Livy took the note with a quick *"Merci,"* and the landlady disappeared into her room like a turtle retreating into the comfort of its shell. Livy unfolded the paper. There, written in a very precise hand, was the address of Paul Cornet's café near Rue Saint-Charles where she'd eaten that afternoon.

Just when she'd thought all might be lost, it appeared her afternoon visit with an old friend might actually bear fruit.

Ten minutes later, Livy found herself back at the café. Then the mystery of the note quickly faded. Grant Duncan, the charming Scot from the French Embassy party, sat at a round wooden table being kept company by a bottle of vodka, two glasses, and what appeared to be a small plate of caviar.

She felt like the naive girl in a Peter Lorre picture, the one who ends up kidnapped or murdered.

"It is a small world," Duncan said. He didn't sound like Grant Duncan at all. Rather, he sounded like he'd grown up eating borscht and reading Chekhov.

"Didn't you used to be a Scot?"

"Didn't you used to be French?"

Ice effectively broken, the tall man stood and offered Livy a seat.

"I have a gift for dialect, as do you," he said, now sounding more like Stalin's educated brother. "But I assure you, this is my natural way of speaking. And I assume this charming British accent is also your own?"

"It is."

"Splendid. Well, now that we have shed our disguises, perhaps you would like a drink. You look like a woman who might appreciate vodka," he said.

"I used to."

"Used to? No, no, you must try this."

The Russian lifted the sleek bottle from the table and poured two shots into glasses in front of him. He pushed one over to Livy.

"Best vodka from Siberia. This is the only place in Paris that has it. It is called Five Lakes. Go ahead. Drink."

Livy had a sip. It went down like smooth acid.

"Yes? Now, *that's* Russian vodka." The man who wasn't Duncan seemed very pleased playing host. "Now try the caviar. One taste for each drink." Livy followed his advice but didn't tell him both the booze and caviar did her queasy stomach no favors.

"At home we have to get three people to buy one bottle," he said. "In Paris, I can have as much as I want."

"So, you are—who, exactly?' she asked.

"I am Andrei Ivanovich Mirov and you are Olivia Nash. The owner here is a friend. He said you wished to speak. But can we not enjoy a simple drink before we talk business? Please. We have no more Hitler, and this beautiful city is free of the vermin. Enjoy."

Livy pushed the glass away, even though this had to be the smoothest vodka she had ever tasted, and leaned across the table. "Look, Mr. Mirov, I've had a long day, so you'll forgive me if I skip the pleasantries. That night at the embassy in London, one of your boys took something of mine and left me with this little bruise right on my cheek. But I'm willing to let bygones be bygones as long as I recover my property."

"I apologize for my nephew's rude behavior. Levchenko is ill-tempered at times. His father was Ukranian," he offered as explanation.

Livy massaged her temples, trying to clear her head. Fatigue and the drink clouded her mind. She knew this moment demanded all her focus.

Finally, she said, "Yeah, your boy packs a wallop. You teach him how to do that?"

Mirov smiled. "He is a fanatic. Like others back home. But I believe we can work together. We do not have to be brutes."

"Well, brutes don't drink this kinda booze," Livy said. "But I'm trying to cut back on the libations, and you're still not saying anything I want to hear."

"We could share the list."

"Then why did your boy take it from me?"

"I had to make sure it was authentic."

"And?"

"It is."

"Brilliant. Then perhaps you'd like to return it."

Mirov's bright eyes danced as he downed another shot. "Even in my position, I can't get a drink like that at home. We sacrifice so much for the state. To create utopia. Hmm. We have a long way to go."

He leaned toward her, as if to share a very spicy secret. "I have the first half of the list, so perhaps I have the upper hand. Other than that, I know nothing. Except I know that you are here to get the rest, and there is something about you that tells me you have, maybe, an idea how to find it. Now, we could each keep our halves of the list and carve up the agents like we have with everything in Berlin and Vienna. Or we could work together. Our countries were allies in the war, yes? I have no quarrel with the British. I respect your spies. I do. You are professionals. We can work together, because we both know who would like to put us out of business."

Livy poured herself another shot. She had no intention of drinking it, but she needed the time to think. Sharing the Mephisto network with the Soviets was a no-go, but she wondered how she might use the offer to her advantage.

"Mr. Mirov, the Yanks may lack subtlety, but at least one of them didn't slap me across the face with a silencer."

"Vance is following you. He's been following you since you left London."

"And how do you know this?"

"Because *we* followed you, too."

"Of course." Her mouth felt dry. Instinctively she reached for the shot, but she just cradled it in her hand.

"Miss Nash, no one knows what the world is going to be like now that the war is over. It's chance. All Vance and the Americans really want is to sell Coca-Cola," he said, pronouncing the name just like an American. "Coca-Cola everywhere. All over the world. That's their highest calling now. Soft drink."

"And what are you selling? Gulags? Bread lines?"

Mirov wagged a finger at her. "Now, now, you will get me into trouble, and we are enjoying each other's company. I am not here to make apologies for world socialism. There are many here in France, and even in your own country, who see its merits."

"Yeah, I heard you were invading Paris by parachute."

"Yes, and a few weeks ago we helped the French communists plan a coup d'etat." Mirov smirked. "Some people will say anything to get the Americans to come to the rescue."

"People like their Coca-Cola."

Mirov leaned back and laughed. "You even make jokes like a Russian. You know, I have a daughter, a few years younger than you. She is afraid of me. Truly, she is." His voice became softer and his eyes fell to the table. "She knows who I work for, what we do, and she—um—she won't look me in the face anymore." Then, as quickly as the melancholy hit him, it disappeared like his Scottish accent. "But you and I, we can work together to do something good, you see?"

"I'll give it some thought," Livy stood. "You don't really have a daughter, do you?"

Mirov shrugged with a grand, theatrical gesture.

The dark circles under her eyes felt like they had weight. "Thanks for the drink, luv."

As she walked back to Madame Riveaux's, Livy stuck to nearly empty side streets, following the breeze from the Seine a few blocks ahead. Despite her exhaustion, she considered her position. Tom Vance wanted her on his side. As did Mirov. But the Russian had made a firm offer. Still, Livy could tell he'd been playing her. That phony story about his daughter. This is what it must feel like to be caught between Scylla and Charybdis. The glow of the lights on the river came into view as she turned on to the Quai de Grenelle. Hands in her coat pockets, she caught herself walking conspicuously fast. A sure sign she felt overwhelmed. Sleep now. Face the two monsters on either side tomorrow. Even Odysseus needed rest.

*　*　*

The next morning Livy woke with a distant hangover that reminded her of mornings when she worked at the P&J. The bitter tang of the alcohol felt thick on her tongue, and she scolded herself for taking even two shots. Her body still craved it, but she knew drinking stood in her way on this job—and the rest of her life, for that matter. Besides, what would Mrs. O'Toole say to a young woman drinking vodka with a Soviet spy in a Parisian café? *Ooh la la.*

She dressed quickly, deciding on the gray suit with a tapered skirt and jacket, fitted at the waist. The outfit came with a matching fedora with a black band and wide brim. When she pulled it over her left eye, she reminded herself a bit of Ingrid Bergman in *Casablanca*. Lipstick on, she admired herself in the bath mirror and grinned. *Eat your heart out, Humphrey Bogart.*

She still didn't know how to handle Vance or the charming Comrade Mirov, but she felt purpose. The one thing neither the Yanks nor the Soviets had was Claude and his information about Nathalie, the Mephisto seductress. Finding Nathalie topped her agenda for the day.

An insistent rapping at her door put those thoughts on hold. She considered picking up the Webley but decided against it. Her press credentials from the Kemsley Group ought to be the only weapon she'd need. No one could dispute that.

She opened the door.

Three men stood in the hallway. The man in front wore tweeds and had a pipe clenched between his teeth. Two younger men in U.S. Army uniforms with black MP armbands around their considerable biceps flanked him.

"Miss Olivia Nash?" the older man said, looking at her through black spectacles. "I apologize for the early hour, but we need you to come outside with us. Now. If you please."

Chapter Fourteen

Minutes later, Livy and the ranking Yank sat on an iron bench overlooking the Seine across the street from Madame Riveaux's. The two younger flatheads stood about ten feet away as if to guard the perimeter, even though only a few older couples passed by on their morning walks.

The professorial type, who identified himself as Charles Gray of the American Embassy, had a lean, studious look. His Harris Tweed jacket, which definitely was out of season, and horn-rimmed glasses gave him an air of academic condescension.

Gray smiled easily and often, although he had a way about him, as if he was used to giving orders and having people follow them. "Miss Nash, it's come to our attention that we might be working at cross-purposes."

Livy returned Gray's smile. "I'm not sure I follow you."

"I'm pretty sure you do. You have inserted yourself in the middle of an ongoing United States War Department operation. So I'm asking you to step back and let us take this one."

"I'm only here to file a story for my editor. About the Grand Guignol theater," Livy said, handing him her press card.

Gray looked it over. "Kemsley? That's Ian Fleming's show, isn't it?"

"Mr. Fleming's the foreign manager, yes."

Gray's smile evaporated as he handed the card back. "Let me be frank, Miss Nash," he said, pulling his pipe from his lips for effect. "I seriously doubt you have any idea what you have gotten yourself into. I knew Commander Fleming during the war. He served his country well, I'll give him that. But even then he had a lot of—how shall I put it?—cockamamy ideas that just didn't pan out. Now you're telling me he's back in journalism and playing spy? Fine. That's none of my concern. But if I may offer you a bit of advice . . . I'd be very wary of whatever it is Mr. Fleming might have told you and sent you out here to do, because you have stepped in the proverbial pile of horseshit. Pardon my French."

Livy didn't miss a beat. "I have several interviews scheduled today, as well as a deadline I have to meet. So I can assure you I don't have time for horseshit."

Gray replaced his pipe and nodded at the young MPs behind him. They walked away in double time. Then he leaned in toward Livy, the morning sun glinting off his glasses.

"You were observed last night having a drink with a well-known Soviet MGB agent. We both know what's going on here, Miss Nash, so let's not play games. Our countries are allies. We have a—a special relationship. Sometimes little miscommunications, such as this, become much larger than they need be. I'm asking you—in a very collegial manner—to step away from what you're doing in Paris. The next time we speak—if there is a next time—I will not ask." He stood up, replaced the pipe in his mouth, and gave a slight awkward bow. "I do hope you enjoy the rest of your time in Paris."

Livy watched the Americans stroll off in the direction of the Eiffel Tower.

First Tom Vance had tried to cozy up to her. Then Mirov. Now some Yank she'd never heard of was trying to give her orders. She looked out over the river and wondered if these same men might try to tell the Seine which way to flow. Of course they would. She stood up, straightened her skirt, and decided—from here on out—to go her own way.

* * *

Later that morning Livy sat behind Allard in his Renault as they navigated the busy streets of the Saint-Germain-des-Prés quarter.

Livy had nursed a dull ache behind her eyes since her meeting with the professorial Mr. Gray. Her thoughts felt jumbled and she hated being chauffeured.

"So, I assume we're being followed? Again?"

"Of course." His dark eyes flashed to the rearview. "Dark-blue Morris this time. I'd say it's the Russians."

"Then lose them."

"I beg your pardon."

If her first day in Paris had taught her anything, it was that she needed breathing room if she was going to get this job done.

"Lose the tail, if you don't mind."

Allard glared at her in the rearview. "I'm not used to taking orders from our correspondents, Miss Nash."

"Look, everyone may follow everyone in this town, but I've had it with people being in my business, so I say we take the initiative and try to regain the upper hand."

"I see your point. It does become tiresome."

Allard flicked his eyes back to the road, then took a hairpin left on Quai Voltaire. He accelerated into the turn. Livy grinned. She turned, glancing out the back window. Cars and bicycles filled the street. It looked like a bloody Grand Prix. But there, flashing out into the far lane, sped a blue Morris.

The Renault continued to accelerate as they sped toward the Champs-Élysées, keeping the Seine on their right. Livy leaned back in her seat as the Pont Alexandre III appeared in the distance ahead. Allard swerved in and out of traffic, moving between lanes. Then, just before reaching the Pont de l'Alma, he veered into the outer lane and spun the steering wheel into a hard right turn. The force of the change threw Livy against the opposite door. He was taking them to the Champs-Élysées.

"Didn't know you had it in you," she said as the car shuddered into a hard left turn.

"You can leave the driving to me, Miss Nash."

A look in the rearview told Livy the Morris was still following, two cars behind.

Allard kept the speed steady so as not to alert the police as the Renault maneuvered through the traffic of the city's most famous street. But instead of heading for more open road, Allard sped toward the worst roundabout in Europe: the Arc de Triomphe. As they surged up the avenue, Allard kept to his strategy of quick lane changes. Up ahead a mass of cars clung to the inner lanes near the arc, four and five cars beside one another. Allard downshifted, creeping toward the pileup. He glanced in the rearview. The cars ahead came to a halt, allowing those coming from the northwest to enter.

Another glance to the mirror.

Allard shifted. The car lurched forward as the engine roared and the Renault sped into the outside lanes, slicing in front of two other slower-moving cars. Horns blared. Livy heard shouts from the open windows, but Allard kept the pedal down. She turned and spotted the blue Morris jammed between two cars on the inside lanes. The Renault emerged from the pack of cars and sped up the Avenue de la Grande Armée. Livy barely had time to catch her breath from that perilous maneuver before Allard jammed on the brakes and turned into the first narrow side street just beyond the notorious Avenue Foch, where the Germans had held prisoners for torture during the occupation.

The car slammed to a halt. Allard turned around, watching the traffic. After a minute, his dark eyebrows relaxed.

"They just passed us," he said. "And now what?"

"Now you let that blue Morris find you again, and I'll have myself a little walk." She gave the older man a genuine smile and eased herself out of the back seat. "And well done, Mr. Allard."

*   *   *

About forty minutes later Livy had walked across the city to the Pigalle district and the home of the Théâtre du Grand-Guignol. She'd taken a couple of detours to make sure no one had followed her, but after Allard's evasive driving she felt certain she was alone.

The approach to the theater felt much less intimidating by day. Last night these doorways had been alive with young women, and a couple of men, offering their services to the theater's patrons. By day, the doorways remained closed. She still had ten minutes before Madame Martel expected her, so Livy found a cozy one, about a hundred feet away from the theater's main entrance, and ducked in. The doorway was recessed so far from the street it felt like an alcove. Albeit one with dozens of cigarette butts underfoot.

So, she thought, *now what?*

She'd been in Paris less than twenty-four hours and had been approached by a Soviet agent and his American counterparts. The Russians seemed to want to work with her and the Yanks wanted her to cease and desist. Cease and desist what exactly? How seriously should she take the warning from Gray? He'd threatened her before popping off, and those bulky military coppers probably weren't his cousins.

Gray's sly jabs at Fleming gave her pause, though. True, he was the sort of cad she'd like to punch, and that office with the ridiculous light-up world map only added to his adolescent credentials. *Just the sort of bloke they like at MI6, actually.*

No, clearly she'd wandered into a minefield and the boys were worried she might make something go bang.

She took a glance down the alley. Livy hoped she'd find answers inside that theater. Nathalie, the contact, had worked there. Plus there was the matter of that fat magician and the ace-of-spades card trick.

Gray was right about the pile of horseshit, she decided. But then she was from Lancashire, and Lanky girls knew how to avoid the piles.

Livy stepped into the alley just in time to see Tom Vance strolling out the front door of the theater headed her way. *Damn him.* Right on her heels again. Taking a hurried step back into the recessed doorway, Livy rattled the knob. Behind the door, a torrent of French curse words erupted. The door opened and a very short, plump woman with red hair, a beauty mark above her lip, wearing nothing but a garter belt on her right leg, stood in the opening.

"Qu'est-ce que vous fais?" The short woman sounded like a munchkin from Oz.

Vance would be passing her in a second. Livy pushed past the little naked woman with a brusque *"Pardon"* and lost herself in the darkness of the smoke and sex-smell of the flat. The munchkin turned her bare ass to the door just as Vance walked past. He glanced in, smirked, and continued on his way.

Livy caught her breath and reached into her purse. She placed two francs in the little woman's hand, at the same time hushing her with a finger over her lips. Just then she heard a shuffling behind and turned to find what had to be the little woman's identical-twin brother—also naked except for a garter on his right leg. The naked man held his hand out as well.

*   *   *

Madame Martel had croissants with whipped butter and jam as well as tea ready for her second reporter of the morning. Livy assumed Martel was plying her with breakfast, especially after her queasy-stomach incident the night before.

Livy graciously accepted and straightaway launched into background questions with the slant of how Martel felt the war might impact the theater's box office. She raved about last night's performance, inquired after the hilariously devilish magician Diablo (of whom she got a useless standard biography), and then, oh so subtly, asked about her American's counterpart's angle.

Smiling the whole time, Martel denied that Monsieur Vance of the United Press had been to the theater that morning.

One croissant later, Livy asked to interview any theater personnel who might be working that morning. The *artistes*, madame explained, gave their all during a long week of eight shows and therefore were entitled to rest during the day. So no Diablo. She did offer Livy the chance to speak to one of the theater's on-site playwrights whose revenge tragedies followed in the line of great English writers such as Webster and Shakespeare.

Livy doubted John Gielgud had ever had his face melted on a stove during *Hamlet*.

After a brief tour of the stage itself, which could not have been more than twenty feet square, Martel showed Livy backstage, where furniture and set pieces for the current shows in repertory were jammed up against a concrete wall. Martel shuttled Livy in the direction of a burly stagehand who looked a bit like a character from one of the plays, as scar tissue covered almost the entire right side of his face. She talked to a woman who did makeup and offered to build a few scars on Livy's face. She declined.

Finally, Madame Martel excused herself to take a call in the box office. Livy accepted her unctuous apologies and wandered backstage until she found a large, nondescript metal door with a sign reading L'ENTRÉE DES ARTISTES. Livy pushed it open.

Daylight stunned her eyes for a second. What a shift, leaving the shadow world of the Grand Guignol's backstage to walk into the brilliant sunlight of a Parisian noon.

The door opened onto a wooden loading dock about four feet above street level. Rubbish bins for the whole block dominated the alley outside the theater. Garbage was stacked up against the opposite wall and for another fifty yards down until the alley intersected with a busy street.

Livy turned to go back inside then realized that a young woman sat on the edge of the loading dock just a few feet to her right. The dark-red check dress she wore camouflaged her slightly against the brick of the adjacent building. She sat kicking her legs, smoking a cigarette, savoring each puff.

"*Bonjour.*"

Livy's greeting startled the girl. She turned as if to stand, registered who had called, then resumed her nonchalant cigarette break after giving Livy the briefest of nods.

This morning's carefully choreographed interviews with Martel and her chosen workers had been a waste of time. Something about the girl's lackadaisical response made Livy suspect that this reticent young woman taking a break on the dock might be worth a chat.

"*Avez-vous une autre cigarette?*" Livy asked.

She didn't smoke, but she knew that you didn't deny a stranger a cigarette if you had a pack.

The girl produced a pack of Gauloises and held it in Livy's direction. Livy took one and begged a light. With a sigh, the girl flicked her a pack of matches. Putting the cigarette between her lips, Livy turned the box over and saw the name of a club printed in faded letters on the outside. It read CHEZ MOUNE.

"*Merci*," Livy said, handing the matchbox back to her. She took a quick draw on the cigarette, which made her gag just a bit. She quickly pulled it out.

"You work here at the theater?" Livy asked in French.

The girl gave her a look. "Where are you from?"

"London."

They both laughed.

"You speak French like a hillbilly," the girl said, picking tobacco from her lower lip.

"I'm a reporter from an English paper," Livy said. "I had to get outside for some air. Martel runs a tight ship in there."

The girl scoffed and turned away. "It's all about the money now."

"It wasn't always like that?"

"Are you writing this down?"

"No."

The girl let out a long puff of smoke. "They are afraid of losing their audience. Maybe now no one is shocked by all this anymore. They sell magazines with pictures from the Nazi camps at the newsstands. That's the real horror show."

A moment passed between the two women then. Just a moment where Livy dropped the mask of the reporter copping a fag and the girl on the dock saw the real Livy. She saw the pain behind Livy's eyes and seemed to recognize that this reporter had experienced the "real horror" that some postwar Parisians craved.

The girl said nothing about it. She only said, "I'm Lorraine."

"Livy."

Livy sat down next to her on the dock and put the cigarette between her lips. She took a short puff and tried not to cough.

"What do you do here, Lorraine?"

"I'm just half-time. I sew costumes, repair them mostly. They get torn a lot. My father works here, so he set me up with this."

Livy nodded, taking another quick drag.

"You don't smoke, do you?" Lorraine said.

"That obvious, is it?"

"We got used to telling who was on whose side during the occupation," Lorraine said. "You had to be careful. Anyone could have been working for the Boche, so you looked for little lies to tip you off.

"My guess is you're not really a reporter, or not much of one, at least."

"Maybe not much of one, no." She dropped the cigarette and crushed it on the street. *Girl couldn't be more than nineteen*, Livy thought, *and she saw right through me*. "But don't tell Madame Martel. I'd hate to see a grown woman cry."

"If she cried, that would mean she had a heart," Lorraine said, rolling her eyes.

"I'm here to find someone," Livy said, hesitating. She didn't know if being direct would work, but it seemed her only option. "A woman who used to work here."

"Do you know how many girls have worked here since the liberation? I can't count. This place has a revolving door, and it spits them right back out into the Pigalle."

"I'm looking for Nathalie Billerant."

Lorraine blanched a bit, nodded, and took the last drag on her Gauloise. "Is she part of your story?"

"I'm looking for her because of a man she knows, a man I need to find."

"Nathalie knows a lot of men. A lot of women, too," Lorraine said, stubbing out her cigarette and standing.

"I've no quarrel with Nathalie. She said she wanted to meet me about this man. It's him I'm here to find."

"They're going to expect me back inside, so . . ." Lorraine said. She stopped, glanced back at the stage door, and softly said, "Listen, you tell me something I want to know and I'll tell you where you might find Nathalie."

"I'll do what I can."

"This man you're looking for—he did something to you?"

"Yes. You could say that."

"Tell me what he did."

Livy hesitated. Lorraine didn't. She turned toward the stage door.

"Hold on," Livy said, sighing as she thought about what to say. God, she was bad at this. The hell with *it*. *This job has been a cock-up so far*. What did she have to lose?

"Yeah, he hurt me," Livy said. "He killed someone I— someone I cared for. Very much."

"This man you want worked for the Boche?"

"Yes, he's French and he worked for the Germans. *Un collaborateur*," Livy said.

Lorraine grabbed the knob of the stage door. She held it hard, and the anger radiated up her arm and through her small body.

What's this girl's story? Livy wondered. She knew that every Parisian, every European had her own pain from the last six years.

"My father moves the sets here. You've seen him, yes? What they did to his face? I'll help you find this bastard—for him.

The Hotel Ritz. It's a room on the third floor, something like three twelve or three fourteen."

* * *

Two hours later Livy had made her way to the third floor of one of the most prestigious hotels in the world and stood outside suite 314. One of the maids on the floor had been nice enough to share a bit of her life story with Livy before volunteering that "that mademoiselle never left three fourteen," making the suite impossible to clean.

Sometimes it pays just to listen, Livy thought.

She didn't exactly have a plan for what might happen when the door opened, but she felt closer than ever now to Edward Valentine, and the bull didn't ask the china if it minded being smashed.

Livy knocked on the door and waited. Three, maybe four minutes passed. The door opened. On the other side stood a gorgeous woman, about Livy's age, with sad blue eyes. She wore a silk dressing gown and held a nasty-looking Beretta, pointed at Livy's chest.

No one spoke for a long moment.

Then Nathalie Billerant's finger tightened on the trigger and she said, "Get out of the hall and close the door, or I'll shoot you where you stand."

Chapter Fifteen

~

Livy eased into the foyer of the suite and closed the door, keeping her eye on Nathalie and the gun the whole time. They stood in a ten-foot-long walkway that led to the room itself. Behind Nathalie, Livy got a glimpse of gold elegance: rugs that gleamed and an opulent sitting area that looked out on a breathtaking view of the city.

"Who are you?"

A complicated question, requiring a very precise answer, or else she might be unavailable for future inquiries.

Like they'd taught her at SOE camp, the best lie had elements of truth. "Olivia Nash. I'm a reporter."

Nathalie blinked. Not the answer she'd expected. She didn't move the gun, though. Livy knew she meant business, and judging by the lack of any perspiration on her brow or her trigger finger, there was a good chance she had used that little pistol before.

Luc could pick 'em, no doubt, Livy thought. This woman looked like she belonged at the Ritz. Even though she'd probably had only enough time to grab her dressing gown and pistol before opening the door, she looked like a million francs.

Her brown hair, cut in a timeless bob, framed a perfectly symmetrical face with lips just this side of pouty and eyes that shimmered even as they narrowed.

"I don't believe you," she said. "Tell me why you're here right now, or I'll shoot."

Livy understood now. Nathalie was scared. That made her dangerous.

"I was sent here to talk to you."

Livy could see she'd said the wrong thing. Nathalie's eyes blazed. Her whole body seemed to stiffen. "Did he follow you?"

"I wasn't followed."

"How do you know? Hmm? He's clever. He knows what he's doing. You could have led him right to me."

A million questions swirled through Livy's head, but she had to focus on keeping this almost hysterical woman from shooting her. She put her hands in front of her slowly to show she meant no harm.

"I made sure I wasn't followed. I promise."

"Then how did you find me?" Nathalie brought the gun up higher, pointing it at Livy's head. They couldn't have been more than six feet apart. Livy had nowhere to hide.

"I asked at the theater, where you used to work. They told me. Look, luv, I wasn't followed and I don't mean you any harm. I came here for you. You asked for help, and I'm here. At your request. Just be a bit careful with that. Guns tend to go off from time to time."

"The British sent you?" She held the Beretta steady, but her trigger finger seemed a tad too jumpy for Livy's liking.

"That's right. Put your gun down and we can talk. That's all I'm here for."

For a brief moment, the hardness left Nathalie's eyes, and Livy believed she might actually put the gun away and they could get down to business. But a thought flickered in the Frenchwoman's eyes, and just like that the moment evaporated.

"Tell me your name again?" Nathalie said, the hysteria back in her voice. The jumpiness shook her trigger finger.

"Olivia Nash."

"*Menteuse!*" Nathalie hissed. "Filthy liar! Get out. Get out now!"

More than a bit confused about what she was supposed to be lying about, Livy backed toward the door. She hoped Nathalie might make the novice mistake of getting too close with the gun so Livy could risk disarming her. But this woman knew how to use a weapon. She held her ground, even steadied it with both hands.

Maybe it was the tension of being held at gunpoint. Maybe it was the thought that if she managed to stay alive, she might leave the room empty-handed. Livy's face suddenly felt hot and her jaw clenched. She'd faced off against rougher customers than this bit o' crumpet.

"Do you know how loud that gun is going to be when you fire it?" she said, snapping. "Have you thought about that? Or what you'll do with my body? Toss it out the window, maybe?"

Nathalie blinked but held the gun steady.

"I don't believe you've thought this through, have you, luv?" Livy went on. Bravado aside, she was one bad decision away from bleeding all over the expensive Ritz rug.

"We're alone, all right? I know your boyfriend, sweetie, and you can be bloody well sure he didn't follow me."

"My boyfriend?" Nathalie asked.

"Valentine."

Nathalie's eyes widened and, unbelievably, the corners of her mouth turned up in a grin. "Edward?" she said. Then she laughed, a sort of exhalation that seemed to release her whole body from the tension that had held it so tight.

She kept the gun aimed, though.

The spasm of relief passed, and Nathalie looked hard at Livy, the smile gone. "I am a single woman, a guest of this hotel—the finest in Paris. You are an intruder. I have a right to protect myself. Maybe you are a communist. They are everywhere, you know. No one would blame me for shooting a communist. So my advice to you, Mademoiselle Nash, is to leave quietly and remember—I will find you."

Livy didn't have much choice. She eased toward the door, her hand feeling for the knob. Nathalie stepped forward, gun ready.

As she heard the click on the latch, Livy stopped. "When Edward does come back, tell him I look forward to our reunion."

That did it. The hard mask of Nathalie Billerant's face fell for a second. Livy saw the recognition and confusion her words caused. The Frenchwoman's luscious mouth fell open and her eyes flashed again. Livy didn't hesitate. She'd spent quite enough time staring at the unpleasant end of *le mademoiselle*'s metal friend.

Closing the door to the suite, Livy trotted across the elegant carpet toward the third-floor lift. Her heartbeat raced and her breath came in staccato spurts. She hoped she'd gone the right direction for the lift; she didn't fancy a double back. Then she heard the ding and the ornate doors opened. She stepped inside the thankfully empty car and slumped against the back wall. Livy pressed the lobby button, trying to normalize her breath.

She had only two floors to get herself together. Livy adjusted her jacket and smoothed her hair. God, she felt so clear. This was how it had felt walking into that Gestapo station. This was what she'd missed. Her whole body craved it, because she knew internally, somehow, how to calm herself when she had no reason to be.

As the lift reached the lobby and the doors opened, Livy relaxed.

Standing in the lobby, waiting to go up, stood the familiar bald, round figure of Le Grand Diablo. Livy stared at him for a second. He looked different somehow. No corny mustache. He stared back, waiting for her to exit the lift. Finally she stepped out, and Diablo brushed past her. He huffed his impatience.

Livy stopped. Her visit to Nathalie might have been for naught, but chance had presented her with another opportunity to get some answers. The doors were about to close behind her. She got back on the lift and pressed the third-floor button. Pivoting quickly, Livy put her hand up to stop an older woman with two shopping bags full of shoes.

"Closed for repairs," Livy said, trying to sound as official as possible.

Before she could protest, the doors shut. The lift lurched upward.

"What do you mean, this lift isn't—" Diablo swallowed his sentence as the flat end of Livy's right hand crashed into his windpipe. A deep gurgle rumbled out of his throat, and he crumpled to the floor. Livy had pulled the punch. Otherwise she would have shattered his esophagus and Diablo would be dead. And of no use to her.

Still, as he was a big man, Livy couldn't very well toss him around. She knelt beside him and pinned his throat to the back of the lift with her forearm. He grimaced. His breathing sounded like a backed-up sink.

"I saw your act last night," Livy said. "I know you can't talk right now, so I'm going to ask a question and you can answer by nodding. Can you do that?"

He didn't respond. Livy added a bit more pressure with her elbow. She repeated the question. This time Diablo seemed a bit more cooperative.

"That card trick with the ace-of-spades deck—did you learn that from a magician called Mephisto?"

After a moment, he nodded.

"The trick was a signal to someone, wasn't it?"

Diablo's eyes widened, but his head didn't move.

"Do I need to repeat the question?" She pressed his damaged neck harder.

Very slowly, he nodded.

The doors opened behind her and Livy stood. The gods smiled on her this time, because no one was waiting for the lift. She stepped out into the hallway.

"Tell him Livy Nash has a proposition for him," she said, turning back to the slumped magician. "Tell him I won't wait forever."

* * *

Livy left the hotel and retraced her steps back across the city. She hated feeling backed into a corner, and that's exactly what Nathalie had done. Valentine's French mistress called the shots for now, so Livy could only wait. She hated that. At least during the war there had been a sense of control. Her job with the Firm had been to attack, to be the thorn in the side of the enemy and to invigorate the resistance. Peter used to laugh at her, saying there weren't enough bridges in France for her to blow up.

Nathalie had information, yet she was so afraid of someone that she might have shot Livy, the person who had come to help her. Why was it so damned hard to get an audience with this woman? Livy'd taken her anger out on Diablo in the lift. The side of her hand still ached. At least he'd confirmed the trick had been a signal. Clearly Nathalie, or maybe even Valentine himself, had been in the theater last night. The trick might even have been a signal to alert someone to Livy's presence. Or Vance's.

By this time she'd reached the Grand Palais and turned toward the right bank of the Pont Alexandre III, which was in Livy's estimation the most beautiful bridge in Paris. Maybe the bridge's ornate statues of the Fames and its carved nymphs overlooking the Seine lacked subtlety, but God, it was gorgeous. She took her time crossing the bridge and watched as the sun began its descent over the Eiffel Tower and the western half of the city.

She stopped a few more times on the half-hour walk back to her flat. She grabbed a crepe at one of the stands near the tower and took stock of everyone who walked past her. Livy finished the treat before finally turning back along the Seine and making her way toward Quai de Grenelle. Her feet ached. She must've walked ten miles today. Rest was what she needed, even on the small bed at Madame Riveaux's.

As she neared the unassuming front stoop of the boarding-house, Livy noticed the particular square-shaped wagon associated with the Parisian police. Two officers, in their blue uniforms and distinctive kepis, stood on either side of the front door.

Livy had run Gestapo gauntlets, so whatever threat these men posed didn't cause her concern. She felt the beginnings of a headache behind her eyes as the tension from her confrontation with Nathalie began to release.

"Mademoiselle Nash?" The larger of the two officers spoke. He had a full gray mustache and hooded eyes, giving him a sleepy look.

As Livy acknowledged her name, the younger officer stepped forward.

"I am afraid, mademoiselle, we must take you to our head-quarters for questioning. You have been charged in a serious matter. Assaulting a French national. Please come with us."

Chapter Sixteen

The French national Livy was accused of assaulting happened to be one Antoine Jabot, who performed under numerous aliases, one of which was Le Grand Diablo.

Livy sat in a small holding room—not so much a cell, since it had a square table and wooden chair—and wondered which had come first: the chicken or the egg. She'd been arrested less than two hours after her tussle with Diablo in the Ritz lift. Maybe he had immediately reported the assault to hotel staff, who had then contacted the police and located Livy's Parisian address. She couldn't rule out that Charles Gray of the U.S. Embassy had made good on his threat and found a way to get Livy off the streets. Diablo just happened to be a convenient method of accomplishing that.

Still Livy wondered at the speed of it all. She'd have bet everything she knew that she hadn't been followed to the Ritz, unless it was by someone far more adept than her. Given her years out of the game, Livy wondered if rust had caused her to miss someone. No, she decided. Spotting a tail required patience, and she'd been extremely cautious, especially given that both Vance and Mirov had followed her earlier.

It didn't make sense.

Livy drummed her fingers on the square table and thought back over the day. She quickly came to a conclusion she didn't particularly like. A woman slaps a man in a hotel lift. So what? Frenchmen weren't known for their subtlety in the presence of women. More than a few men got slapped in this town, she reasoned.

No, someone had the ear of the Parisian police. Perhaps it was Gray. The Americans wielded considerable power in liberated Paris. But it seemed more likely that Nathalie had made the call.

Unless Valentine had been at the Ritz with Nathalie that morning. Could that have been why Nathalie threatened her, and the reason for the recognition the Frenchwoman registered when Livy repeated her name? Valentine would want to be prepared for a confrontation with Olivia Nash. He'd want a meeting to be on his terms. That theory made as much sense as anything, even though sense had been decidedly lacking since her arrival in Paris.

Livy put her head down on the table and tried to rest. She kicked her shoes off and thought back through what had happened since being picked up by the police. Naturally, Madame Riveaux had made an appearance. She'd stood on the doorstep, wearing her ubiquitous Oriental dressing gown, and told the police she'd always known Livy was trouble.

At the station, the officer with the hooded eyes offered her tea, which she declined, while asking her the sort of routine questions you'd ask a foreigner who'd been arrested. The whole thing took no more than a half hour. Then he escorted her to a bland waiting room and left, adding, "Someone will be with you shortly."

Not *my superior,* not *an officer from the British Embassy,* not anyone specific. *Someone.*

As ominous thoughts gathered in Livy's head like heavy rain clouds on a May afternoon, she heard movement outside the room. The door at the end of the hallway opened, and boots clattered on the floor in her direction. An armed gendarme took a position outside. So *someone* had brought the military police along.

Dear God. She'd caused an international incident on her first assignment.

Then came the sound of a much different pair of shoes on the floor. Livy guessed the wearer of these soft-soled, probably expensive shoes must be the *someone* in question.

He'd worn a similar suit the last time they'd met, but that had been almost two years ago. Then she'd known him by a different name. But now Livy knew that the man who stepped into the room was not named "Luc." Some knew him as Mephisto, others as Edward Valentine.

"Well, you have gotten yourself into a jam, haven't you?" He spoke in English. Perhaps he didn't want the muscle outside to understand their conversation.

Valentine stood on the other side of the table near the wall. His easy smile and relaxed manner betrayed no hint that he knew the woman sitting at the table desperately wanted to kill him. He had the upper hand and didn't need to say it.

That didn't stop Livy from wishing she had a pencil or something very sharp that she could shove into his eyes. God, she could rip his eyes out with her fingernails. If Sergeant Pierre in the hallway then unloaded his clip into her, she'd die satisfied.

There would come a time for that. *Just hold on, girl*, she told herself. *Hold on, and wait. The time's coming.*

"Pity that our reunion has to happen in such a disagreeable place," he said.

Livy took a long look at him and wondered how she had ever found him trustworthy, even under the guise of Luc, the simple mechanic and *résistant*. Valentine's long, angular face and wiry frame gave him an elegant silhouette. His tailored double-breasted suit fit him perfectly. The creases in his face—Livy guessed him to be in his midfifties—curled upward as he smiled, giving him a puckish air. But his brown eyes, which Livy had once found comforting and stalwart, now sparkled like a schoolboy who'd pulled a whole term's worth of pranks and gotten away with them all.

The man is a performer, Livy thought. *His line of business is misdirection and trickery, and he's good at it.*

How she hated him. He'd taken Peter from her. At the worst possible time. One night together and then never again. Livy still loved him. She couldn't deny it, here in the presence of his murderer. She knew it in the very core of her being that she'd loved Peter Scobee as she'd never loved any man in her life, and this slick bastard had taken all that away.

"I understand your taking offense at Diablo's performance of the ace-of-spades deck," he said, grinning. "After all, you've had a chance to see me do it, and he is a bit of a bumbler."

Livy forced herself to look at the table. Looking at his hideous grin right now would provoke her to do something stupid.

"It's a shame you never had the chance to see me perform. Onstage, that is. The bullet catch—that was the piéce de résistance of my act. Do you know it? It's elegantly simple but quite dangerous. Someone fires a gun at the magician and he catches the bullet. It has been done a million different ways, of course, but I always caught the bullet with my hand. More impressive than catching it on a plate, yes? You have to be careful with it. The great Chung Ling Soo was killed doing it. Houdini was afraid to even try."

Livy kept her head down as tears pushed at the corners of her eyes. Her pulse thumped in her temples as Valentine droned on about his act.

"This isn't the time for boasting though, is it? You've come here to—what—make us a business proposition for my network on behalf of His Majesty? How awkward it must be. Negotiating with the likes of me."

He lowered his voice. "I know you hate me, Livy. Of course you do. But you also must understand the war was a different game. Played under different rules."

"A game?" she said, her voice harsh and breathless.

"Oh my dear, we are still playing it. The only difference is there is less shooting. And, of course, the sides have changed. You came here to bring me over to your side, didn't you—dear Olivia?"

Livy finally peeled her eyes from the knotholes in the tabletop and took him in. His eyebrows arched, waiting for an answer.

"You were lucky to survive the last war—Luc," she said, trying to keep the emotion out of her voice. "I'm trying to give you a chance to survive this one."

He took a step in, unbuttoned his suit coat, and stretched out in the chair opposite her. Valentine's long legs reached the other side of the table, nudging hers as he made himself comfortable.

"How very difficult this must be for you. I imagine most women of your sort are back home. Getting married. Saving their ration coupons and trying to keep the larder stocked. But not you. Dear Livy Nash, sent back out into the field, and her first assignment is me. How you must feel. I can only imagine."

Then his joker's smile vanished and something like shame flashed across his lean features.

"Do you remember that old Citroën I repaired for you and Peter to drive to Paris? Got the car started, changed the flat, and sent the two of you on your way? Do you remember I sweated all the way through my shirt? It was so hot that day I nearly passed out. You see, Livy, I had to get you on your way so the roadblock could stop you and Peter. They were expecting you at a certain time, and I had to make sure you got there." He leaned forward, less than a foot away from her face. Livy could see the nicotine stains on his front teeth and smell the espresso on his breath.

"I know our shared past is—complicated. But if we are to work together, on the same side, we have to put all that behind us," he said. "Don't you agree?"

Livy didn't mind the proximity now. She could see the large pores in his cheeks. More signs that Valentine was just flesh and bone and could be torn apart almost as easily as skinning an animal.

"Yes. Let's put it all behind us," Livy hissed. "Why don't you start by telling me how you are even alive? That shell should have at least left a few marks on you."

Valentine shrugged his shoulders. "When they dragged you away, Faber and I started for his car. He heard the shell just before it hit. Pushed me down. The worst of the blast was several meters away. I did, however, chip a tooth." He glanced at his watch and stood up. "Oh my, it looks as if my time with you is almost up. The gendarme outside has other engagements," Valentine said, jerking his head at the armed officer outside the door. "Money can buy anything in free Paris. You'd do well to remember that."

He rebuttoned his jacket and turned to go, but Livy's voice stopped him.

"Why should anyone buy the services of a second-rate magician?"

Valentine tapped on the small window, and the gendarme opened the door. The man known as Mephisto held up a finger and turned back to Livy.

"That's where you are wrong, my dear. I am an excellent magician."

*   *   *

Minutes went by and Livy didn't move. She stared at the door long after Valentine and the guard had left and replayed the entire conversation in her head. Each time she came to the same conclusion. All this was about money. Valentine had paid to put her in jail so they'd have a safe spot to begin negotiations. He'd said, "Money can buy anything in free Paris." His services and the entire Mephisto network would go to the highest bidder.

Fleming's orders had been clear: retrieve the list and confirm its authenticity. He'd authorized her to pay Nathalie for the list. Livy guessed the same would apply to Valentine.

She could promise him a nice estate in Hampstead, tickets to Covent Garden, and an audience with King George. Frankly, the thought of giving the bastard anything made her sick.

At some point in her ruminating, Livy fell asleep in the small chair, her head resting on the square table.

"Mademoiselle." The officer with the hooded eyes stood in the open doorway, gesturing outside. Livy had no idea how long she'd slept. She rubbed her eyes and followed him back to a small waiting area where a police officer presided over a long desk with rows and rows of keys positioned behind him in a wire cage. The officer gave Livy's name to the guard and waited while he found her purse and passport.

"So Diablo or Jabot or whatever that round little magician calls himself isn't pressing charges, then?" Livy said.

"I have no idea, Mademoiselle Nash. I have been asked to release you into another's custody," he said, with more than a hint of annoyance. "You are out of my hands now."

Just then the door to the street opened and sunlight flooded in. A man in a suit and fedora stepped inside.

"Please wait outside, monsieur. We are almost done with her."

"Will do, officer," Tom Vance said, giving Livy a wink. "I'm in no hurry."

Chapter Seventeen

❧

"At some point, you're going to have to say something."

Since leaving the jail and hopping into a waiting cab, Livy Nash had given Tom Vance the deluxe silent treatment. Vance, who apparently enjoyed the sound of his own voice and, on occasion, the sound of others, had kept up a steady litany of comments about the scenery, all in an attempt to get Livy to say something more than the address of her room, which she had grunted at the driver upon entering the cab.

Vance sighed and adjusted his blue silk tie as the taxi bounced along the narrow Paris streets. At last the driver left the Trocadéro district and turned on to the Pont d'Iéna, another of the city's historic bridges that spanned the Seine.

If Livy's silence angered Vance, then so be it. He'd gotten her out of jail as the emissary of Charles Gray, the American who'd warned her to stay out of his territory. Back in London, she'd felt reasonably certain that Vance fancied her. The way he kept his eyes on her all the time and smiled whenever she looked at him. A woman could sense these things. Now she felt like a fool. All Vance's talk of being an ally felt even emptier now, since he appeared to be nothing more than Professor Gray's errand boy.

"All right, you can give me the cold shoulder all you want, but we need to talk before you run off," Vance said as the taxi slowed a block away from Madame Riveaux's.

"On the left now," Livy snapped at the driver.

The taxi stopped, and Livy leapt out like a hostage escaping captivity. Vance hopped out of the far side of the cab, shouting in his broken French for the taxi to wait. The driver protested but kept the engine running.

Vance caught her about ten feet from the front door, grabbed her right elbow, and spun her toward him. Livy came to a stop about a hand's width away from Vance's nose.

"I've already assaulted one man today. Shall we make it two?" Livy said.

Vance released her elbow and took a step back. "I'm sure you mean business, Livy. But so do I. And right now your business is my business."

"I think we've had this conversation once or twice before, Mr. Vance."

"I know you think I'm the bad guy here, but I'm not. You've probably also figured out that Gray had something to do with me bailing you out. He did. But the only reason Gray knew you'd been arrested was because he's pals with the prefect of police. Turns out that officer was worried about you."

"Worried? He arrested me."

"He had no choice. His orders came from higher up."

"So he arrested me, then got worried and called the Yanks to bail me out?"

"Something like that. It's—complicated."

Livy snarled. "I speak and understand English, so why don't you try explaining yourself."

"Okay. Okay. The prefect got in touch with Gray, because he knew you had a visitor."

"If the police didn't want me having visitors, why didn't they stop it?" Vance opened his mouth to speak, but Livy cut in. "And don't you dare say it's complicated!"

"Look, will you wait while I pay off this cabby? Just one minute?"

"Fine."

Vance handed a stack of francs to the disgruntled driver, who wasted no time leaving. Livy waited, feeling as if the Americans were treating her like a third division team trying to compete with the first. Vance took the time to straighten his tie and pat his hair down as he walked back to her. Always so cocksure, these Americans. Maybe that's why they bounced.

"Can we go somewhere—less in the open maybe—and talk?" Vance said, still playing the contrite and attentive suitor.

"I think here will do."

"All right, I'll make it quick. Who was your visitor today?"

"Me auntie from Preston."

Vance didn't laugh. "Livy—I am not your enemy. We're here for the same thing."

"You keep saying that, Mr. Vance. Shall we compare notes about the Grand Guignol?"

"Let's start with Nathalie Billerant," he said, stepping closer to her. "Or maybe the magician you beat up at the Ritz this afternoon."

"What can I say? I don't like rubbish magic acts."

Vance looked down, and for the first time Livy thought he might actually get angry.

"I really am trying to work with you, and—well—protect you. And before you interrupt and tell me you don't need protection, let me just say that Charles Gray has the clout to put your behind on the next plane back to London if he wanted. As far as I know, he may be arranging that right now. This operation is very important to him. He wants Valentine. We may not have much time."

"We?"

"I've known Fleming for years. He worked in Washington trying to push the U.S. into the war. I know how he thinks. We, you and me—my country and yours—we want the network. We want Valentine. Once we have it, we share it. We're allies."

"Is that why you took me to dinner in London, Mr. Vance? Because we're allies?"

Before Tom could consider a reply, Madame Riveaux's door opened and the dragon lady herself stood on the stoop, laughing alongside the tall and perpetually smiling Andrei Mirov.

The two men regarded each other for a moment before the Russian broke the silence.

"What is the saying? Three's a crowd?"

Livy watched the tall, older Russian and the young, bouncy American size each other up like peacocks preening. Mirov finally broke the silent battle of egos

"Forgive me, Miss Nash. I was just talking with your charming landlady here," he said, without a trace of irony. Madame Riveaux blinked at the tall Russian coquettishly as Mirov bid her good-day. She gave Livy yet another glare and disappeared inside.

"And you, my friend, I do not believe I have had the pleasure."

"Tom Vance," he said, smiling cautiously. "And you are?"

"Andrei Mirov. A pleasure, Mr. Vance," he said, laying on the accent a little thick so that the American's name sounded more like "Veents."

"What brings you to Paris, Mr.—um—Mee-roff."

"My name, ha, it is challenge for the American tongue. I am a writer. Many writers come to Paris for inspiration. Your Hemingway and Scott Fitzgerald, for instance."

"Not too many Russian writers can get away these days."

"Maybe they love their country too much to leave. And what do you do, Meester Veents? Maybe you work for Coca-Cola?"

"I'm a journalist. Miss Nash and I are colleagues."

"Ah. A fellow seeker of the truth, then."

"Something like that."

"I wish you luck in finding it. The truth can be— dangerous." Mirov let that hang in the air for a moment before going back to the stumbling-foreigner routine. "Oh, maybe I use wrong word. Dangerous? Is right?"

"You're laying it on a little thick, comrade," Vance said.

Livy'd had enough. "You're both exhausting. So, if you're planning to continue your little pissing match, you'll be doing so without me."

Both men turned and looked at her.

"My apologies, ma'am. The gentleman and I got carried away," Vance said, pivoting toward the street, where he whistled at an idle taxi on the other side of the *quai*. "Besides, work calls. Nice to have met you, Mr. Mirov." He put on his fedora

and adjusted the brim as his eyes met Livy's. "I hope you'll think about our story, Miss Nash."

Livy watched Vance's cab drive away with a trace of sadness. The American had been outclassed by the Russian's banter, and their verbal jousting had only made Vance's thing for Livy that much clearer. She liked that about him. Truth be told, she liked a lot of things about him.

"I thought he'd never leave," Mirov said, a mischievous grin spreading across his long face as he broke the silence. "You must be quite hungry, my dear," he said, holding up a brown paper bag. "I just happened to have brought a bit of Paris with me."

Minutes later they sat on a bench on a raised path overlooking the Seine just north of the small Statue of Liberty replica near the Pont de Grenelle. The sun had started to set, and the city glowed in its dim light. A long tourist boat, with a handful of people on board, made its way south. Mirov had brought along a bottle of French red wine, complete with corkscrew and two small glasses, as well as a pair of chocolate pastries.

"Is this supposed to be romantic?" Livy said, laughing as the Russian uncorked the bottle.

"Of course not. I am far too old for you, Olivia. Besides I have someone back in Moscow."

"Oh, and how old is she?"

"Ummm, twenty-five. No, no, twenty-six. Wonderful girl."

Livy laughed and declined the wine. She hadn't eaten today. The churning in her stomach reminded her of those mornings after a bout with Polish vodka where her head felt like Waterloo station. She didn't miss that feeling, or the drink.

Mirov offered her one of the pastries. After one bite, she had to remind herself to take her time. Her appetite had other ideas.

The Russian chewed and stared out at the water. "The Germans didn't deserve this place. You know, the French hid the *Mona Lisa* from them. They kept it moving. Think what the fascists would have done to the treasures of London or Moscow."

Livy grunted affirmation but kept eating.

Mirov kept his focus on the river. His eyes looked glazed as he ate. "I spent far too much time in Vichy during the war and not enough in this beautiful place. Comrade Stalin's Order Number Two Twenty-Seven? Do you know it? No? Back then we were NKVD, and he had us tracking down Red Army deserters and giving their whereabouts to soldiers, who found them in the vineyards of Bordeaux or the ports of Toulon and—passed judgment. I suppose we all had to follow orders during the war. Who knows? One day someone may pass judgment on me." The Russian wiped bread crumbs from his coat and turned to Livy, the moment of melancholy passed.

"So Mr. Vance is your—friend?" Now he pronounced the name effortlessly.

"I wouldn't say that," Livy said, clearing the bits of chocolate from the corners of her mouth. "He just shows up from time to time. Like you."

"He and I, we are not the same. His clothes are better. Mine hang on me now a bit," he said, tugging at his jacket. "I lost weight recently. One thing war is good for, I suppose. But now I need new clothes."

"You know, I'll probably get in a lot of trouble with the Americans if I'm seen with you again."

"Yes. I expect you will. They are angry, because I have half of what they want."

"Half of what I want as well."

"But you have something we both want, Olivia."

"Is that why you're trying to win me over with wine and chocolate?"

"Well, you refused the wine, so I'm forced to rely on my Russian charm."

"Russian charm? Your friend who clobbered me with his pistol could do with a bit of that."

"I am a bit of an antique, you might say. Maybe I talk too much. Yuri Sergeevich Levchenko uses his gun. I'm afraid there are many more like him now in Moscow than men like me."

Livy ate the last bite of pastry. She looked out across the river and wondered which building across the way housed the MGB surveillance.

"And what is it exactly that I'm supposed to have?" she asked.

"Edward Valentine."

Livy laughed. "You're misinformed."

"You know him. You have history. Am I wrong?"

I knew Luc, she thought.

"The rest of us—at least those on my side—only know what kind of man he is. What he is capable of. The information from his agents brought down operation after operation during the war. We had people in Berlin in the run-up to Stalingrad. All of them—twenty-six men and women—arrested by the Gestapo and sent to camps. Dead. Because of him and his people. Then an operation we launched into the Crimea. A hundred men parachuted in at night to track Hitler's 6th Army. But the Germans—oh, they were waiting for us. All those young, young boys were met by machine gunners on the ground. Most of them died in the air. The ones that didn't were shot in the fields. The operation was blown by one of Valentine's agents in Sofia, which coincidentally had just hosted the magician Mephisto.

"The list," Mirov went on, his anger building, "contains the names of men and women who caused good Russian boys to die in the icy fields of Stalingrad, and to be ripped apart as they fell from the sky. Now, I suppose we could find these people and force them to work for us." Mirov's long face suddenly looked old. "But I did not come to Paris to recruit murderers. I am asking you to help me find him, Olivia. If you know how to contact this man, I am asking for your help. Bring him to me. You see, I do not want Edward Valentine to work for us. No, my loyalty is to my countrymen. I want him to see him in the Lubyanka. On trial for his crimes."

Livy studied the Russian's face. His eyes never wavered. She had to take him at his word.

"And should I help you, what's in it for me?"

"I told you I do not want the list of Valentine's spies. I want him."

"Your man with the mustache took half of the list from me in London. Am I supposed to believe he'll stop there?"

"Levchenko is hardheaded, I grant you. But I outrank him." The Russian leaned forward conspiratorially. "And besides, he is my nephew. I can make family gatherings very difficult for him if he doesn't do what I say."

Livy didn't smile at his joke. She knew he could be playing her. She also could see how this might work out in her favor.

She rather liked the idea of Mirov and his boys having a go at the bastard with hammer and tongs back in Moscow. But that wasn't the job she'd been given.

"Tempting offer," she said, standing. "Have your man Levchenko return my property first, and then we might have something to talk about. You can leave a message at the brasserie for me."

*   *   *

Two hours later, Livy stood in front of the small dresser mirror in her room. She turned from side to side, looking for bulges in this very tight mermaid gown. The black satin dress tied behind her neck and then plunged dangerously low. Just below her chest the designer had sown a row of fleurs-de-lis, which served to enhance what was she'd always thought lacking above. The gown hugged her hips tight all the way to her knees and then expanded, finlike, to the ground.

Livy doubted whether she could walk in it, much less swim. Tonight, however, all this glamour served a purpose.

She spent a good half hour trying to wrangle her brown hair into something that didn't resemble cousin Bessie out for a night on the town in Blackburn. Eventually she gave up and took another look at herself in the mirror. Not half bad. Throwing her coat over her arms and grabbing her larger-than-average black clutch, she made for the stairs.

As expected, she had no trouble hailing a taxi.

The drive gave her just enough time to think through this decision. Vance and Mirov had made their intentions clear regarding the Mephisto network. More importantly, the two men had been specific about what they intended for Edward

Valentine. Vance wanted the magician on the U.S. payroll. Mirov would have Valentine interrogated, probably tortured in an MGB prison, and executed for war crimes.

The last thing Livy wanted was to have to take Mirov at his word. She'd be a fool to trust him. No, the key to all this was still Nathalie, and Livy was going to make damn certain she had a face-to-face with the Frenchwoman before she decided anything.

Now, as the taxi rumbled through the Paris night heading for the first arrondissement, Livy thought of how her father used to tease her French mother with some of Lord Nelson's more inflammatory quotes. She remembered one that had sent her mother into a flurry of Gallic hysterics: *Firstly you must always implicitly obey orders without attempting to form any opinion of your own regarding their propriety.*

Good advice, your lordship, Livy thought.

Her father had gone on to finish Nelson's quote, which went, *Secondly, you must consider every man your enemy who speaks ill of your king; and thirdly, you must hate a Frenchman as you hate the devil.*

Livy smiled at the memory of the mock fights her parents staged, which always ended in some sort of embrace and an early bedtime for their little girl.

England expects that every man will do his duty, Livy thought. She popped the clip on the clutch to check that the Webley could be removed quickly.

Chapter Eighteen

⁓

The doorman gave her a knowing smile, tipping his hat as she sashayed through the front door of the Ritz. Livy assumed no one would give a second thought to a well-dressed, well-lubricated young woman arriving in a taxi after midnight. After all, this was Paris.

She also assumed that anyone who'd been working earlier in the day when she'd left a roly-poly magician lying in a heap on the floor of the lift would not be around for the late shift. If they were, she didn't think they'd recognize her now. She'd transformed from frumpy reporter with unmanageable hair to vixen in a mermaid dress with hair somewhere in the vicinity of manageable.

Unfortunately, she had about thirty yards of marble-floored lobby to clear before she reached the gilt-edged lifts. Livy resisted the impulse to hoof it as she got closer. Rich socialites in body-hugging satin dresses who'd had too much champagne were in no hurry. Her heels clicked on the floor as she walked the lobby gauntlet.

"Mademoiselle, *excusez-moi.*"

Livy looked around for the voice before her gaze landed on the clerk at the desk, a large man with a hawk nose and a very thin mustache, who smiled as he stopped her progress.

He will expect less of a drunken guest, Livy reasoned. So she played it to the hilt. She pointed to her chest as if to say, *Moi?* and then wobbled ever so slightly.

Undeterred, the clerk came around the desk toward her. He wore a dark, unassuming single-breasted suit with a fluffy pocket square. His black oxfords made no sound as he glided over.

"Mademoiselle, please forgive this intrusion, as the hour is very late, but if I could just confirm your room number, then I will be happy to wish you a very good-night."

Livy had two choices. She could play the indignant guest, complain that she didn't have time for this and would be sure to bring this intrusion up with the manager in the morning. In an instant she decided the confrontational approach might cause too much suspicion, and that her gown and the tipsiness could do the work for her.

"Ah, of course, I am not thinking clearly at the moment," Livy said, suddenly worried about her "hillbilly French." She hoped the drink might also account for a bit of slurring. "Forgive me, let me think," she said, tossing her hair around like Rita Hayworth while flashing her best smile. "Ah yes, suite three ten. Is that all you need from me tonight?" she said in a tone that was a little more than playful.

"*Merci*, mademoiselle. Please let me check the register." The clerk scurried back across the floor to the desk. Livy peered at her nails, trying to look a little more impatient.

The clerk came back, but this time with the bulky register under his left arm. "Mademoiselle, you did say suite three ten, yes?"

"*Oui*, three ten. *Au revoir*, monsieur."

"I do beg your pardon again, mademoiselle, but Monsieur Dufort is our guest in suite three ten."

Livy had expected this. She gave the clerk a shy, knowing smile. "And Monsieur Dufort is expecting me. I am a little late, because I was enjoying the night with a friend of mine. It was her birthday, and she has excellent taste in champagne—"

"Madame Dufort and their children are also our guests in the suite." The clerk glared at her.

Livy blanched; her hand went to her mouth. Tears pooled in her eyes. "*Mon Dieu* . . . the bastard. He told me he would be alone this time. He promised me. I have not seen him since the war, and this was to be our—reunion."

"Please, mademoiselle."

Livy wiped her eyes, stamped her heel, and whirled on the clerk. "You are trying to protect him? Is that what you are doing?"

"Of course not, mademoiselle, but you must understand, I cannot allow our guests to be disturbed—"

"Disturbed? Monsieur Dufort is expecting me. He would not have asked me to come to your hotel and meet him if his wife and family were also here. Do you understand my meaning, monsieur? So if you would like to throw me out of your hotel, fine. But what will you say to Monsieur Dufort tomorrow morning when he asks why his guest was not admitted? Hmm? Believe me, when I speak to him, I will tell him the truth."

By now the clerk's face had reddened all the way up past his considerable widow's peaks. "Mademoiselle, I am merely trying to protect our guests. Of course I am not trying to—interfere with your evening. I will just call Monsieur Dufort and let him know you have arrived."

The clerk turned on his heels and made for the desk. Livy considered letting him make the call. Dufort, or whoever, would probably say a guest was not expected, and that would be that. The clerk might interpret that as a gentleman being discreet, but Livy had no interest in taking that risk.

So by the time the clerk reached the desk, Livy had dropped her head to her chest and begun to sob. Her keening caught the attention of the doorman, who stepped away from his post to see what was happening. The sound of the crying alone ensured that the clerk couldn't make his phone call.

"Mademoiselle, please—" the clerk said, scurrying around the desk again.

"What did you say to her?" the doorman said.

"It doesn't concern you," the clerk snipped. Livy opened her clutch, ostensibly looking for something to wipe her eyes. The small gun and silencer remained neatly tucked inside.

The doorman produced a white hanky from inside his voluminous coat as Livy continued to moan and sniff.

"I will go. Please tell Monsieur Dufort I tried to keep our appointment," Livy said to the clerk, throwing her shoulders back as she wiped the last tears from her eyes.

By now, the clerk stood at her side and practically bowed before her. "Mademoiselle, I am sure that won't be necessary. Forgive my concern. I did not mean to cause you so much distress. Please, enjoy your evening."

Livy cleared her throat before speaking. "You, monsieur, are a credit to this hotel," she said to the clerk. Then she smiled at the doorman and offered the hanky. He demurred. She smiled, blinking her wet eyes at him. Livy could see she owned the doorman.

"*Au revoir*, then," she said, and walked slowly and a bit more steadily toward the lifts. She felt their eyes on her, so she took her time. As the doors opened, she gave the two men a little wave.

After the theatrics she'd had to employ in the lobby, Livy felt grateful to find the third floor empty. She required a minute, perhaps two, of quiet in the hallway. Then the real work would begin.

She kept up the stumbling-party-girl act from the lift and down the hall to suite 314. Giving a quick look to both ends of the corridor, she knelt down and took a long look at the door. The gold knob rested just above a standard pin-and-tumbler lock. Livy assumed it would be of a certain quality—perhaps tougher to spring than one in an average flat. Still, burglary had been on the curriculum at the SOE camp, and she'd picked more than a few locks in her day, though never while wearing a tight satin dress in a hallway in one of the best hotels in the world—but there had to be a first time for everything.

Livy popped the snap on her clutch and reached under the gun to find her metal pick and small tension wrench. With another quick look down the hall, she inserted the wrench into the lock and pushed the tumblers to see which way it opened. *Clockwise it is.* Keeping the tension wrench inside, she inserted the pick and guided it along the lock's pins. She was able to push each of them up except one. *Yes, this is a good lock*, Livy thought. The Ritz would want to keep its guests safe and secure.

She could feel her body getting warmer, and her hand started to sweat. The pick felt slippery in her hand as she slowly pushed the last pin up, waiting to hear the telltale click that it was set and the lock could now be opened. The pick slipped in her fingers and the pin reset. Livy wiped her hand on her dress and set about trying to reach the stingy pin again. Finally, she made contact using the edge of the pick and gently pressed the pin upward.

With a *click*, the final pin set. Livy inserted the tension wrench and turned the cylinder. She gripped the doorknob with her free hand and felt the second *click* as the lock opened and the knob turned.

As she stood, holding her breath, Livy heard the distinctive *ping* of the lift opening and the shuffling of feet headed in her direction.

Livy put her hand carefully over the unlatched door and waited for the approaching guest to turn the corner and see her. She reminded herself to breathe and pantomimed futzing with the door.

A middle-aged man in a brown suit stepped into the corridor.

Suites 309 and 310 were the last in the hall. Livy prayed this man wasn't Monsieur Dufort. Surely the clerk would have warned him that a confrontation waited outside his door.

But the man only gave Livy a curt nod and yawned quite loudly as he walked past. Relief washed over her as the man in brown stopped outside suite 312. The moment of release must have caused Livy's grip on the door to slacken, and when it did, the tension wrench and pick fell out of the lock and landed on the soft carpet. The rug muffled most of the sound, but the metal clanged together as the tools collided. The man in brown turned, raising his considerable eyebrows. Livy shifted her left foot, hiding the tools with her shoes. At the same time she yawned, covering her mouth quickly in embarrassment. Realizing he'd caught a lady in an indelicate moment, the man quickly disappeared inside his suite.

The second his door closed, Livy scooped up the tools and dropped them back into the clutch. She held the door open with the toe of her left heel as she removed the Webley and silencer.

Livy's first cautious steps into suite 314 assured her that its occupants had either turned in or were away. Only a sliver of moonlight from an open curtain lit the foyer and the adjoining room. Still, Livy took her time easing the heavy door shut before moving farther into the suite.

She remembered the plush rug and the detailed carving of the baseboard from earlier when Nathalie Billerant had held her at gunpoint. This time she needed to go farther than the entranceway.

As Livy edged toward the end of the foyer, she became aware of every sound in the room. Her satin dress swished lightly with each step. In the distance, even through the thick glass of the room's picture windows, she could hear traffic on the streets three floors below. Otherwise, the room was cloaked in darkness and silence.

Livy eased around the corner and stopped. She let her eyes adjust once more to the minimal light and took in the layout of the suite. She stood on the edge of a large sitting area with a sofa and two armchairs. Thick, embroidered drapes had been pulled about halfway on either side of the large window, allowing the outside light to peek through. Behind her was a large dining area with an ornate long marble table and four tall chairs.

Straight ahead Livy saw two sliding wooden doors pulled together. Without question, the bedroom lay beyond. Closed doors might be a sign that a guest, or two, had turned in for the night.

Livy held the Webley before her and made for the bedroom. The swish of the satin seemed louder now, but she'd come too far to stop. Soon, things might be getting very loud.

The stifling smell of smoke from far too many French cigarettes invaded her nostrils as she gripped the handle of one of the slatted bedroom doors and slid it open slowly. The curtain in the bedroom hadn't been closed, allowing a theatrical wash of moonlight that gave the silk sheets of the sprawling bed a light-blue hue. The rumpled sheets had been tossed aside. A light glowed beside the bed.

Livy found the light switch on the wall to her right. The wall sconces flickered into brightness as she latched the sliding doors from the inside.

Nathalie Billerant sat in the cushioned chair beside the bed, draped in a powder-blue silk robe, calmly smoking. The ashtray on the bedside table overflowed with a night's worth of smokes, all tipped in red lipstick. She watched Livy without a trace of surprise. The Frenchwoman looked as elegant as ever except for the fresh welt, purple and swelling, under her right eye.

"You have a talent for showing up at the worst possible times," Nathalie said, picking tobacco from her bottom lip.

Livy had hoped to catch Valentine in the room. Instead she faced this icy, gorgeous woman who, even with a black eye, looked like she belonged on the big screen.

Keeping the silenced Webley pointed at Nathalie, Livy turned over the room, looking for the small automatic she'd encountered on her first trip to suite 314. She found the weapon stowed under mademoiselle's lace things in the bottom drawer of the bedroom bureau.

"Really, you should have looked there first," Nathalie said, crushing another cigarette.

"So, what happened to you?" Livy said in English, dropping the second gun in her coat.

"What does that say?" Nathalie deflected. "On the gun."

Livy angled the silencer slowly so she could see the inscription. MORT AUX BOCHES.

"Very cute. Did you do that yourself?" Nathalie's words dripped with irony, but her voice remained level.

"It was a gift from a girl in the Resistance," Livy said. "She was killed at Vercors. And what were you doing during the war?"

Nathalie held Livy's accusing stare. She didn't blink. Instead she reached for an ornate silver-and-enamel art deco cigarette case. It must have cost a small fortune. As Nathalie lit another of her smelly French cigarettes, Livy noticed an inscription on the edge: L'HABIT NE FAIT PAS LE MOINE.

"'The habit doesn't make the monk'?" Livy asked.

Nathalie let the smoke escape from her finely drawn lips and glanced at the case. "'Don't judge a book by its cover.' N'est-ce pas?"

The air in the room felt thick with cigarette smoke, but there was another scent underneath. It smelled a bit like wood with a touch of spice.

"What is that smell? Seems a bit heavy for you," Livy said.

"It's Zizanie. Cologne," Nathalie replied, as if speaking to a child.

"Ah, and where is your boyfriend tonight?"

Nathalie put the cigarette to her lips and inhaled.

"He the one who did that to your eye?"

The Frenchwoman allowed the smoke to escape from her mouth slowly. Her eyes were hooded and opaque. The thin silk robe Nathalie wore fell just above her knees, her creamy skin blemish free. She dangled her bare legs and pedicured feet in front of her so casually. If she had any concern about being held at gunpoint, she didn't show it. Judging by the darkening bruise under her eye, Livy figured Nathalie had had a rough night already.

"You sent for me," Livy said. "Here I am."

Nathalie's upper lip curled in a mocking smile. "I arranged a meeting. That's all."

"And you didn't show."

"Because it was not safe."

"Well, we're all alone now. Safe as houses. Plenty of time to chat."

"I said I would contact you. This is not the time. Now, get out of my hotel room."

Livy shook her head, marveling. This bit of croissant had made overtures to His Majesty's government and so far had played everyone for thickheaded prats. Her and her little teasing games. The *French*, Livy thought. *Always so bloody superior.*

Not tonight.

"I have the gun this time, luv, and this isn't exactly a social call."

"*Vous ne comprenez rien.*"

Livy stepped closer, pushing the gun forward. "No, you're wrong, I understand plenty. What I understand is I'm done playing games."

Nathalie crushed out her cigarette and stood up. For a second Livy wondered whether she might try to take the gun from her. Instead Nathalie held her ground.

"You know the kind of man Edward is. You know what he is capable of. So do you really think I would be afraid of you?"

As much as she despised Nathalie as a wartime *collaborateur*, Livy had to admit this woman had steel in her spine.

"He did that to your face, didn't he? Valentine was here earlier and hit you. Tell me why."

Nathalie turned the bruised side of her face away.

Livy sensed an opening. She pressed her advantage. "Tell me where he is. Take me to him. Once I have him, then we can negotiate. Just you and me. I can pay for the list. It's money you want, isn't it?"

"Edward is gone," Nathalie said, reaching for her cigarettes again. "But I can't talk to you now. We have to wait."

"For what, exactly? *Je ne comprends pas.*" She grabbed Nathalie's arm—hard. "I'm through waiting."

"What are you going to do? Shoot me?"

"I'll do worse. I place one call to the prefect of police and make a formal accusation of collaboration. And I have proof, too. A sworn statement of a man by the name of Claude who you seduced into working for the Germans. Think Valentine was rough? You know how the French justice system feels about people like you. They still hang collaborators, you know."

The words struck Nathalie for an instant. She took a deep breath and shrugged out of Livy's grip. She opened her case and lit another cigarette. As she inhaled the first smoke deep into her lungs, her sneering demeanor returned.

"You want Edward? Okay, *ça marche.* I can take you to Edward tonight," she said, practically spitting the words.

"I want him and I want the list. The full list."

Natalie laughed. "You will have to wait for that, *petite anglaise*."

The time for playing about is over, Livy thought. She had come to do a job, and so far she'd done nothing. She walked around to the other side of the bed and lifted the phone receiver. She waited a moment, and the familiar voice of the front-desk clerk answered.

"Good evening, monsieur," Livy said. "Please connect me with the local police. Yes. It is an urgent matter."

Livy glanced across the bed. Nathalie's right foot bobbed nervously, but she seemed every bit as defiant as before.

The line rang. Ten times and counting. *Bugger this*, Livy thought.

"Yes, I need to speak to the officer in charge this evening, please," she said, despite the continued ringing. "This concerns a matter of national importance and cannot wait—"

Nathalie suddenly turned, jabbing out the cigarette. "Stop!"

Livy put a hand over the receiver.

Nathalie said, "Listen to me. I don't care about the list. The network. It means nothing to me. I just want it over. That's why I reached out to you. Edward was here this afternoon. He found out I had contacted you."

Livy replaced the receiver, still ringing on the other end. "But he asked for me, didn't he?"

Nathalie held up her hands, pleading. "No. Not Edward. I did. I sent for you. It was me. When he found out, he became so angry. He kept me here all day with him. He made phone calls and then he went out. He's made a deal."

"A deal?"

"With the Russians. They're leaving Paris tonight."

Chapter Nineteen

Whenever Marion Nash rode a train—any train—she would regale her daughter Livy with stories of the intrigue surrounding Paris's legendary Gare du Nord. One story in particular—about an American heiress in the twenties who decided to shoot herself and her British lover inside one of the terminals—fired the imagination of her little girl more than all the others.

So, in this grand building where journeys began and ended, Livy Nash hoped she would be in time to keep Edward Valentine from being taken to Moscow. Just as she thought she had gained the upper hand at the Ritz, Livy again found herself chasing the game.

She had allowed Nathalie to get dressed, and then the two of them set off for the station. Livy felt like a gangster in an American film as she kept the Webley in the pocket of her but toned overcoat, pointed in Nathalie's direction.

The taxi made the normally ten-minute drive from hotel to station in just over seven minutes. Livy felt a bit queasy as the cab braked in the Place de Roubaix, about a hundred feet from the station's massive facade.

Nathalie leapt out of the car first with Livy right behind. The driver angrily protested, so Livy turned and tossed him the fare plus a hundred extra francs. The cabby tipped his cap and drove away.

Livy felt relieved to see that, far from considering escape, Nathalie stood on the sidewalk, scanning the front of the station and surrounding area for Valentine.

"We'll have to check the departures," Nathalie said, still keeping her gaze ahead. "He told me they were taking the last train to Dieppe tonight. Then aboard a freighter for the Black Sea in the morning."

I'll never find this bastard in another city, Livy thought. It had to be tonight.

Livy grabbed Nathalie's arm, and the two women hurried toward the station. The five-hundred-foot facade of the Gare Du Nord towered over them, its row of double pilasters separating the three bays inside the station. By day, Livy knew the station would be a madhouse, filled with commuters trying to make trains as they ran through a veritable gauntlet of black marketeers and prostitutes. But at this time of night, the station was calm.

They hurried through the center front doors, making their way toward the giant blackboard with its three words, Départ, Departure, and Abfhart, in huge letters across the top. Over their heads the curved iron-and-glass ceiling of the station glowed with moonlight and the dim interior lighting. The only sounds came from the hiss of train brakes and the steps of a few passengers sleepily making their way toward idling engines.

Livy sighed when she found the departure at the bottom of the great board. The night train to Dieppe was scheduled to leave in just over an hour.

"We have time, then," Nathalie said, seeming relieved as well.

"They won't be waiting on the platform. They'll come in at the last minute, just before it pulls out," Livy said.

"So, what's your plan?"

"My plan is I'm the one with the gun. Keep moving." Livy grabbed Nathalie's arm, steering her back to the front doors.

They'd have to bring Valentine in through the main entrance, she reasoned. The front of the Gare du Nord spanned almost the width of the Place de Roubaix, more than five hundred feet. Livy would have to rely on Nathalie to help her spot an approaching car or group of people in a hurry.

The lights of the station only illuminated the walkway outside, so every flash of light or set of headlights could mean that Valentine and Mirov might be at hand.

Would it be the tall Russian? It had to be. To Mirov, Valentine was a prize prisoner, and the MGB wanted him back in Moscow. What about the Mephisto list, though? It still gnawed at Livy how she'd let the other Russian, the one with the busted nose and the bad breath, take half of the list from her that night at the French Embassy.

Livy knew she'd have to improvise once they arrived. Whether by train or car, she was determined to leave the Gare du Nord with Valentine. She felt the coming confrontation in her body, the desire to climb the walls of this place, but outwardly Livy appeared calm. She'd felt the same way before a battle during the war, and just before she and Peter had been stopped by the Gestapo. Anxiety knotted her insides, and yet her mind again went to Peter. In this moment where an impulsive decision could change or end someone's life, she felt him beside her.

"Don't worry." That would be his advice. The words alone wouldn't calm her; it was his smile, the brightness in his eyes, the sense he carried that nothing could ever get in their way.

Livy's grip on the Webley tightened. Any moment she'd be face-to-face again with Peter's killer. What would he have done in her situation? Carry out the orders. Complete the mission. *England expects nothing less.*

*   *   *

Minutes seemed endless. The hot tension Livy felt when she arrived at the station had settled somewhat. So after more than twenty minutes of waiting, Nathalie wandered over to a small bench just inside the main doors and sat. Livy moved back so she could keep an eye on both the front doors and her companion.

"Clear something up for me, luv," Livy said, her voice hushed. "You sent for me, but Valentine didn't know?"

Nathalie didn't speak for a moment. Then, "He told me about you. How he knew you from the war. I saw . . . a way out." The defiance was gone from her voice. She sounded tired.

"You must wake up in the morning and wonder whose side you're on that day."

"I gave Edward everything. For four years. You see how he treats me."

"Then why did you do it?"

Nathalie looked up. The hat she wore pulled down over her bruised cheek covered nearly the entire top half of her face. "What?"

"Work with the Germans."

The Frenchwoman sighed. "Why does anyone ever do anything? For money, I suppose. For love."

"A bastard like Valentine?"

Nathalie tilted her head up to look at Livy. Her eye was nearly swollen shut. "You and I—we are more similar than you would like to think."

Before Livy could respond, lights from outside the front doors crossed her face. She inched forward. The pair of head lamps that eased into the square slowly became four. Nathalie stood and moved beside Livy as the two cars slowed and then parked about twenty-five feet from the doors.

"This has to be them," the Frenchwoman whispered.

"You don't move unless I tell you to," Livy said. "I'll shoot if you run."

Nathalie nodded. Her right eye twitched slightly. Livy wondered if somehow she'd become Nathalie's protector now.

Both cars looked to be large black Citroën saloons. The rear doors of the first car opened, and two men in long coats and hats stepped out. Both carried traveling bags. One of the men waved to the driver, who pulled away as the two made for the front doors. Livy tensed and eased the Webley out of her coat as the men pushed through the doors about ten feet to her left. They were of average height, with mustaches and thick noses Brothers, by the look of it. Maybe Italians.

Nathalie shook her head and let out a deep sigh. Livy watched the mustache boys until they disappeared inside the men's room; then she whipped her head back to the front in time to see the second car turn off its lights.

It was too dark to make out how many people were inside. One back door opened, and a tall figure unfolded from the car and walked to the back. The man wore a long coat, collar up, and a homburg. He looked both ways before opening the boot. He disappeared from view for several seconds.

Livy couldn't take much more of this.

Then the man in the homburg closed the boot. He wore a messenger bag around his shoulders. With more speed now, he dashed to the other side of the car and helped someone out. Another tall man.

Nathalie caught her eyes and nodded, but Livy already knew. Mirov and Valentine had arrived.

Livy knew she couldn't let them get into the station. Too many variables came into play once they crossed the station's threshold. The decision calmed her.

She grabbed Nathalie's elbow and hissed in her ear, "Stay next to me. No matter what happens." The Frenchwoman nodded. Livy opened the doors and moved out into the square to meet the two men, gun drawn.

Mirov saw her first and grabbed Valentine by the arm, mirroring Livy's position with Nathalie. The two men stopped, still in the street, about fifteen feet away from the women. The black saloon's engine purred behind them as if ready to drive away. A match inside the car flickered, illuminating a face Livy had first seen some time ago outside the French Embassy. The boxer's nose, the thick upper lip, the mustache that curled down the sides of his mouth. Levchenko glared at Livy through the windshield as he lit his cigarette. Then the match flickered out and the darkness cloaked him again.

"Olivia," said Mirov, his long face drawn and tired, "this isn't your battle anymore."

"You're right. It all ends tonight. I've got Nathalie. She's got the list, and I'm taking that bastard back with me."

"You had your chance, Livy," Valentine said, smirking. Then to Nathalie, "And you. You're being played for a fool, girl."

"You shut it," Livy said, turning the gun on the magician. "Give me one reason to shoot, Luc. I've been waiting here a long time and I'm feeling a bit jumpy."

Mirov stepped forward. "Olivia, this will not end the way you want. You have to let me take him. You have to trust me. You have to trust that we want the same thing."

"Trust you?" Livy scoffed. "Back away. Now. This doesn't need to be messy."

The Russian kept getting closer to her and was now about ten feet away. Livy knew he wanted to appease her. She'd experienced his charm in a variety of accents, but it wouldn't work tonight.

"We both have orders, but we don't have to be enemies, Olivia. That's what he wants," he said, jerking his head at Valentine. "Look at what we—our two countries—accomplished together. Just because the war is over, we don't have to tear it all apart—"

The next moment happened so quickly Livy barely registered it. She turned back to Valentine to see he had a small automatic in his hand. At the same moment Mirov reached for her. Then a chunk of his gray hair hit her coat and fell to the ground. Livy looked down and saw a pile of gray, now red mixed with blood and brains. Instinctively she whipped the gun to Mirov. Somehow the Russian was still standing, even though a chunk of his forehead lay at Livy's feet. He staggered forward, one wobbly step, until another bullet hit him square in the back. His arms flung out to the sides, suspending him for a moment, before his lean frame crashed face first to the pavement.

Nathalie screamed. Livy spun toward Valentine.

But he looked back toward the square, searching for something. Suddenly he swung around, pivoting toward Nathalie, the gun extended in his right hand. Livy squeezed the trigger of the Webley twice. The first bullet hit Valentine in the stomach. The second caught him full in the chest, spinning him around. He teetered for a moment, and then Valentine's head snapped back as if he'd been punched in the face. His black fedora toppled into the square. For a moment Livy saw his bare head and the hole where the third bullet had entered, and he looked vulnerable. Peaceful. Like Luc. Then he crashed hard, facedown, into the street.

A third shot. From where?

Livy's mind grappled with the new immediate danger. She and Nathalie had no protection. If a sniper lay out there in the darkness, they'd be next. No way to protect themselves.

Livy tensed, waiting for the bullet. She expected death.

Nothing happened.

She looked at Valentine. The magician Mephisto, the man she knew as Luc, lay completely still.

Then the black Citroën's engine revved. The big car spun away from the curb, its wheels whining as it left the Gare du Nord. At the same time Nathalie, who by now had stopped screaming, began to run. She kicked off her unwieldy heels and dashed awkwardly into the square.

Without a second thought, Livy took off after her, but the gathered fabric of her dress restricted her gait. She trampled on satin with each step. Stopping, she ripped the bottom of the dress off, just below the knee.

Nathalie had a head start of maybe twenty-five yards. Livy shoved the Webley in her coat and ran. Her strides at first matching Nathalie's.

In the distance, a siren began its wail.

Livy pushed forward, her breath coming in hard fast bursts. Legs churning now without the damned skirt's restriction. Nathalie began to lose ground as they reached the unlit portion of the square farther from the station.

The siren's insistent scream drew nearer as Livy caught up to the fleeing Nathalie. She lunged for her coat but grabbed only air. With one burst from her legs, Livy threw herself at the Frenchwoman, grabbing the collar of Nathalie's expensive overcoat, and dragged them both to the hard street. They toppled over each other, grunting. Nathalie pushed and flailed, trying to get free, but Livy held tight to the coat collar. The tumbling stopped with Livy kneeling over her back. Nathalie thrashed like a captured animal under her, repeating *"Non"* over and over.

With the wail of the siren only a few streets away, Livy dug her knee deeper into Nathalie's back. Placed a hand over her mouth to quiet her cries. As the police car's cry began to fade, so too did Nathalie's will to resist. Livy took a moment to catch her own breath and then used what little strength she had left to get Nathalie on her feet. She put her arm around the Frenchwoman's shoulders. They limped into the darkness as the blinking light of a police car lit up the square behind them.

Chapter Twenty

Livy dragged Nathalie through the backstreets near the Gare du Nord, gun rammed into her side, until she found a café that was still open. There she rang Allard. He listened, without interruption, as Livy explained what had happened. Quite calmly, he told her to find a dark corner near the café, somewhere where the two of them wouldn't be seen, and that he would pick them up shortly.

Livy and Nathalie sat side by side in the back doorway of a butcher's just off the main road about a mile from the rail station. Waiting. Again. They had not spoken since the shooting. Livy broke the silence.

"What was that about? Running into the square back there? You could've been killed."

Nathalie spun toward Livy, her battered eye swollen and red from crying. "You should have let me go."

"You promised me that list. So, I'm keeping you safe and right by my side."

"Let me go now, and I will give it to you. Edward is dead. There is nothing stopping us now."

"Not the way it works, luv. Some folks in London would like a chat with you."

Nathalie stood suddenly, her voice loud and shrill. "London? No, I can't. I won't." The sudden burst of raw emotion caught Livy off guard. She scrambled to her feet, pushing the barrel of the gun into Nathalie's side.

"You're going to sit down and be quiet," Livy said, hissing. Nathalie tried to pull away. Livy wrapped a hand around her throat. "Don't make me do this, Nathalie. A car will be here soon. Both of us are leaving Paris. Tonight."

The fire seemed to leave Nathalie instantly. She sank back to the sidewalk, crushing the hat over her face as she sobbed quietly. Livy sat next to her, listening to Nathalie cry, hoping Allard would be there soon.

Ten very long minutes later, he arrived. Despite having been awakened in the middle of the night with the sort of news no head of station wants to hear, the Englishman looked rested and polished. His suit and shirt were so pressed they crackled.

He took Nathalie first and put her in the front seat of the Renault. Livy followed and sat in the back. Livy expected Nathalie to try to get away again, so she kept her hand on the gun. But Nathalie seemed too spent to try anything. She leaned her head back against the door, fidgeting with her opulent cigarette case, and closed her eyes. Apart from the occasional siren, the time passed quietly.

Livy's eyes darted back out to the main road, looking for the police, who would be searching for the killer of the two men at the station. The travel bag she'd left at Madame Riveaux's sat on the seat next to her. Allard had thought of everything.

She held the Webley tight during the drive. She couldn't take the chance that Nathalie might try to make a run for it at a stop sign.

Livy slumped into the automobile's leather. She still wore the torn satin mermaid dress, which felt dirty to her skin now. She craved a bath and clean clothes. As the sun came up, she undid the top buttons of her overcoat. She noticed a curled strand of Mirov's gray hair that clung to the coat's lapel. She left it there.

Allard drove not to the airport but to a small airfield about ten miles out of the city. A green guardhouse stood at the entrance, and the British soldier inside waved them through upon seeing Allard. At the end of the unpaved runway, a green Lodestar transport plane with the RAF insignia on its side sat idling.

Allard stopped the car just beyond the guardhouse and helped Livy out of the back seat. Her legs and arms ached from her tumble in the street, and her right elbow burned, as if she'd been cut. He asked for her gun. She handed over the Webley and silencer. Allard placed it in a green travel bag and shoved it under his seat.

Allard didn't say anything else. He could have said many things. He could say she'd been reckless and damned near gotten herself killed. He could say she might have caused an international incident in a city and country still trying to find its way two years after liberation. Instead he methodically went about the business of transferring the two women from his car to the waiting plane.

Allard helped Nathalie on board first, into the waiting arms of an RAF guard. Then he turned to Livy.

"I'll take care of everything on this end," he said, handing her the travel bag. "If I were you, Miss Nash, I don't believe I'd return to France in the foreseeable future. *Bon voyage.*"

Livy nodded and found a seat inside the warehouselike interior of the cargo plane. She sat on one of the facing benches opposite the Frenchwoman. A few minutes later they took off. Nathalie's head lolled against the side of the plane. She sobbed as the plane surged upward.

"He's dead now," Livy said. Truth be told, she had begun to pity Nathalie. "You don't have to worry about him again."

"Edward has been dead to me for a long time," she shot back, turning her head away. Within minutes she fell asleep.

Now he's dead to us both, Livy thought. She remembered how Valentine's body lay in the street, the way it flopped like a broken toy. There'd been a time when she might have felt like dancing over the traitor's corpse. But it had all happened so quickly. How she had wanted the chance to . . . what? Enjoy the moment? The reality was, she still felt empty. Killing Valentine didn't erase her past. It only reopened the wound. What had she expected? That Valentine's death would be the salve to ease the pain of losing Peter? God, she'd still give anything to talk to him again. To see Peter's face light up as she told him about all of it. Valentine was dead, but so was Peter. Despite the soothing drone of the engines in flight, Livy never closed her eyes.

*   *   *

The next day Livy sat in one of the guest chairs next to Penelope Baker's desk in the Kemsley News office in London. Even though she wore her brown suit, which had only recently been pressed, Livy felt haggard next to the fresh and very manicured Miss Baker.

Livy remembered the first time she'd sat in this chair, waiting to see what would come her way once she crossed to the inner office. Hard to believe it had been only days ago. Fleming's offer had seemed like a life preserver thrown to her after she was sacked from the P&J.

On the surface, she'd accomplished what she set out to do. Nathalie had been taken into custody. Valentine was dead. But still it felt all wrong. One thought nagged at her like a bad toothache: *Who killed Andrei Mirov?*

The *whoosh* of the interior office door sounded as Fleming appeared. He nodded at Livy and went back inside.

"Good luck," Pen whispered as Livy passed her desk.

Inside, Fleming lit a cigarette but didn't speak. He picked up a folder from his crowded desk and thumbed through several sheets until he found what he wanted. Behind his desk, the map of the world pulsed with dozens of bulbs representing Kemsley's foreign correspondents. The light in Paris still burned.

"The French police have taken over the investigation of the Soviet national Andrei Mirov," Fleming said, eyes on the report. "I take it you knew him prior to his death?"

Livy nodded.

"'Deceased appears to be in his midfifties with two gunshot wounds. One to the head and the other through the chest. Documents cleared through the Soviet Embassy in Paris. Believed to be a longtime member of Soviet state security, also known as the MGB.'" Fleming looked up. His blue eyes were dark and hooded. "I don't suppose you saw who shot him?"

"No," Livy said. "The shots came from the square. I never saw anyone else."

"You told Allard there was a third man there. Another Russian?"

"The same man who took the list from me at the French Embassy. He drove the car. But I don't think he could have shot Mirov. The angle wasn't right."

Fleming nodded, considering her explanation, then sat behind his desk and placed the folder on top of the smallest stack. His wide mouth was a flat line. "What happened with Valentine?"

Livy didn't know what to say. She'd asked herself the same question many times since it happened. "Valentine had a gun. Then Mirov was shot. I didn't have time to think about it. He turned toward Nathalie and I fired."

"Valentine threatened Miss Billerant?"

"I don't know what he intended. I didn't give him time."

"You just shot him?"

Livy blinked. Her mouth felt dry as she remembered the night. She pursed her lips and tried to sound calm.

"A man's brains had just landed on my coat. Here's another man with a gun and he's turning in our direction. So, yes, I just shot him."

Fleming took a long drag of the cigarette. "And Miss Billerant ran from you after Valentine was shot. If she wanted to give us the list, then why would she try to get away?"

"I don't know. She wouldn't tell me. Just pleaded to stay."

Fleming leaned across the table. Clearly, the sequence of events confused him as much as Livy.

"Is Nathalie being cooperative?" Livy asked.

"Not in the least. She's refusing to talk unless we send her back to Paris. Apparently the Americans are having a go with her today. We shall see what they can get out of her."

Fleming picked up the folder again and looked it over. "We have to assume the Russians have the half of the list they took from you. Until Miss Billerant decides to keep up her end of the bargain, they still have the advantage, I'd say."

Livy tried to disguise what she felt inside. Her stomach lurched and tears pushed at the corners of her eyes. She'd cocked it up but good. She tried denying it to herself, but she knew it now. If Fleming registered her discomfort, he gave no indication.

"You broke into the Billerant woman's hotel room in the middle of the night. What made you force her hand?" he asked.

"She was stalling. It didn't feel right to me. Plus I knew the other side was closing in and Valentine was playing both sides to see who'd give him the best deal."

"How do you know?"

"He as much as told me."

"Valentine contacted you?"

"When I was in jail."

"Jail?" Fleming let the word hang in the air. "I see." He smoked and didn't speak for at least a minute. "You hated him, of course?"

"Yes sir, but that's not why I shot him. I couldn't let the Russian take him. I had my orders."

"So, now we just sit and wait to see what, if anything, the Russians do with the Mephisto network." Fleming's wide mouth turned down. He tossed the folder on his desk in disgust. "Thank you, Miss Nash. I think that will be all."

His words seemed to stop time. *That will be all?*

She had to leave, but her legs wouldn't move just yet. She had no air. Had her heart stopped? She forced herself to stand, managing a nod in Fleming's direction. His eyes never left the desk. Livy hoped she'd make it outside before the tears came. He'd taken a chance on her and she'd delivered a right royal mess *and* an uncooperative source. Well, she'd had a go. Now it was time to bow and get off the stage.

Somehow she made it to the door, through the outer office, and out of the brown, unremarkable building on the Gray's Inn Road. Livy stood on the sidewalk, as people purposefully hurried past and around her, and realized she had no idea where she was headed.

Chapter
Twenty-One

～

Three days after her meeting with Fleming, Livy walked to the *Press and Journal* building in central London. She had no real plans for the day. In fact, she had no real plans for any day, but in the middle of the night she'd been struck by the realization that she had unfinished business, and finishing required a bit of help.

Beyond that she'd spent the last two days sitting in bed thinking, not even changing out of the gown she'd worn to bed, a gown her mother had worn. Moths had eaten through much of the hem and the elbows, but it felt like a second skin to her. Despite the curt dismissal, Fleming had sent round a very generous stipend for her work in Paris, but that wouldn't last forever. She'd settled up with Mr. Langham on her rent, paid the bills, and avoided Black Market Billy and his access to the booze of the world. But she'd need a new job and soon.

Sleep had been sporadic. She'd nap for an hour or two and then be woken by a nightmare. The dream was always the same: She stood on a platform at the Gare du Nord as a train approached, Valentine and Mirov in front of her. As the speeding engine reached the inside of the station, the Russian's head would pop like a balloon. When it did, Livy screamed and shoved Valentine into the path of the oncoming locomotive. The engine raced on through the station, and once it cleared, Livy would walk to the edge of the platform to look at the body, but it was never Edward Valentine lying on the tracks. It was always Peter.

She'd wake up then.

Always the same dream with perhaps a slight variation. It shook her at first, especially in the middle of the night, and then made her feel ridiculous in the warm light of morning. She didn't know what to make of the last moment in the dream—Valentine suddenly becoming Peter—but somehow she knew it meant unfinished business.

She reached the old brick P&J building. Its anachronistic modern electric sign spun slowly over the front door, the name of the paper written in an Old English–looking type. The juxtaposition of styles jarred.

Livy considered just popping in and taking a quick tour of the old office, with lots of backslapping and "Oh, remember when . . . ?" and "Well, don't be a stranger." Part of her worried she might break down and ask for her old job back. *Correction— strike a line through* ask *and substitute the word* plead. *Much stronger choice of words and, in this case, far more accurate.*

But the closer she got to the front door, the more she could smell the lingering odor of the butcher's shop that had occupied the ground floor. That gave her pause. So she found a bench on the sidewalk near the front glass doors and waited.

Lunch arrived and Myrtle Dickinson bounded out the front door in hot pursuit of a quick meal that would have her back at the desk in plenty of time. Dear sweet Myrtle from Burnley. Livy had to say hello.

"Oh my oh my oh my, it's Livy," Myrtle said, grabbing her old coworker and hugging tight. "I've missed you so much. I'm lost up there without you. You know I am."

"Are you keeping them all honest, luv?"

"I don't know about that." Myrtle blushed a ripe shade of pink under her cat-eye glasses. "But I am working on 'The Ladies' Front' now. Mrs. O'Toole gives me a bit more responsibility each week, and oh, I just hope I can do it justice the way you did."

Livy could have said any number of things to that, but she just smiled—her first in days—and said, "Mrs. O'Toole is lucky to have you. She may not know it yet, but she is."

"You're so good to me, Livy. Oh, and what about you now? Working for the big pants, we hear."

"Well, I'm not so sure about that."

"You're a foreign correspondent, isn't that right? For—um, for—is it *The Times*?"

"Just sort of a fact finder, really. Who knows, they may not even keep me on, you know."

"They're lucky to have you. *They* may not know it yet, but they are."

After being ensconced in a world of lies and trickery, the simple, unassuming pleasure of a chat with Myrtle felt like a spring day in the park. Livy grabbed the little woman and gave her a long hug and kiss on the cheek. "You're a peach, Myrtle."

"Come on, it's my lunchtime and we can catch up. I don't have all that long. Mr. O'Toole likes me back in the office a few minutes early in case he needs me to proof something."

"However long you have. It's my treat. But there is something I'd like you to find for me in the news files. I need an address."

* * *

It took Myrtle less than an hour to find the address Livy wanted. For some reason Livy had expected it to be farther away from London, but the street Myrtle gave her was in Chiswick. Livy thanked her friend and promised to ring her for dinner and drinks later that week, though for Myrtle "drinks" meant ginger beer. Part of her Lancashire charm.

Livy made it to the nearest Underground stop a few minutes after three and took a deep breath. She couldn't move forward without putting the past behind her. Livy also knew that if she waited until tomorrow, she'd spend another sleepless night dreading it.

Chiswick, an area of London frequently visited by the Luftwaffe during the war, was famous primarily as the birthplace of the artist William Hogarth. A chipped sign, possibly hit by a stray piece of German shrapnel during the Blitz, reminded travelers of the direction of the great man's birthplace once they exited the Chiswick Park tube station. Livy went the opposite direction.

She walked past the usual shops and cafés. It didn't take long to figure out that this had to be the right place. The sidewalks teemed with mums and prams, going to the park, going home from the park, et cetera, et cetera.

After about a fifteen-minute stroll, she arrived at the address on Wilton Avenue, a few blocks off the Chiswick High Road. The house needed a bit of work. It looked to be a fairly standard two-story walk-up sandwiched between two other duplicate homes. Each had a small iron fence, a small garden, the same basic two steps up to the front door, and two front windows, one on top of the other. However, the window and doorframes all needed a good coat of paint and the fence had started to rust a bit.

Livy saw the boy first. He sat on the bottom step drawing something on a sheet of paper on top of a schoolbook. He had thick dark hair and the clear blue eyes that only young children seemed to have. Five years old now, Livy guessed. As she opened the gate, the boy looked up, called "Mum!" and ran inside, leaving the drawing on the steps. She looked down at the budding Hogarth's work. He'd drawn a police constable with a tall hat and big badge.

"Can I help you?"

Clara Scobee stood just inside the door. Livy had seen her only in photographs, but they hadn't half done her justice. She was about Livy's height, five and a half feet, with a very small build. She had golden hair and bright brown eyes. A few lines had developed at her temples and next to her mouth. The result of many sleepless nights, Livy reckoned.

"I'm—I'm sorry to just stop by . . . um . . . my name is Olivia Nash, Mrs. Scobee." Livy wanted to apologize and run away, but she had to be here and see his wife and son, face-to-face.

Clara blinked at the name and looked as if she might speak, but then her son reappeared, clinging to her knee.

"I served in the war. With your husband," Livy said, trying not to sound pathetic.

"Oh—in France, with Peter?" Clara asked, clearly confused. "But I don't—"

"You see, we were together near the end of the war."

"Ah, yes," she said, beginning to understand but not really looking as if the thought pleased her. "Miss—miss, is it? Yes, um—Miss Nash, I'm not really sure this is—"

"I was there with him—at the end of it, you see. I wasn't able to make the presentation at the palace, and I just wanted to—meet you, I suppose."

"Please, Miss Nash, I'm sorry. Won't you come in?"

Clara put the kettle on, and the normality of two English-women sitting down for afternoon tea began to play out. The tension of the doorstep remained, however. John, who didn't seem to say very much, sat at a makeshift desk in the kitchen, drawing away. Clara sat in a small upholstered chair with lace coverings to hide the threadbare armrests. Livy sat opposite her on a love seat across from a bookshelf where Peter's George medal sat, still in its bright-red box.

"Won't be a moment on the tea," Clara said, her smile forced, clearly hoping the kettle would boil and this visit could move forward.

"You're very kind to invite me in, Mrs. Scobee," Livy said. "I just—I don't really know why I wanted to come see you, but you see, Peter and I became—well, he became someone I looked up to—in France. He taught me—"

The kettle's whistling interruption of Livy's rambling monologue was like the bell saving a punch-drunk fighter.

Clara excused herself to the kitchen, stopping to satisfy John's request for his own drink. This gave Livy a chance to think through—again—what she wanted to say to this woman, and what she hoped would come from this visit. Was she there to size Clara up, see what sort of woman Peter had wanted at home? She told herself that was rubbish, but she had to admit to herself that could be part of it. There was more, though. Guilt, maybe? She'd slept with this woman's husband. That's what she'd be to Clara. The other woman. She felt her face redden as shame consumed her. Livy resisted the urge to bolt out the front door.

"Do you work, Miss Nash?" Clara returned with the pot.

"Um, yes. I work for a newspaper."

"Ah, I see. An independent woman."

Livy tipped the milk into her cup and stirred. "I want you to understand, Mrs. Scobee, that Peter meant a great deal to me."

"Did he?" Clara said, her jaw clenched as she went through all the motions of the genteel hostess.

Why did I ever come here? Livy wondered.

"And he meant a great deal to others in our unit," she added. "Mrs. Scobee, I'm sorry—this is hard for me because . . . oh God. Your husband and I—and others—what we did during the war was very . . . *isolated* work. Dangerous, necessary work, but—but lonely. God, I'm making a mess of this—"

Clara's back seem to stiffen. Her voice hushed. "Miss Nash, I'd be careful what you say to me with my son in the other room."

Livy stopped. She saw herself through Clara's eyes now, and she felt stupid and selfish. Livy put down her cup.

"I've nothing to say that might upset him . . . or you, for that matter. I'm sorry I'm stumbling, but Peter and I—and everyone in our small unit—had to trust one another. I've never been married, but I imagine it's like the trust a husband and wife have to have. Absolute. We all had that for one another, but Peter, you see, he was our leader. He was a born leader, Mrs. Scobee. Even in the worst of times—the very worst—we took strength from him. Look, I don't know what I'm saying or why I want you to hear this, but he—your husband—" Livy's voice began to crumble. "Peter was loved by everyone who knew him, Mrs. Scobee. He was a good man. You'd have been very proud of him."

Clara Scobee fought to hold back the tears that pooled in her eyes.

"Mum, I can't find the green pencil," John said, tugging at Clara's shoulder, his eyes fixed on Livy.

"Just give us one more minute, John. One more. Miss Nash was just leaving."

After a bit of *ooh*ing over John's latest drawing—a giant, rampaging Frankenstein's monster—Livy made her goodbyes. Clara saw her to the door, her tears now dried.

"Look, I'm sorry again for the bother, Mrs.—" Livy began.

"Miss Nash, you didn't come all the way out here to tell me that my husband was a brave man. I'm quite aware of that. The king gave me a medal saying as much," she said, her lips tight. "I don't know why you came here, honestly, and I don't need to know." Clara leaned back in her chair. Her eyes hardened, "I don't need to know what happened, or didn't happen, between you and my husband in France. That is the past." She shook her head and sipped her tea. The moment of anger seemed to have passed. "My son and I have to move forward. We weren't given a choice in that matter, but we are making do and moving forward. The war is the past, Miss Nash, and whatever happened then is just that. Just—memories." She put her cup on a table and leaned forward. "But some memories will drown you, Miss

Nash. If you don't mind my saying so. You might do well to remember that."

After leaving the Scobee's scruffy house, Livy meandered back in the direction of the Chiswick tube stop. She'd hoped the visit to see Peter's widow would offer some form of clarity. She couldn't have expected understanding from the woman. Instead she felt chastened. Foolish, even. Clara was right, though, Livy thought. *The past is drowning me. And no rescue in sight.*

She took a circuitous route, unconcerned about time, nowhere really to be, and tried to see the future that lay head of her.

Chapter
Twenty-Two

⁓

"He's got enough going right now, darling. We do have actual foreign correspondents who work for us, you know."

Penelope Baker sat next to Livy on a bench outside the Chancery Lane tube station. Livy had called and asked for a meeting with Fleming but been told the boss was too busy. That didn't deter her. After two more calls on the same day, Pen agreed to an "informal lunch chat." So there they sat, given cover by the lunchtime bustle around the tube stop, sharing chips. Despite her cool, professional exterior, Pen devoured the warm chips as if she'd given all her rationing coupons away.

"Of course," Livy said. "I just wanted to know if they'd gotten anything out of Nathalie. So many questions still, you know?"

After her visit to the Scobee house, it had taken Livy the better part of a very long sleepless night for her to realize she couldn't move forward just yet. Not until a few things made more sense to her.

"Listen, Livy—do you want the last chip? No? Thanks so much." Pen cleared it in two concise bites. "Now, I'm in no position to give advice. I mean, I had my little fling with

Ian—Mr. Fleming. I knew his type going in, of course, but like a stupid git I thought I'd change him. Stupid, stupid! So I learned. And what I learned was there comes a time when you have to let the past be the past."

"I've been hearing that a lot lately."

"You did your job. Now let the other chaps do theirs. Whatever that might be," she said, glancing down at her expensive wristwatch. Cartier, Livy guessed. "Got to be back, darling. I'll give you a shout if I hear anything."

Pen Baker merged with the others crossing the street to catch buses, make a train, or do whatever normal people did. Livy didn't move, her mind fixated on two disparate days in France when people had died. She kept seeing Peter's death. Then Mirov and Valentine dead outside the Gare du Nord. Nathalie running in the direction of the gunshots. Something connected those two days, but she couldn't see it yet.

* * *

The next morning, Tom Vance showed up on Livy Nash's doorstep in Camden Town. Hat, literally and figuratively, in hand.

"Is this an official visit, Mr. Vance?" Livy had nowhere to be and looked it. Untamed hair, rumpled gown, and quilted robe to cover it all up. Allard had been right; she wasn't exactly Rita Hayworth.

"You might say that." He, of course, was dressed to the nines in a cream pinstripe suit, brown wing tips, and a straw trilby. "So, if you need time to get dressed—oh, and please, call me Tom."

"What's on your mind, Mr. Vance?"

Vance grinned. "Maybe I could just step inside? I have a confidential proposition for you."

Vance got to the point once Livy shut the door.

"We might have a break on the Mephisto network. We have a walk-in back in Paris who claims he has the whole scoop. The day before, there was a murder in Montmartre. A talent agent was killed in a flat. Next day a gunman comes after our walk-in. He escapes, but is so hysterical he turns himself in. He claims this talent agent was part of the network and that the murder is some sort of message. He's terrified. Says he'll give us everything for protection. Anyway, I think you know our walk-in. His name is Jabot, but he's that magician Diablo, the one we saw at the theater. If I'm not mistaken, you also had bit of a run-in with him at the Ritz."

"Interesting," she said. *A Mephisto agent is killed and then someone goes after Jabot.* The news intrigued Livy—although she had no intention of letting Vance know that. "But I'm out. I'm just an unemployed journalist sitting in her dressing gown in the middle of the day."

"Tell me about Jabot. What do you know about him?"

Livy nearly laughed in his face. "He needs to work on his act. Thanks for the chat, Mr. Vance. The door is behind you."

Vance didn't move. "Valentine's dead, but the list is still out there, Livy. Now, you know this operation better than anybody. We can still finish this job, but I need to know what you know."

"We?" she said, scoffing. "Oh, did your Mr. Gray change his mind about me? Last I saw of him, he told me to leave Paris for good."

"I'm not Gray. This is your operation, too, Livy, as far as I'm concerned. And so I'm asking for your help."

Livy turned away. Her eyes roamed over the walls of her confining flat. If she told Tom Vance to get the hell out and he did, then what? Paris practically beckoned her. It would give her the chance to answer those nagging questions that kept her up at night. And with Nathalie still uncooperative, she might just be able to finish her job and persuade Fleming to give her a second chance.

She turned on him, arms folded, head tossed back. "Take me to Paris, then."

Now it was Vance's turn to look incredulous. "I don't want to assume too much, but there was a double murder at the Gare du Nord last week, and I imagine you are someone the French authorities would, at the very least, like to question."

Livy felt exposed suddenly, as if what had happened at the station had been private. The notion felt personal and ridiculous at the same time. But her bravado never wavered.

"They have to find me first," she said.

"My God, do you have any idea the kind of risk I'm taking by even being here? Gray warned me that if he found out that I had so much as talked to you, he would disavow all knowledge of me. And if he ever saw your *limey ass* again—and that's a direct quote—he'd hand you over to the police himself."

"All that tweed makes him itchy, I'll bet."

Vance ignored the sarcasm. "I think this Jabot is the real deal. If what he says is true, then this may be our last chance to get the Mephisto list. The Soviets can't start calling the shots on this."

"You may be right, but I'm through having these little chats so you can find out what I know. You want my help? Then get me a plane to Paris and let's go back like proper colleagues. I'm not just some girl you snog at the Dorchester. When I'm there, then you have my help."

"All right, but I'll put you up somewhere safe while I have a look around the murder site in Montmartre and interrogate Jabot. Then you can take a look at my notes and advise me. Okay?"

"Mr. Vance, I have no intention of being a kept woman during this trip. If you want my help, it's on my terms."

"And those terms are what exactly?" Vance said, seeming more than a little hesitant.

"First, I fully intend to let my people know I'm working on this again." Livy planned a courtesy call to Dennis Allard upon arrival. His pencil-thin mustache might curl, but she felt an allegiance to the man, and also—even though he had unceremoniously sacked her—to Fleming. After all, she hoped to have her job back after this sojourn.

Livy went on. "Second, I'll do everything I can to help you, but I want to see where this talent agent was killed, and I want to talk to Jabot as well."

"You don't want much, do you?"

"Yes or no?"

"So your plan is to just walk into a French police station?" he asked.

"I walked into a Gestapo headquarters during the war. Getting into a Paris police station will be easier than eating crepes suzette. Finally, whatever happens as a result of our interrogation of Jabot will be mutually beneficial to both our governments."

"Do you realize what happens to both of us if the police pick you up?"

"Those are the terms. Take 'em or leave 'em."

Their eyes held each other's. Searching. No smiles. Silence. Waiting. Livy's stomach flip-flopped. Outside a car horn echoed down the lane. Finally, Vance spoke.

"Fine. Like you said, we're in this together. Proper colleagues. But if something happens—something neither of us can see right now—then it's every man for himself."

"And every woman, luv."

* * *

During the flight, Vance thumbed through a worn copy of *Look* magazine with Gregory Peck on the cover. Livy tried to sleep, but unanswered questions plagued her like the ghosts of the dead. Still, she put her head back and did not stir until the plane touched the tarmac.

She used a phone at the arrivals desk to call Allard and let him know she'd returned. "I'm doing a bit of freelance work at the moment, but it ties in to the previous story I filed for Kemsley. I hope you'll pass this message along to the editor. He might be interested in this new piece once it's finished."

Ever the professional, Allard said her work "sounded interesting" and promised to "keep her in mind if his Paris contacts developed an interest in her." But his usually unflappable BBC radio voice stumbled a bit as he spoke. Livy imagined Allard ringing up Fleming immediately. She wondered how the news might be received at the Kemsley office in London. Would Fleming welcome the news? Or was it more likely his wide mouth would turn down and he'd light another cigarette while ruing the day he'd ever walked into that pub?

As they walked through the airport, Livy felt a familiar surge, part adrenaline and part fear. She and Vance steered clear of police officers and their military counterparts, the gendarmerie. Livy linked her arm with Vance's as they strolled, like a couple on holiday. Livy pointed at the signs in French, leaned on his shoulder, and even gave him a kiss on the cheek as he hailed a taxi. Her exterior masked the anxiety that gripped her. The police could be trouble, but Livy knew seeking answers to the questions that plagued her was a dangerous route.

They approached the customs desk, arm in arm. She offered her passport to the blue-uniformed officer. He looked it over and then smiled up at her.

"Bienvenue, mademoiselle."

Livy took back her passport with a smile and wondered if she'd ever see London again.

Chapter
Twenty-Three

Just over an hour later, Livy and Tom stood in front of a four-story building of flats in the Montmartre district of the city in the eighteenth arrondissement. This area of the city had always been Livy's favorite. It was the part of Paris that seemed the most Parisian. She loved the great hill from which the district derived its name, as well as the vibrant art culture, the night-clubs and cafés, the funicular cable car, and of course the Sacré-Coeur.

But on this particular sunny afternoon, her focus rested on the architecture of the building before her.

"Very nice place," Livy said.

Vance nervously looked up and down the street.

"Stop twitching, Tom."

"He was shot inside, you know. We might find out a little more in there. Plus, we'd be less conspicuous than standing here on the street in the middle of the day."

Livy smiled at him. "You're cute when you're nervous. Look at this place, though. How much do you think one flat might cost? I'll lay you ten to one the Germans occupied this whole block during the war. They took all the best spots."

"So what exactly are we to make of this, Miss Marple?"

"Come now, Tom. You told me yourself that the man who was shot—Milos—was in his forties, with a wife and three little ones all under ten. And here he goes and buys a flat in oh-so-posh Montmartre? I feel certain the missus would much rather he have spent the money on food or maybe a maid to help around the house."

"This feels like his little romantic getaway. Somewhere discreet for a mistress or two."

"Could be. Place like this doesn't come cheap."

Vance blinked at her. "The car. He bought a brand-new car the day he was shot. The police towed it in. Nice one, too. Red. Soft top."

"And didn't you tell me he was just a midlevel talent agent? So where does he get all this money to buy a car and rent a flat in this part of Paris?" Livy could feel it. The well-kept secrets of the Mephisto list were starting to spill out into the open.

* * *

The flat in question was on the right at the top of the second-floor landing. Vance had given the concierge a wad of francs that afforded them ten minutes to look around.

Since it was the middle of the day, the maid seemed to be the only one in the building aside from the concierge. She gave them both a quick nod as they entered.

Everything about the building said money. The floors in the lobby had the sheen of marble, even if they weren't. The banister appeared to have been hand carved, with deep detail in the woodwork. Livy reckoned a building this elegant must have been an enclave for the Germans during the war. Maybe that's why everything looked so new and shiny inside; the owners had wanted to scrub away any trace of the former Nazi tenants.

They stood outside flat number fourteen. Livy tried the door. Locked.

"You have a key, then," Livy said to Vance.

"Are you kidding? We have no jurisdiction here."

"So the francs you gave the concierge got us in the building but not the flat?"

Vance shrugged.

Livy leaned against him, her voice a whisper. "You got taken. Everyone thinks you Yanks have all the money in the world."

"We do," he said.

The maid on the floor below gave the wall sconce near the door one final swish of her dusting rag and turned toward the door when Livy called to her from above. She hesitated. Her eyes narrowed as Livy bounded down the stairs and approached her slowly.

"*Excusez-moi, s'il vous plaît,*" Livy said, switching to French. Suspicion clouded the maid's face as her gaze flicked up to Vance and back to Livy. She'd have to be won over. Livy smiled at the woman and asked her name.

At first she hesitated; then said, "Alis."

"I'm sorry to be holding you up from your work, Alis. I know you have things to do, but I'm a journalist from a British newspaper in London. I write about Paris for my paper. I came here to find out more about why the man was killed in flat number fourteen."

"I don't know anything," the maid muttered.

"I know you don't. Of course. And frankly, from what I know of him, he seemed like a pig. God rest his soul. But why he was killed might be very important."

Alis shrugged as if to say, *What do you want from me?*

"If you have a passkey, would you let my friend and me step into the flat for two minutes? Two minutes is all we need."

The maid shook her head and turned away.

Livy went on. "I know you could lose your position here over something like that. But you could stand with us the whole time. Two minutes and we're gone."

Alis's tight lips didn't budge. This one would need more convincing.

Livy leaned in closer and lowered her voice. "I would never do anything to jeopardize your position here. I wouldn't ask if—well—my position is at stake, too. See the Yank up there?" She nodded over her shoulder at Vance. "He's in line for my job. My editor thinks a man can do it better. So you see, I need to see the room, Alis. Where it happened. Then maybe I can write something good enough to convince them to give me another chance."

Alis's stare could have melted the polar ice caps.

Livy nodded. "Right. How does fifty francs sound?"

Alis held out her hand. Livy dug into her purse and counted out the money. The maid watched her carefully and then stuffed the cash into her apron.

"You are not with the police?" she said.

"No, not at all. We're journalists."

"I will tell you, but not him," Alis said, with a look up to Tom on the landing. She lowered her voice. "I saw him."

"Who?"

"The man who did it. I think it was him, at least. No, it had to be. I was in another flat. I heard a loud crash on the floor above, and I walked out into the hallway here and looked out through the front door. I saw a man hurrying away."

"You haven't told this to the police," Livy asked.

"No. No police. They're all communists now. I don't trust them."

Livy seriously doubted her claim but didn't argue. She had to keep the maid talking.

"What did you see, then? What did he look like?"

"He was short, but strong. He had one of those mustaches like this," she said, drawing down a finger on either side of her lips. "I could even smell his cigarettes after he left. That's all I have to tell you." She picked up her bucket and mop. "I have work to do." Before Livy could say another word, Alis was down the hall.

"I thought you were getting us in the room." Vance stood behind her now. Livy grabbed his arm and pulled him through the entrance and onto the street.

Vance shrugged her away and stopped. "Mind telling me what the hell happened back there?"

"I know who killed the talent agent," she said, her eyes scanning the streets for a free taxi. "I don't know why, but I think the Russians are killing the Mephisto agents."

*　*　*

Vance hailed a cab that took them from the eighteenth to his flat on the Left Bank. Ever the southern gentleman, he explained that he would stay at the U.S. Embassy. The murder and the walk-in had put everyone there in a state of alert, so his presence wouldn't be suspicious.

Vance's one-room flat was downright utilitarian. A single bed, which had been made up at least, occupied one corner across from a small wooden desk pushed against the wall under the room's sole window. A toilet about the size of a closet opened at the foot of the bed. Despite its size, the flat did boast a spectacular view of Notre-Dame and the Seine, made even more remarkable as the sun set over the centuries-old cathedral. The view calmed Livy. Her last memory of Paris had been death at the Gare du Nord and waiting in a dirty alley as Nathalie sobbed next to her.

Vance interrupted her contemplation. "If you need anything else—food, whatnot—you let me know. I can't risk you out on the streets alone."

"I can take care of myself, Tom."

"I think you've made that abundantly clear." His southern bonhomie suddenly had teeth. "But what you seem to miss is we are working together on this."

"Never said we weren't."

"Okay, well, maybe you might want to remember that. You left me in the dark back there at the flat, so from now on I am keeping you close. I have plenty at stake in this little game of ours, too. Are we clear?"

Livy had sensed his tension on the drive to his flat. She took her bag from him and held his hand for a moment. Vance rubbed the back of his neck and sighed.

"I need to be up-front with you about something, I guess. Gray got a letter from my daddy about two weeks ago. My old man is—um—not without some pull back home. Says he's been to his congressman, his senator. Even threatens to go to the president, or at least pull his money from Truman's next campaign, if Gray doesn't send me home."

Livy looked up and wrinkled her brow.

"Wants me back to run his tobacco business when he retires. He took over for his daddy, and so he figures it's my turn. Doesn't matter to my old man that I'm working for the Central Intelligence Group. Or whatever the War Office is calling us this week. You see, the problem is, Gray's holding that letter over my head. Right before I came to get you, he took his pipe out of his mouth—that's how you can tell he's about to pontificate—and said, 'Thomas, go get me that list and I will burn this letter from your father.' So, I'd appreciate it if you'd let me do the shopping," Vance said, his old swagger returning, "and thanks for calling me Tom. Mr. Vance was making me feel old. No, the real risk is keeping you in Paris too long. We need to move quickly. I'll see if I can't get us in to see Jabot tonight."

"I've been giving that some thought, actually—"

"Hold on, now. Like I told you, Gray has contacts with the prefect of police here. Jabot's in a French cell, but he is under American jurisdiction. So, you just can't walk past the guards, right into his cell, and expect to have a little chat."

"Fortunately, that wasn't my plan, luv. No, I'm going to need a U.S. Embassy credential—"

"Whoa, whoa, whoa! Who exactly do you think I am?" Vance stood in the doorway of his flat, Livy's travel case at his feet, and held his hands out in front of him.

"—a few things for my hair, a clipboard and steno pad, and possibly something in the way of an American military uniform. I'll write down the size for you since you'll probably muck it up. Or I could wear just a business sort of suit. And, I think, glasses. Something plain. After all, you did offer to do the shopping." Livy placed one hand on his lapel and gave him the same look she used to give to Gestapo guards when she had to pass through a checkpoint. Tom Vance was considerably more charming than those blokes, though. "I have faith in you, Tom."

"Well, that makes one of us."

Livy gave him her very best pout. "We're proper colleagues now."

"And for that, you should be eternally grateful."

And just like that, his hand was on her hip. She didn't push it away.

"Oh, I am. And I think you are, too?" she said with a slight grin.

"Seems to me like you're just trying to get me to do what you want."

"It's what we both want, isn't it?" She became even more aware of the faint scent of lavender in his hair oil and the almost sea-green color on the outer edges of his eyes. She looked up and his face was closer. Vance's eyes flickered down to her lips. Another kiss was inevitable. But this time it wasn't on the street outside a hotel. They were in his flat. Alone. The sun setting over Notre-Dame. *If this were a film, the score would crescendo right about now.*

But that's the pictures.

Livy knew that tension heightened desire, pulling two people closer to shield them from what might come. She'd felt that during the war. With Peter. The past—still her constant companion—had her its grip again and guarded her jealously. That's why this felt so wrong.

For now.

She pushed slightly against his chest with both hands. He hesitated, the moment already diminished. Vance looked confused, scanning her face for an answer, but Livy had no words. Something held her back, and would keep holding her back until she put it to rest. No matter what she felt for this man, she had nothing for him tonight except the job at hand.

"As you said, we need to move quickly," Livy said, turning away from Vance. "You might want to take notes."

*　*　*

Three hours later Vance and Livy stood outside the Paris Police Prefecture. Most of the items on Livy's list had proved easy to find, except the military uniform, so she'd settled for a dress suit. She'd opted for gray, which she felt might fit her character best. The credentials had proved impossible to acquire on short notice and would have required significant alteration. So Vance had told Livy to disguise herself as much as she could and they'd bluff their way in.

She'd managed to make her rat's nest of brown hair look a bit tidier. Small pieces of tape just under the edges of her hair pulled the skin around her eyes up enough to give them a slightly altered shape. Add cat-eye glasses to that, and Livy thought she could be Myrtle Dickinson's sister.

"Can you sound like an American?" Vance had asked as they waited for the cab, his manner now cool and professional after whatever had almost happened between them last night.

"'Course. *Awwwl* I have to do is take every bit of life out of my voice and sound as flat as the prairie." Livy smiled.

"Charming." Vance shook his head. "Let me do the talking this time."

Minutes later the cab pulled up to the station and Vance led them through the side entrance of the flat gray building. Livy remembered the last time she'd been there. Then she'd been a guest of the police after her face-to-face encounter with Diablo/Jabot. Now she returned in the guise of an American stenographer accompanied by the same man who had sprung her. She remembered the long, dark hallway and the scuffed brown floors that led to the holding cells. At the end of the corridor, a tall, lanky guard, wearing a kepi and a khaki uniform, did paperwork behind a desk. Livy didn't recognize him from her earlier visit, but still she quickened her gait and tried that American "bounce" she'd noticed in Vance's walk.

Vance plopped down his ID badge and told the guard they had more questions for Jabot.

The French guard barely looked at the credentials and pointed to a closed door behind them. Vance opened the door. Livy looked up. An American MP sat behind a small desk at the end of the hall. A soldier with a rifle over his shoulder stood at his flank.

The Yanks had taken charge of this particular prisoner. Livy knew she was now officially on their territory.

Vance stepped up to the desk and handed his ID to the MP, whose jaw looked like it had been chiseled from granite. He looked it over quickly and said, "We've been expecting you, Mr. Vance." He looked up, his eyes roamed over Livy slowly. "She your secretary?"

Livy started to speak, but Vance interrupted. "I can't type to save my life, and shorthand is way above my pay grade. That's her job. Don't worry," Vance said, good-old-boy irony dripping from every word, "she don't bite."

The MP fretted. "My captain says I have to get his okay on any unauthorized visitors. And it's a little late."

"Listen, the ambassador wants this report on his desk first thing in the morning," Vance added. "And he has a lunchtime call to Washington. We all got regulations to follow, but I don't want this to bounce back on either of us."

"The ambassador, huh?"

"And he's the impatient type," Vance said, shaking his head.

The MP nodded at the soldier beside him. "I'll clear her, then, but make it snappy." The soldier plucked a key from a large ring on his belt and led the way to the holding cells.

Antoine Jabot, or Le Grand Diablo, as Livy knew him, sat in the back corner of his cell on a folding bed attached to the concrete wall. His right arm hung in a sling, tight against his body. His head whipped around as the door opened. He scrutinized the two new arrivals.

If Jabot saw through Livy's disguise at all in the American soldier's presence, they were sunk. Anticipating this, Vance kept his body between Livy and Jabot, speaking over his shoulder at the soldier to tell him they would need only fifteen minutes.

Jabot straightened up. He shot a look at Vance and sat forward, studying Livy closely. She didn't want to seem suspicious and look away, so she walked to the small square table in the room, put down her steno pad, and prepared to take dictation. Jabot leered at her, even as Livy kept her eyes on the desk. Could he possibly recognize her through the glasses and all the rest?

Finally, the soldier closed the door. Vance stepped around the table behind Livy. "Mr. Jabot, I'm Tom Vance with the American Embassy," he said in French.

"Who is she?" His voice, so clear at the theater, now sounded raspy. No doubt a lingering effect from Livy's chop to his windpipe the week before at the Ritz.

"Secretary. We need a record of everything."

"I don't want to talk now. My arm hurts. I told that guard I want to see a doctor."

Vance took a look out of the small window in the door. The soldier had walked back down the hall.

"Mr. Jabot, my secretary has some questions for you. I suggest you answer them carefully."

"What is all this? Who is she?" Agitated now, Jabot stood up. His jowls jiggled as he spoke.

"Keep your voice down," Vance warned. "I wouldn't want to have to ask the guard to step back in here and move you to one of the less comfortable criminal cells on the other side of the building."

Jabot sunk back to the bed.

"How long have you been part of the Mephisto network?" Livy said, trying to speak French with an American accent.

Jabot put his fists on the table and gave Livy a long, hard look. "I know you," he said, his voice a croaking whisper.

"That's right, you do, you little weasel," Livy said, dropping the American accent and returning to her native directness. "So sit down and maybe I won't kill you this time,"

"You—that woman! I knew it," Jabot said, and then turned to Vance. "What is this? I will talk to you. But not her."

For all of Vance's breezy southern attitude and fancy suits, he had a presence. Right now, he seemed to swell up a bit in the chest as he crossed his arms and glared at the little magician.

"Mr. Jabot, my friend here nearly broke your windpipe once. Do you really want to provoke her a second time?"

Jabot fell back onto the little bed, his good arm held out in front of him like a white flag. "Please. Please. Ask your questions. Just—just keep her away from me."

Livy took off the glasses. "Right then. How long have you known Valentine?"

"Since before the war. I toured with him. On the same bill."

"So, he recruited you?"

"He was a great magician. I wanted to learn."

"Like that ace-of-spades trick?"

"Yes."

"Do you remember recruiting a Claude D. who worked on the docks in Nice?"

Jabot scoffed. "Yes, but the only reason I know him is because he talked. And someone made sure he paid for it, too."

Vance stepped into Jabot's space, arms crossed, glaring.

"But it wasn't me," Jabot protested. "I just gathered information and passed it along. I had my own people who reported back to me."

"And now you think someone tried to kill you?" Livy asked.

Jabot held up his arm. "Can you not see? I was shot. He would have finished the job, too, but I was lucky."

Livy sat back at the table. "Tell us how it happened. All of it."

Jabot was more than willing to play victim for his two interrogators. "It was two nights ago after the last show. Barely any audience. I went up to my dressing room on the second floor, and he was waiting inside. I smelled the *connard* first.

Those disgusting cigarettes they smoke. But still I opened the door and flicked on the lights. I saw him—just for a second—and I knew. He was there for me. After what happened to Milos, the talent agent, I was nervous anyway. So I turned the lights off and ran. He fired through the door and hit me right here. The doctor said he missed the bone, but still it's so painful, you can't imagine." Jabot gripped his arm and moaned like a mourner at a wake. "Anyway, I ran backstage. There were a few people there, and I never saw him after that, but—"

"You got a good look at him, then?" Livy said, interrupting.

"I told you—for a second."

"And what did he look like?"

"He had a hat and coat, so I didn't see much except that big mustache of his. And a nose that looked like he'd run into a brick wall a few times. Other than that he looked like all the rest of them. Russians."

Livy looked away for a second. So Levchenko had killed Milos and tried the same with Jabot. He had half of the Mephisto list, but what was the point in killing them off one by one? Something was missing.

"And how do you know it's the same man who killed Milos?" Vance asked.

"They shot him in the face," the magician said to Vance. "That's how they do it. To send a message. All Milos did was pass on information. Like me. The talent he hired for parties and big gatherings passed on what they heard. Back to me. To Valentine. That's how the network worked. Milos wasn't important. Just another link in the chain. I tell you, they are going to kill all of us," Jabot said, his hoarse voice painful to hear. "You think the Nazis were bad, heh? Now the communists are murdering men right under your noses. We would never work for them. No!"

"I hate to break the news to you, but that's exactly what your boss had in mind," Livy said. "He was selling you all out to the highest bidder—Moscow."

"My boss? Who are you talking about?"

"Valentine," Livy answered.

Jabot's entire demeanor changed. His face erupted into a wide grin and he chuckled quietly. Livy and Vance exchanged a look.

"Did we miss a joke?" Vance said through gritted teeth.

Jabot shook his head, the chortle rattling in his throat. "You really don't know, do you?"

Their blank faces only caused him to laugh more. "Valentine? Ah, no, no, no. He hasn't been in charge since before the war ended. And we would *never*," he said, drawing the words out slowly, "work—for—*communists*."

Livy felt as if the table had been upended. She didn't want to ask the obvious question.

"Who is it, then?" Vance said.

Jabot narrow eyes flicked with glee from one to the other. "And if I tell you, what will you do for me?"

Vance stepped closer to the magician. "We won't throw your fat ass back on the street for the Russians."

Jabot's grin faltered. "Okay. Okay. I was just surprised you didn't know. That's all. I've only met him maybe twice—three times. That's the way it works. No names. I only know Milos because he got me a few bookings."

"This other man, you must call him something," Livy said.

Jabot shrugged. "No one knows his real name. But they call him Marcel."

Chapter
Twenty-Four

≈

The plot to ensnare Marcel, the real leader of Mephisto, began that very night. Jabot refused to take part, at first. Even after Vance threatened him physically, the rotund magician vocalized his reluctance, fearing that his would-be assassin might take another shot. Vance assured him he would be protected and that his cooperation in the matter would be the only way to ensure he remained in U.S. custody.

Jabot agreed to set up a meeting with Marcel in the usual way. He instructed Vance to take out a small advertisement in tomorrow's *Le Monde*. The ad indicated that a Madame Dupuis sought a one-bedroom flat in Paris, required immediately. One bedroom meant meet on the same day. The last bit indicated urgency. If all went according to plan, then Marcel would be in the audience at the Grand Guignol the next night.

It was well after midnight when Vance took Livy back to his flat. Vance lingered, fussing over her, making sure she knew where the extra blankets were kept if she became cold overnight. Then, with a promise to be back shortly after sunrise, he left.

Livy couldn't eat. She didn't sleep either. She sat and looked at the silhouetted outline of Notre-Dame framed by the moonlight. Thoughts flickered across her mind like a movie edited out of order. Valentine leaving Paris with Mirov. Mirov shot from behind. Valentine with a gun. Valentine dead. Nathalie running into the square toward the sniper.

Then, for reasons she didn't understand at all, Livy remembered a time when she was very young, maybe six or seven years old. Her parents had been fighting. She never knew why, but there had been yelling after dinner back in their bedroom. Her father came out, but her mother stayed in all night. Livy went in to say good-night. Her mother's eyes were still swollen from crying.

That night, while she lay in her bed, Livy's mother came into her room and crawled into bed next to her. She hugged Livy very tight. The affection made Livy sadder and more scared. The tension in the house lasted two more days until suddenly everything returned to normal. Like magic. No gradual change. One day her parents were ignoring each other and the next they were smiling and hugging, and slept together again in their own bedroom.

Livy never knew what had happened during that terrifying week, but her mind devised countless scenarios, reasons for the near breakup of her parents. In each imaginary situation, the cause of the disintegration of her parents' marriage was their young daughter. Like many only children who believed they kept the world spinning, Livy blamed herself.

She had the exact same feeling now.

Sometime around three AM she fell asleep in the chair in front of Vance's window. She woke up a few hours later as the sun streamed in. Vance would be back soon. Livy had little time to think this through. Quickly she threw her things back in her travel bag and put it out of the way under Vance's desk. She knew that after tonight, she might never see Vance again.

*   *   *

That night, foreign correspondents Tom Vance and Livy Nash paid a second visit to Le Théâtre du Grand-Guignol. Madame Martel, of course, took this as a high compliment. She fawned over them and offered them house seats, second row aisle. Livy declined, saying they preferred the boxes at the rear of the theater so they could observe the audience's reaction. Madame Martel was only too happy to oblige.

The curtain rose promptly at eight on a play aptly named *The Bloody Trunk*. It began innocently enough, with two French students losing all their money in a poker game. Of course, then they had to murder a young woman for her money, dismember her, and place the bits and pieces in the titular box.

Livy scanned the audience. She found the same mix of Parisian couples looking for cheap thrills and American servicemen lured by the temptations of the Pigalle district. They laughed at the excessive gore, as well as the severed arms and legs the two students shoved into the large trunk.

Livy knew she also shared this theatrical experience, if you could call it that, with the man called Marcel. A man who'd flown under everyone's radar, even Fleming's. The fact that this Marcel had been the shadow leader of the Mephisto network alone made him a more formidable enemy. More dangerous. Her mind returned to the not-so-subtle fate of the informer Claude: tongue ripped out, throat cut, and the other inmates scared silent.

The Grand Guignol's plays had nothing on this Marcel.

The audience quieted down as the play moved to its conclusion. Guilt gnawed at one of the students. Livy had to admit the actor played this quite believably. He confessed his crime to another person, and his fellow student, incensed at this betrayal of their crime, shot his friend in the back of the head. As the guilt-ridden student died, his friend knelt over him and sobbed.

The stage went black, and the audience, still stunned by the unexpected reality of the final scene, didn't applaud.

"Mesdames et messieurs, je vous présente Le Grand Diablo!"

The curtains billowed, and Jabot—aka Le Grand Diablo—appeared, stepping into his spotlight. He took a slow, ostentatious bow before the crowd, which gradually broke into polite applause. Livy imagined the wound in the magician's right arm smarted under his tuxedo.

Even from the back, she could see a line of sweat running down the magician's forehead. A tall, lanky MP had remained with him during the journey from the Paris jail to the theater. The MP has been instructed to remain just offstage while Jabot performed. Still the round Frenchman had worried that he would be exposed during his stint onstage.

"Like in that film *The 39 Steps*," he'd said. "They shoot the mind reader."

So Diablo dispensed with the warm-up tricks and started with the grand finale, Mephisto's card trick. Again he asked for a volunteer from the audience, and again a young American soldier answered the call, bounding up onstage.

Diablo made small talk with the GI, who seemed to fancy himself a young Humphrey Bogart, with his stoic demeanor and tight-lipped grin. As the soldier prattled on about life during the war, Livy watched Jabot search the audience. Her eyes followed his. Was Marcel here?

The smirking soldier picked his card, let the audience see it, and replaced it in the deck. Diablo's hand trembled as he pulled the gun. His voice even shook when he said, "Now, find your *kart* or—*bang, bang.*"

Laughing, the soldier pulled the wrong card out of the trick deck and showed it to the audience. Livy moved to the edge of her seat. The ace of hearts. The deck was nothing but aces of hearts. Another signal. If the deck had been spades, it meant the meeting was off. Hearts, Jabot had told them, meant the meeting was a go. Marcel was here.

Jabot fired the trick gun and the audience laughed. Most of them. Livy's eyes landed on a man in the fourth row on the aisle who didn't seem amused. He sat across the theater from her, so she could only make out a shock of blond hair and a dark suit. The low light obscured his profile.

Onstage, Diablo took his final bow and made his exit. The magician had said Marcel always met him at the stage door after the second play. All Vance had to do was walk around to the door and, along with the MP, take the mysterious Marcel into custody.

But Livy had other ideas. She had to talk to this Marcel first. Livy knew the answer to the questions that had been plaguing her might very well be answered in that alley. Whatever the risk, she had to confront him.

As the applause died down, Livy leaned over to Vance. "I'll step into the alley and make sure no one leaves by the stage door."

Vance put a hand on her arm. "By yourself?"

Livy smiled. "If I need a big, strong man, I'll yell for the MP." She kissed his cheek, adding, "Thank you."

As the next play began and the lights dimmed, Livy dashed out into the street, turned to the right, and walked about half a block until she reached an alleyway lit only by dim streetlamps. She hurried past the lit portion of the alley toward a small bulb at the end of the darkness, which hung just over the stage door.

There she stopped and waited. She stood in the alley, just off the loading dock where she'd shared that bitter French cigarette with the seamstress Lorraine. The sounds of a night in the Pigalle fell silent in this dark corner. Through the walls of the theater, Livy heard the occasional gasp.

Soon enough, Vance would come to check on her. Soon enough, the MP, who had been positioned backstage in plainclothes, would step outside in anticipation of the meet.

She heard the footsteps first. Boots. They crunched on the gravel at the alley entrance. Then a tall figure, silhouetted by the streetlamps, slowly ambled toward her. Livy moved away from the pool of light at the stage door. She didn't want to be seen until the last second. The steps drew closer. Cautious. Deliberate. There would be a great deal at stake for him, she knew.

It must have taken only half a minute for him to walk the length of the alley, but to Livy it seemed interminable. Finally, fifteen feet away, he stopped, as if sensing her there. She stepped into the light, and they looked at each other.

Livy had known it would be him. She'd sensed it since the Gare du Nord. The name Marcel confirmed it. Now, here he was. Living. Breathing. The man she'd really come to Paris for. Alive and in front of her.

Peter Scobee had changed more than Livy had expected. His thick hair had been dyed blond, but even in this dim light she could see the dark roots. A deep scar ran from under the dyed hair across his forehead to the left of his eye, ending at his nose. The cut must have needed stitches, because even now its width and jagged edges made it stand out against his sunburned face. Otherwise he seemed much the same. His brown eyes, although guarded, flickered on seeing her, and the corners of his mouth turned up as if to smile before stopping.

They looked at each for several seconds. His cologne smelled of wood and spices. Livy thought he might speak. His lips parted, but he said nothing. Then Livy remembered the time. She had no interest in this ending here.

"Peter," she said. His name caught in her throat. *Goddamn it!* "You have to leave. Now. They'll be coming for you."

"I didn't know . . . it would be you, Livy," Peter Scobee said.

"The Pont Alexandre in one hour. Under the bridge. But you have to go now."

His eyes looked heavy from lack of sleep. How much of the last two years had he spent on the run? she wondered.

He pivoted and hurried back down the alley.

Livy watched him go. Unconsciously she held her breath until he was gone. Then her body convulsed. She gasped like she'd been underwater for minutes. Putting a hand over her mouth to mute the sound, she regained control of her breath. Livy wiped a patch of sweat from her brow and hurried away from the theater, Jabot, and Vance.

Chapter
Twenty-Five

～

It had taken Livy almost an hour to walk from the Pigalle district to the Pont Alexandre III. She knew she'd need sanctuary until this was over. A safe place to think and plan. There was only one spot in Paris open to her now.

After leaving Peter, she walked up the Champs-Élysées until she found a café still open. She feigned an emergency and begged to use their phone. The moment required little acting under the circumstances.

The line on the other end rang and rang.

"Hallo?" A man's voice—completely alert.

She spoke quickly and rang off before he could reply. She left the café and headed for the bridge.

As she walked, she wondered about Tom's reaction to her going missing. No matter what feelings he might have for her, the American would by this time assume he'd been duped. And he wouldn't like that. God knew Mephisto was enough of a priority for the Yanks they would swarm Paris to find her. She tried to push the thoughts away. Right now she didn't have room in her brain for Tom Vance.

She approached the Pont Alexandre from the Champs-Élysées side, past the Grand Palais, and walked across the bridge to the Eiffel bank of the river. It had to be almost midnight. The bridge and the walkway below were deserted. She made her way down the stairs, pulling her coat tight. It felt like winter with the water lapping just a few feet away. The wind along the Seine was almost constant and at night could penetrate the thickest of coats, even in summertime.

The lights from the ornate bridge glowed above her head, but darkness shrouded the pathway. That's where Peter stood. As she drew closer to the river, he stepped away from the support beams. He held his hand out, beckoning her to move toward him, nearer the foot of the bridge and the shadowy part of the walkway. Livy followed.

They stood several feet apart, like strangers, unsure of how to respond to each other. Their eyes met; then Livy looked away to be certain she hadn't been followed. She hated looking at his face. He'd changed so much. Not just the hair and the scar, but the look in his eyes. He had weight on him now. Not physical weight; something different. He even smelled different.

"How did you get the scar?" she said, almost casually.

"The shell. At Fresnes."

"Oh. I wondered how you—" She stopped herself. What could she say? *I thought you were dead before. But no, you escaped with just a scar from a mortar while almost everyone around you was ripped apart.*

"I did what we were taught during training. Lie flat. Keep your head down. There was a stone enclosure around the wall. If I'd been standing or kneeling even, things would have turned out very differently. Valentine and the German Faber walked away while they dragged you off. We were lucky that day."

"The others weren't," she said without emotion. "It was the bullet catch, wasn't it? The magic trick."

Peter looked away, as if the question was beneath him. "That was Edward. I mean, yes, of course, the bullet was a dummy. A blank like they use in pictures. Onstage the magician pretends to actually catch a real bullet. But I just had to sell it, you might say." Peter shook his head, impatient. "Surely that's not why you did what you did tonight. Just to find out the logistics of that—that episode."

"Episode? I watched you die," Livy said, her voice as cold as the night air. "I believed it. I bought it all. I deserve to know how you did it."

"Livy," he said, putting his hands on her shoulders. She let them stay there. "I'm sorry. If I could have warned you, I would have. But that was part of it, you see. They had to make sure you didn't suspect. I couldn't say anything. Leave any sort of message. It had to be convincing."

"Did it? Why all the show, Peter? Just to work for the Germans."

"No! My God, of course not!" He raised his voice. Catching himself, he pulled her deeper into the shadow of the bridge. "I never intended to work for the other side. I can't make you understand how it felt then, what was in my head. But you know what it was like for us. How many of our people died in prison or concentration camps. You know what they did to them there. So, what did that make us? Hmmm? Human sacrifices? We were supposed to 'set Europe ablaze.' Isn't that what the great man Churchill himself said? Instead we were pigs sent to the slaughterhouse. Most of us never even had a chance. I made a very hard decision. I'd given everything, Livy. Almost everything I had to give."

"You weren't the only one."

"I know," he said.

She could see the weight he carried. Was it guilt? Fear? She couldn't tell yet.

He went on. "After the invasion and Vercors, the war was over. We all knew that. Edward had been running the network so long. Most of his agents were bloody-minded anticommunists. The network was fraying, and Edward didn't have it in him to make it work after the war. You see, none of his agents knew one another. They passed their information on directly to Edward or Jabot. It had to have leadership. I saw an opportunity to take over, Livy. But Bulldog had to go. It had to be clean. No loose ends. I'm sorry," he said again.

Peter looked at her, and for a moment the years seem to contract. They'd had many moments like this in nettled fields or outside burned-out farmhouses. Nights that passed with intimate conversation because they could never be sure they'd even see another sunrise. Fear hung over them tonight as well.

"That woman in the prison, she hurt you, didn't she?" he said.

Livy turned away.

"I know this is impossible to understand." His voice comforted her, even now. "But I'm not the villain here, Livy. I saw a way out of the hell they put us in. We had a deal, Edward and I, with the German Faber. In exchange, Edward gave him a new passport so he wouldn't be rounded up as the Allies moved through France. But I made him promise to transfer you to a hospital unit. You would have been safe then."

"But then that little shell went and fell right on your plan, eh?"

His hand touched the long scar that ran down his forehead. "It could have been so much worse. For both of us."

Livy leaned back against the steel truss. She didn't know what to say. He sidled up against her, their shoulders touching. Again, she didn't move away.

"When did you know it was me?" he asked.

Livy shook her head. "I don't know. I felt it more than knew. Jabot told us you were calling yourself Marcel. Maybe that sealed it."

"You could have let the Americans arrest me," he said quietly. "Why did you warn me?"

Livy's mind went back to Tom, but only for an instant.

"I wanted to see you," she said. "I've wanted that since they separated us at Fresnes." Her voice dropped to a whisper. "Sometimes that's all I wanted."

Peter put his arm around her. The gesture felt protective, soothing. He'd done it many times during the war. On occasion, she'd returned the favor.

"I'm here because I wanted to see you, too," he said. "I know you have questions, and I'll do my best to answer."

Livy moved away, shoved her hands into her coat. The wind became more insistent, cold, stronger.

"What do you want me to say, Peter?" she said, her voice too loud for the night and the moment. "That I loved you once? Fine. I did. Do you want to know about the presentation of your George Cross by the bloody king? Maybe how your wife and five-year-old son are coping without you? But that's not it, is it? So, what is it exactly you want from me, Peter?"

Peter physically crumbled as he listened to her. By the time she finished, he looked like a fighter at the end of fifteen rounds. Livy knew she'd hurt him. She took no pleasure from it. One look at the lines at his eyes and the sagging in his cheeks and she could tell his life since the war had been hard. Maybe his own sins weighed him down.

Yet Livy still cared for him. That hadn't changed.

He threw his shoulders back and cleared his throat. "I can't expect you to condone my choices. I did what I needed to do. I had my reasons. But I didn't sell my soul to the Germans, and I won't sell out to the damn communists either. I'm not a traitor to my country, Livy."

"Do you really believe that, Peter? Does it comfort you? You've betrayed everyone and everything. Your country, your wife, your son. Me."

"Stop it," he shouted, grabbing her shoulders. "Listen, this is a new world now, Livy. There are new rules. New opportunities. Were we just supposed to drop everything after the war and go back to the factory or the farm? Pick up a check on Friday, fill the larder, feed the family, and get pissed at the pub on Saturday night? Is that what we fought for? We gave our hearts and souls. Why shouldn't we profit now that it's done?"

Livy watched dispassionately. *He's such a convincing speaker,* she thought. *Under different circumstances he could run for Parliament.* Brave operative behind enemy lines. Decorated war hero. Devoted family man. No, that was the old Peter. The new one seemed familiar but had different skin.

"The group Edward built is powerful," he went on. "They're spread out all over Europe, even the East. It's the perfect network, Livy. Whoever wants control of Europe must have my people on their side. We can control what happens next. Do you see?"

"We?"

He'd recovered from her blows. The old smiling, confident Peter Scobee tried to break free from the facade of badly dyed hair and scarred face. He stood in front of her now, not touching her, but his eyes bored directly into hers.

"I need you with me, Livy. Edward's gone now. There's no one else I can rely on. What am I saying? There never was anyone else I could rely on. If I could have said all this to you back at Fresnes, I would have. I would have asked you to come with me, but it was—too complicated. You must understand that."

He reached for her hands. Livy didn't resist.

"This is our chance to do what we used to do. The Allies— the Americans and our government—they're the only options left. They were always the only option for me. I want what's coming to me, and I want you to be with me again."

Livy believed him. She recognized a hint of desperation in his eyes, a flicker that seemed to indicate he knew this was a long shot. The hopelessness registered in his wet palms and the sweat on his upper lip.

"I think you know it isn't that simple, Peter."

"I know what I'm asking for is insane, so what can I do? Tell me. I mean what I say, Livy. I need you."

Livy stepped back, hearing the laughter of a young couple on the bridge above. Peter retreated into the shadows, but she didn't join him. She stared at the river, listening as the couple's voices diminished.

"You have to help me trust you again, Peter," she said simply.

He stepped up to her again, and she smelled the mix of his cologne and sweat.

"What can I do? Tell me." Her words had made his chest swell and his smile return.

"You need to be honest with me."

"Livy, I've been honest with you. You see me for what I am."

"Who killed Mirov?"

Peter didn't flinch. His eyes remained on hers, but Livy could practically see the gears turning in his head. He licked his lips, blinked rapidly, and said, "I did. I shot him."

Livy's expression didn't change, even though she remembered how the Russian's gray head had erupted. The chunk of it as it struck her. "You killed him to control Valentine? You didn't want the network in the hands of the Soviets?"

"Yes, yes, that's right. Edward forced my hand. I never expected it would get that far."

"You shot Valentine as well."

"I finished him off for you, Livy. You didn't know it, but we were working together that night."

Livy began to feel sick, listening to him. She turned toward the river, feeling the cold breeze against her face. "It was you who asked for me, wasn't it?"

"Of course. I wanted to see you again."

She turned on him. "You knew I'd be easy enough to manipulate."

"I wanted someone I felt I could trust," he said, his voice low and calm. "There was no one else. Talk to your people. Our people. Tell them I have the list and I'm willing to make a deal but I won't wait long. Look, Livy, I know I'm asking too much of you. After all that you've been through. All our history. But if Fresnes had never happened, who knows how it might have been with us. We can still have that."

Livy watched his eyes as he spoke. They never wavered. At least they looked the same. So much of him was different now. She tried to imagine the rosy future he painted for her. She followed its path, but it always came back to the same ending.

"I need—time," she said, hesitantly. Words eluded her.

"I don't have that, and neither do you."

"What do I tell them?"

"They get the list. All of it. In exchange, I want complete immunity. But they can't cut me out, you understand. I'm part of the deal. Top man. Tell them that."

"I'll tell them."

They agreed to meet the next night at the same place. Before he left, Peter actually smiled, and for a moment he looked just like he did when Livy had first seen him that night in the field when her plane landed.

"Tell them I need an answer by tomorrow." His voice dropped suddenly. "And Livy, I'll be watching. Anyone comes with you tomorrow night and I'll leave. No deal then. I'll leave Paris for good. This is their only chance; tell them that." He grabbed her arm. Not too hard. He just held it. "And don't even think of betraying me, do you understand? I've gone through too much. I wouldn't let you get away with something like that."

He delivered his threat in the same tone of voice he'd used to admonish members of the old circuit when Michelle would run late or her brother broke curfew. Like a parent giving a child a minor scolding.

"I'll have an answer for you tomorrow," she said.

Without a word, Peter turned and disappeared into the long shadows cast by the bridge's under-girders, leaving Livy alone again.

Chapter
Twenty-Six

Once Peter was out of sight, Livy scurried off the Champs-Élysées and down an alleyway, moving past the back doors of cafés and brasseries. Piles of bagged trash cluttered doorways. Tom and the other Americans wouldn't be sitting around waiting. They'd be out looking for her. She couldn't afford dreamy sentimentality right now. She had to move.

She put her hands deep in her coat pocket and found—among ticket stubs and a bonbon wrapper—a rubber band she'd taken from a copy of *Le Monde* on Madame Riveaux's doorstep. She grabbed her tangle of hair and corralled it into a ponytail that she pulled along her shoulder. But she needed more to change her appearance. Anything. A woman walking the streets of Paris this time of night would have to be either a prostitute or a spy.

Taking a quick glance around, she spotted an Italian restaurant at the next corner. Even in this most exclusive part of the city, the backstreets smelled of piss and wine. Just behind the restaurant were two metal trash bins. She dug through the wet, half-eaten pasta and bread until she found a handful of newspapers. Opening her coat and jumper, she shaped the trash into something like a ball, shoved it against her skin, and closed her coat. Not bad. A little pooch that would only collapse if someone touched it. Or if it started to rain. Finally, she took a half-eaten crust of baguette and put it in the heel of her right shoe. She hoped the slight limp and her paunch might throw off any American patrols looking for her.

Livy looked up at the sky. Alone again in Paris. Walking the streets at night, fearful of being picked up by a patrol. Just like the war. It all felt so very familiar. *And Peter. Alive.*

The disguise bought her time to think as she walked. She went back over her conversation with Peter. How he'd taken over the network from Valentine. And that brought her back to the murder of Milos, the talent agent, and the attempted shooting of Jabot. It had to be Levchenko. The descriptions from the maid and Jabot matched perfectly. Livy felt certain the Russian was doing more than taking out the list one at a time. He'd shot Milos inside the Montmartre flat. He'd been waiting for Jabot in his dressing room. He could have killed them anywhere, but Levchenko needed privacy because he wanted something from them. But what?

The sound of two military jeeps rumbling down the Champs-Élysées abruptly ended her contemplation. She'd have to take the backstreets and cling to the shadows.

* * *

It took Livy a little more than half an hour to walk to the Rue Saint-Honoré in the first arrondissement on the right bank. The neighborhood was home to fashionable shops, designer boutiques, and Parisians with money. She approached the final block of her walk through an alley that ran between two three-story buildings. Livy edged out near the street and glanced both ways. Across the road was her final destination: a taller building of flats with a small courtyard at the side that appeared to lead to fire escapes running around the back of the structure.

Two cars were parked out front. A blue Citroën with dusty tires and a scratch or two down the side, and a gray Peugeot that looked as if it had been bought yesterday.

At this time of night, foot traffic on the street was almost nonexistent. Some young people, probably university students, strolled in the direction of the Avenue de Marigny, perhaps headed to restaurants near the avenue. They laughed as they walked, more concerned with the conversation than a destination. Just behind them a single man in a gray hat and coat walked purposefully, his hands shoved in his pockets. Livy eased back into the shadows.

A second later the street was empty. Livy hugged a dirty brick wall and counted to herself. When she reached twenty-five, the man in the gray coat and hat came back into view, walking quickly in the opposite direction, hands still shoved in his pockets. *Got you*, she thought. *Subtlety has never been the Americans' strong suit.*

At that moment, the rusty gate of the courtyard in the building across the street opened and Dennis Allard stepped out. Tall and polished even at this time of night. She watched him scan the streets and then walk back into the courtyard and fiddle with something around back. A back entrance. When she'd rung him from the café, Livy had had no idea how Allard might receive her plea for help. But now it looked as if, at the very least, he was offering her a way into his flat if she could make it past the Gray Man.

Then the older man checked his watch and moved out onto the street, heading east toward the Place de la Concorde.

From her vantage point in the shadows, she watched Allard walk briskly for a block and stop in front of a tobacconist. He looked through the window, seeming to pay particular attention to a display inside. As he did, the man in gray came into her view again, walking back toward Livy.

Slowly the Englishman turned away from the tobacconist and retraced his steps. The man in gray moved briskly down the other side of the street. *He's got him now.* Allard's long strides soon caught up with the man. By the time they were within twenty yards of Livy, Allard lagged only a few paces behind the Gray Man.

"*Monsieur, monsieur!*" Allard called from across the street. "*S'il vous plaît.*"

The Gray Man stopped. He cupped a hand to his ear, the fedora covering the top of his face.

"*Quelle heure est-il?*" Allard called, tapping the face of his watch and shrugging.

The Gray Man shook his head.

Allard shrugged in disbelief. "*Parlez-vous francais?*"

To which the man across the street waved his hand dismissively and continued eastward.

Livy had no time to stay and admire Allard's tradecraft. He'd given her the cover she needed.

Minutes later she opened the door to Dennis Allard's warm, comfortable flat and collapsed into an armchair. She removed the bread crust from inside her shoe and put her head back. She'd just started to get comfortable when the door swung open.

"I thought I told you to stay away from Paris."

Livy's eyelids felt heavy. She wanted to get rid of the greasy newspapers against her skin and take a long bath. His voice, however, felt like a smack across the face with a velvet glove.

Allard stood ramrod straight, looking down at her. The wind at the river wasn't as cold as his voice. "Do you even begin to comprehend the position you are in, Miss Nash? Or perhaps the position in which I now find myself and, by proximity, the British government? Is that at all clear to you?"

"Well, you made the choice to let me in, didn't you?" she lashed back. Even the sound of her own voice made her head throb.

"Who says I'm not going to send you packing?" he said, the whisper of a grin creasing his mouth. "I'm quite sure the Americans would give you a place to stay the night."

Livy fell silent.

"Fortunately for you, they are still infants in this game we've been playing for four hundred years."

"I saw you on the street. Nice work that."

Allard huffed. "They have the block covered, apparently. I thought Vance brought you back. Why are they looking for you?"

Livy ignored the older man, stepping to the curtains.

"I wouldn't do that if I were you," Allard cautioned. "I just let one of their men know he'd been blown. We have to be careful."

Livy gave him a look. Exhaustion made her want to lash out. Allard registered the hint of anger.

"I call the shots here, Miss Nash. Are we clear?" She nodded. "Capital. Now, it's a bit late, but I'm having tea. Feel free to join me."

Allard stepped into the small kitchen area, sandwiched between the sitting and back rooms. Livy paced, trying to shake some of the stiffness in her legs. "Did you let Fleming know?"

The gas burner flickered on under the kettle. "Of course."

"And what did he tell you?"

Allard put the tea in a small pot and plucked a single white china cup from the cupboard above the stove. "He said, 'Let's hope she doesn't muck this one up.' But there is something you should know, Miss Nash."

"Yes?"

"I don't work for Fleming." The kettle began to hiss, and Allard let it.

"So you won't let me do my job."

"I didn't say that." He poured the hot water into the kettle. "Sugar? Milk?" Livy shook her head. "I am most concerned that my employer—the British government—is not humiliated when one of its citizens is arrested for murder."

"We work for the same people, Mr. Allard."

"Not quite. I am an indentured servant. You, my dear, *were* an independent contractor." He placed a spoon on her saucer and gave her the cup.

Livy felt like tossing the lot into his smug face, but she had to have Allard's help or she'd be in the hands of the Americans and probably in jail. "We have the same goal, then."

"Perhaps, but our methods are decidedly different."

Livy put the tea back on the counter. "I know you think I'm reckless. I have been. During the war, you didn't get style points. We hid bombs in dead rats when we had to. We just got the job done. This is different, I know. But we want the same thing, and I need your help."

She sounded like Peter. Desperate. Justifying reckless behavior.

Allard made himself a cup, adding two lumps of sugar and milk. "The job? We have the woman, Mademoiselle Billerant. We've questioned her in London almost a fortnight now, and she's been absolutely no use whatsoever. Apparently all she does is beg to come home. Are you telling me there is someone else out there we might recruit?"

For a second she felt tempted to tell Allard about Peter. She longed to be rid of the burden. But how she could make this man understand and see that her way was the only possible choice in these circumstances?

"No. No other recruits. But we can keep the rest of the Mephisto list out of the hands of the Soviets."

"Your tea is getting cold," Allard said, nudging the cup and saucer toward her. Livy took the tea but didn't drink.

"I can't do this without you," Livy said.

Allard sighed. "You came back with that American, Vance. Apparently that didn't work out, because they're out there looking for you. Why shouldn't I expect a similar outcome?"

"Things happened. Once I talked to the magician, Jabot, then I knew there might be a chance for me to finish what Mr. Fleming sent me here to do. And I *will* finish this job, Mr. Allard. There's nothing else for me, whether you can see your way clear to help me or not."

The older man took another sip of tea. Allard's clear blue eyes fixed on hers, his expression unchanged.

"My flat, my rules. Clear?"

Livy nodded.

Allard put the saucer on the counter. "What do you need, then?"

Livy reached into her coat and handed him a folded piece of stationery she'd lifted at the jail. Earlier she'd scribbled several lines on it in pencil. His eyes scanned the paper, then widened as he looked up at Livy.

"Are you quite serious?"

"You have to trust me, Mr. Allard. I promise I'll keep it brief."

"If you're meeting with a Soviet agent in my flat, then you're damned right you'll keep it brief. May I ask the purpose of this?"

Livy couldn't possibly tell him the real reason. If it all went wrong, then Allard would be culpable. This had to be her decision. And she'd have to live with the consequences.

"I'm going to propose an exchange of information."

*　*　*

Allard insisted she take his bed. After changing out the linen, he said good-night and retired to the sitting room.

Allard's bed felt like a soft nest. The thread count of the sheets had to be astronomical. The mattress cradled her body, but her mind resisted comfort. Too much was at stake. Too much could still go wrong. Despite Allard's strong tea, Livy fell asleep almost immediately, but she woke several times in the night, the pieces of the puzzle flitting around in her head.

An hour later she woke to the sound of running water. Allard in the bath getting ready for the day. Livy knew it would be a long one. Maybe the longest she'd ever had.

When she'd left Peter the night before, they'd promised to meet again—tonight—at eleven. Now Livy lay in Allard's cushy bed, staring at the drawn curtains over the window.

Sleep still buzzed in her head but gradually cleared. Peter had warned her against betraying him. Even said he'd be watching her. She felt sure she'd left that alley clean, no tails. But Peter Scobee was a man who'd arranged his own death. Left his wife a widow and his young son fatherless. The man was smart, capable, and perhaps more ruthless than even she knew.

She resisted the impulse to get out of bed, draw back the curtains, and look at the street below. Was he out there? Wherever he was, he probably felt exactly as she did. Wondering if he could trust her. Considering that he might have to do her harm if things didn't work out.

God, Peter, she wondered. *How did we ever come to this?*

Allard gently rapped on the door.

"Yes?"

"Morning," he said, opening the door. The man was completely dressed. Pressed, polished, and scrubbed. "Help yourself to breakfast. I have several things to do today. Should be back this afternoon. I'll knock three times. Pause. Then knock twice more. Don't open the door to anyone else. No matter what. Oh, and be ready. I may have someone with me."

"Someone?"

"Per your request," Allard said. He closed the door. Livy listened to him leave.

She got out of bed, went to the sitting room. More curtains drawn. The street outside a mystery to her. Livy sat in the armchair, curled her legs under her, and tried to focus. She had to concentrate now and see the entire story, from first to last.

Livy knew now Nathalie had been nothing but bait. Her resistance to meet with Livy until that night in the hotel must have been part of the power play going on between Peter and

Valentine. So when Valentine had found out about Nathalie and Peter's plans, he'd decided to give Mirov the whole network. Peter then must have decided to shoot Mirov and Valentine, but would his plan have changed when he saw Livy at the Gare du Nord?

"You didn't know it, but we were working together that night," he had told her.

Peter would know—better than anyone—how much Livy hated Edward Valentine. He'd reeled her in perfectly. She saw him now so clearly. Her Peter.

She looked at the clock on Allard's mantel. Hours to go before he'd be back. Everything hinged now on Allard making contact with the Russians.

But now she needed food, even though her stomach churned and her mouth tasted like acid. Livy forced herself. She fixed toast with jam and brewed a pot of strong tea. What she had to do tonight couldn't be done on an empty stomach.

Chapter
Twenty-Seven

~

Just after three PM, Allard knocked on the back door of the flat. Three long knocks, a pause, and then two quick ones. Livy had been dressed since breakfast. She wore her navy suit, which she'd taken the time to steam-clean by leaving it in Allard's bath with the hot water on and the door shut. She then pressed her blouse. He kept the flat equipped with all manner of laundry supplies. Allard would make a first-rate wife.

She'd paced a rut in Allard's frayed Turkish rug that morning. Going over and over the plan while she chewed her nails ragged. So many ways it all could go wrong. More than once she'd considered dipping into Allard's well-stocked liquor cabinet.

Now, finally, here they were. She hushed her breath and opened the door. Allard had not come alone. The man standing next to him looked like the lone Russian they'd pulled out of Central Casting.

"May we come in, then?" Allard said, huffing. Livy stood aside as he quickly closed the door. "This is Mr. Varlamov from the Soviet Embassy."

The Russian looked to be about forty. Little round glasses amplified his narrow eyes but couldn't hide his heavy Slavic features. He knew how to dress, though. Gray pinstripe suit. Solid blue tie that could have come from a Jermyn Street tailor. Nothing too flash that might upset his worker's pedigree, but his clothing didn't make Moscow look cheap either. He smelled like he'd had a shower of sugar water. Despite the finery, he looked every bit as uncomfortable as Livy felt.

"I told him you would be brief," Allard said. A command.

"Of course. Thank you for your time, sir."

The Russian sized her up, his eyes narrowing before he smirked as if to say, *Who is this girl?*

Livy gave Allard a sideways look. "I'll let you know when we've finished."

A dark cloud crossed Allard's face. Livy knew the Englishman could shut down this whole thing, then and there. Protocol, however, kept him from making a scene, and he retreated from the flat without comment. One had to know how to use the English class system in one's favor. Mrs. Sherbourne would be proud.

The Russian was a different matter. He stood close to the door as if the floor of the flat were mined. Allard had probably driven all over Paris to make sure he didn't have a tail before bringing the Russian in through the back door. Livy knew the clock was ticking.

"Mr. Varlamov, would you—"

"You have information about murder of Andrei Mirov?" His thick accent butchered the vowels, but his voice carried weight.

"I do. I'm willing to make an exchange with you."

Varlamov sighed, looked at his watch.

"A trade for information about his killer."

Varlamov took off his round spectacles and rubbed his eyes. "We do not—trade."

"I think you will for this."

"Excuse me, please. But Andrei Mirov was victim of murder. The French police investigate."

"And they will not find this person, Mr. Varlamov, I can promise you."

The Russian chuckled, as if humoring the farfetched story of a child. "We shall see. Is that all?" Varlamov turned to go, his hand on the doorknob. Livy knew she'd cocked it up. If the Russian left, it all ended right there. She'd be back at the P&J inside a month. Copyediting Mrs. O'Toole's rubbish. She had to speak her mind. No other option.

"I was there the night they shot him." Livy let it land. The Russian hesitated.

She went on, feeling oddly vulnerable with this brick wall of a man. "I liked him, Mirov. He didn't deserve to die that way."

Varlamov took his hand off the knob, waited.

"I wasn't alone that night. Your man Levchenko was there, too. You might say we're acquainted as well. Look closely at my right cheek and you'll see what's left of a bruise he gave me."

The Russian's eyes betrayed nothing, but Livy could feel the gears turning as he tried to make sense of it all.

"Exactly, who—are—you?"

"I'm your only chance. Your people think they'll get an answer about the killer, but they won't. No one knows. Just me."

Varlamov looked somewhere between scandalized and angry. "Go on," he said softly.

Livy's nerves jangled, but she knew she'd hooked him. "Levchenko is in Paris right now. If you go back to the embassy and tell him what I'm about to tell you, then you're going to make your fellow comrade very happy."

The Russian's lips twitched as if he wanted to speak but didn't know how. "This man you speak of—"

"Levchenko."

"I, of course, do not know him. Many citizens work in our embassy. But if you have something important to say to this man—"

"Levchenko."

"Yes. Then I would help you."

"Good." Livy allowed herself a smile. "If, *by chance*, anyone at your office does know Mr. Levchenko, this is my offer."

*   *   *

Allard came back about an hour later after escorting Varlamov safely away from the flat. He locked the door and turned to Livy, his jaw set.

"Do you have any idea how difficult that was? How many favors I had to call in just to get one of those damned Reds to come to my flat?" Allard's genteel pretense had been thrown out the window to make way for some out-and-out bluster. Livy knew he wanted her gone.

"I have a very good idea, actually."

"At the end of all this, we shall have a full accounting of the operation, I assure you," her unhappy host said, huffing. Allard looked like a man who had nowhere else to put his frustration. Livy understood. He had years of experience, and in the last eighteen hours he'd found himself harboring a fugitive from the Americans *and* the French police. On top of that, he was taking orders from a woman more than twenty years his junior. Livy admired the older man. He was doing his best.

"I look forward to that," Livy told him, meaning it. What happened after tonight didn't matter to her. Finishing the job was all she had. She glanced at the English bracket clock sitting on the mantel. It had just turned five PM.

Six more hours.

"Right, then. I have the other item you asked about," he said, turning to the bedroom.

Livy followed and found Allard holding a cloth bag.

"It's lighter than the one you gave me that night, but it should have enough stopping power if you need it." He pulled a small black automatic pistol from the bag and handed it to Livy. "It's a Beretta .32 automatic. Eight rounds. Manual safety and another on the hammer."

The gun felt light, easy to use, though not exactly comfortable in her hand. But the Webley hadn't either.

"It's the Italian version of the Walther," Allard went on. "This particular one was taken from an Italian infantryman, so there's no chance of it being traced to us . . ." He hesitated until she looked up at him. "If it has to be used."

His glare said he thought that a distinct possibility. And why shouldn't he look at her like that? She'd killed two people, the German guard at Fresnes and Valentine. Is that what Allard saw in her now? A dangerous woman? Cold and—what?—a killer?

"It's compact and easily concealed," Allard went on. "Did you hear me?"

"Yes. I got it," Livy said.

"Good. You look tired. Perhaps a bit of dinner might help us both."

Chapter
Twenty-Eight

~

The plan seemed simple enough. At 10:15 PM precisely, Allard went down the front steps to draw the attention of the American contingent watching his apartment. At the same time, Livy took the rear stairs to make her way out of the building. She had on her blue suit, with the Beretta in the same clutch purse she'd carried the night she broke into Nathalie's room at the Ritz. The Beretta actually fit better than the Webley and its bulky silencer.

The back door squeaked as she opened it and stepped into the courtyard. She closed the door quickly to minimize the creak of rusty hinges.

The gate at the end of the courtyard looked even older. Livy unlatched it, pulled the gate back, and heard nothing. She stepped into the alley. The night felt still between the high walls of the adjacent buildings. The glow of lamplight from a few upper rooms couldn't penetrate the darkness below. Only the glimmer of a streetlight about twenty-five yards away allowed her to see her watch. Half an hour to the Pont Alexandre. That gave her fifteen minutes to spare.

She sensed the presence before hearing it. She felt as though fingers were gently tickling the back of her neck. Then the heavy feeling in her stomach returned.

"Don't try to run, because I'll call the others in. Do you understand?" Tom Vance said.

He stood in front of her, about ten feet from the court-yard's rusty gate. The brim of a brown fedora hid his engaging eyes, and the soft southern voice had turned hard. He stuffed both hands in the pockets of his tan overcoat, making Livy wonder whether or not he had a gun. She stole a quick glance at the other end of the alley. Unless someone was hiding in the shadows, Vance had come on his own.

"If it has a front door, chances are it has a back door, too," he said, a faint sneer on his lips. "I knew you really had nowhere else to go."

Livy ran through her options quickly. She had the Beretta in her purse, but what possible good could it do her? She bloody well wasn't going to shoot him. And she had no chance if she started running. The block teemed with Americans. No clear way out presented itself at the moment, and her time was limited.

"What do you want me to say, Tom?"

Vance expelled air, laughing. "Well, we could start with how sorry you are for leaving me in the middle of an operation after I put my neck on the line for you with my bosses. Which, by the way, makes me look like a goddamn fool. You could start with that."

"I think you just said it for me."

"Okay. We'll do it my way, then. Come on." He held his hand out.

"Tom, I have to go. Now."

Vance smiled. "Then we'll go together."

"It won't work that way." At the moment all she could do was stall.

"Livy, I don't think you understand the situation you're in right now."

"What are you going to do? You can't arrest me."

"No, but I have four guys out front who can pick you up and take you wherever I tell them to." His smile wasn't so nice now.

Her stomach clenched. She'd had enough of the boys telling her how to run this show. "Very impressive, luv. But I need to take care of this mess. And I have a deadline," she said. "Tom, you have to trust me that we're on the same side here. We want the same things."

"Do we? Then tell me where you're going."

Livy shifted the purse to her left hand. She couldn't possibly tell Tom about Peter. Tonight would be dangerous enough for her. Vance and the U.S. Calvary would only make it worse. No, this was her job. It was personal and she had to finish it.

"I can't do that," she said.

"Then we're going for a ride. Right now." He stepped in, holding his right arm out for her. Livy swatted it away with the purse.

"You got a little heft in that bag, don't you?"

"Tom, you need to trust me."

"You gotta be kidding me. Let's go." He reached for her again.

Livy stepped back, putting her hand out. "I'm doing this alone because I have to. Can't you see that? If you or anyone else is there, it's blown."

"We'll talk about this when we've got you under lock and key. Understand?" Vance grabbed her left shoulder hard.

Livy responded instinctively; the flat edge of her right hand slashed at the base of his throat. Vance put his hand up just in time to deflect the blow, releasing her shoulder. Livy quickly bashed the side of his head with her heavy bag and watched Vance stagger into the courtyard, falling against the gate. She pivoted and ran toward the opposite end of the alley. She'd taken all of three long strides when she felt Vance's hand on the nape of her jacket. She lunged forward, and they both fell clumsily on the uneven paving stones.

Livy's nose and cheek crashed hard into the ground, and Vance collapsed on top of her. The stones smelled of piss and week-old wine.

"Are you all right?" he asked, rolling off her and struggling to his feet. Ever the southern gentleman.

She touched her forehead. Blood streaked her hand. Livy got to her knees while Vance leaned against a big, square refuse dump, trying to catch his breath.

"This is really how you want it to be?" Livy said, getting to her feet.

"You're not leaving without me."

Livy faced him. Time had left her with no choice. "Then I suppose you should follow me. Just you."

"You're not in a position to dictate terms, Livy."

"All right then, we can stay in this alley for another half hour tossing each other around, or you can follow me and let me do my job."

Vance rubbed his right shoulder and winced. Livy knew this scuffle had taken a toll on him. She didn't want to hurt him in any way, but his opposition had to end here. She absolutely must be at the bridge by eleven o'clock.

"You can watch it all from a distance, Tom, but this is my show, all right? It has to be this way."

Vance mulled it over, snarled, and then nodded. "But I'll decide what I do when I see what I see. I can't trust you anymore. You're not getting away from me again."

"Right, then," Livy said. She glanced at her watch. What had been an extra fifteen minutes to spare was now only five. "I hope you can walk fast."

She turned and headed toward the end of the alley, about fifty feet away. Vance followed a couple of paces behind. Nervously, Livy looked at her watch again. She quickened her steps. Vance kept up.

Allard's gray Renault appeared out of nowhere. The engine's roar echoed off the walls of the narrow space. Head lamps flashed in her eyes as it pulled into the alley. The sudden appearance of the car split Livy and Vance to either side of the backstreet. She pressed herself against the jagged wall as the big car squeezed between the two.

The driver-side window rolled down, and a familiar voice barked, "Get in."

Livy grabbed the right rear-door handle and wrenched it open as Vance did the same on the opposite side. Thankfully, Allard had unlocked only Livy's door. Vance yelled something as Livy flung herself into the back seat.

Allard reversed, the big wheels trying to find purchase on the uneven walkway. The squeal of tires drowned out Vance's shouts while he tried to hold on to the passenger-side door handle, as if trying to keep the car in the alley. But the Renault whipped back into the street and hesitated briefly—then the tires screamed again and the car lurched forward. Vance threw himself at the door, fumbling for something to grab on to, but the car surged away, leaving him in a cloud of exhaust fumes and gravel.

The Renault's engine whined and Allard drove hard, intent on getting away from Vance and the other American agents. Livy righted herself, checking to make sure she still had her purse and the Beretta inside.

"Took you long enough," she said.

"I'd say the timing was perfect," Allard countered over his shoulder. "You might want to fasten your lap belt."

Chapter
Twenty-Nine

~

Exactly twenty minutes later, Allard dropped Livy off on the other side of the Champs-Élysées, half a mile from the Grand Palais. She reasoned that the Americans would have other cars out looking for his, and their parting company ahead of schedule made sense. Before she left the car, Allard promised to return in one hour.

"If I'm not here, you might try the American Embassy," he said. The joke gave Livy a moment of calm. "Oh, and Miss Nash?"

"Yes?"

"Be quite careful, won't you?"

Livy managed a nod and closed the door. The Renault, head lamps off, turned away from the world's most famous street and disappeared into the night.

Now I am alone. Hamlet's line seemed apropos as she began the long walk toward the Seine and the bridge. She glanced at her watch—10:47. She would be just on time.

Livy knew she ought to feel uncontrolled anxiety. The next hour loomed with too many variables. So much could go wrong. Much of the outcome revolved around her own reactions. Which Livy Nash would show up at the bridge?

Livy didn't pray. Yes, she believed in God. Well, she believed in something somewhere that had a say over the world, but that didn't mean she believed you could necessarily have a direct chat with it whenever you felt like. Still, as the lights of the bridge came into view, she closed her eyes and asked—whoever, whatever—for composure, reason, and strength. The last most of all.

Now the bridge lay just ahead. Despite the postwar layer of dust that seemed to cover much of Paris, the Pont Alexandre III bridge retained its grandeur. Its beauty was striking, especially at night. The gold inlay along the bridge gleamed bright, and the serene faces of the gilt-bronze statues of the Fames on the Right Bank settled Livy's nerves.

As she approached the stairs on the left side, she looked down to the walkway along the river. Darkness shrouded the area where she and Peter had met the night before. About fifty yards away, a figure with the unmistakable shape of a kepi on his head walked away. The police must keep regular patrols. Livy worried the officer might return later.

Another glance at her watch—10:58. She took a quick breath. The cold wind that whipped along the river gusted around her as she edged closer to the foot of the bridge. Livy couldn't see anything from the stairs. Taking a step closer, she checked again to make sure the police officer wasn't turning around, but his figure only grew smaller in the distance.

Where was he? For a solid minute Livy feared Peter had made good on his threat and left Paris. She stood there for another four minutes. Alone and vulnerable. A target herself, like Mirov at the rail station.

Now it was 11:07. She shuffled closer to the bridge girder. Then she saw him. Peter Scobee stood at the edge of the darkness under the *pont*. His thick blond hair still gave her a chill.

"Livy, we can't stay here. The police —" he said.

"I saw him. We won't be here long. Don't worry."

Peter nodded. He seemed anxious, less sure of himself than he had the night before.

"So—do you have an answer?" he asked.

"I do," Livy said. "I gave them your terms. They agreed. To all of it."

"Just like that?"

"They want the list. It's that simple."

Peter visibly relaxed for an instant. He put his head back and sighed.

"But they need assurance first."

"What sort of—"

A peel of laughter in the distance interrupted them.

"Over here." Livy led him back into the darkness under the bridge. "Just to be safe."

"We shouldn't stay here long. I have somewhere we can go. Where we can talk."

"The Ritz? Are you still there?"

The question seemed to land between Peter's eyes. He shook his head as if to clear the cobwebs before replying. "You knew?"

"I smelled your cologne when I broke in the night you killed Mirov. Zizanie," she said, naming the scent in an imitation of Nathalie's purr. "You were in the room that day as well, weren't you? I imagine that's why Nathalie held a gun on me. Couldn't have me finding you there now, could she?"

"Where is she now? Nathalie?"

"We have her back in London."

"And she hasn't said anything?"

Livy shook her head.

"She's loyal to me," Peter decided. "She'll keep her mouth shut."

"You sure about that?"

"Livy, I know you're bound to have questions," Peter said. She could almost see the gears in his head turning as he looked for the right words. "I have questions, too. You know the chance I'm taking by even being here. The only reason I'm taking this risk is for you. What other reason could I have?"

They stood there, in the wind, in the shadows, light flickering across their faces. These were the worst possible circumstances to try to determine someone's sincerity, but Livy believed him. She knew Peter wanted the partnership again. He needed it. The damned thing was that a part of Livy wanted it, too.

She pulled her coat tighter. The wind hadn't changed, but she felt it penetrating her clothes, her skin. "You have questions for me?"

Peter nodded, his eyes darting around the walkway over to the stairs before landing back on hers. She could tell he didn't want to say it. "Why are you even here? You should hate me. All the pain you described. I don't understand."

"I told you before."

"I need to know," he said, his tone suddenly aggressive. The big scar on his forehead seemed to throb as he became more animated. "This isn't like what we did before. We work for ourselves now, and the only people we can trust are each other. I need to know I can trust you as well. Trust you with my life."

The blood pulsed in her veins. She'd kept him alive in her heart for two years. Drinking to survive with the pain. Suddenly, the past and what was to come became too much to hold inside. She slapped Peter hard with her right hand. The smack echoed under the bridge like a gunshot. Peter's head wrenched to the right from the blow, but Livy wasn't finished. She grabbed his shoulders and shoved him back, pushing the much taller man to the ground.

"You bastard. Can you fucking trust *me?*" Livy said. Her fury now unconfined, she didn't really care about being heard. She didn't really care about the plan, her own plan. "Who do you think you are? You've betrayed everything and everyone who believed in you. How long do you think it's going to take your son to get over your death? Which, by the way, was just a magic trick. Even Nathalie, poor little Nathalie—did you take her from Valentine? Was it ugly? Or did she just sleep with whoever was boss?"

Peter didn't move. He didn't try to get up. He listened, his face expressionless.

"Can you trust *me?* I grieved your death in a bottle for over a year. I came back to France for Valentine. For revenge. For *you.* So do I have to answer your stupid question, or can you answer it yourself?"

The rage now satiated, Livy felt her pulse regulate. The calm when she needed it most. *Play the part now*, she thought. *The end is in sight.*

She held her hand out to help him, and he took it, standing up. Again he towered over her. His impassive expression hadn't changed.

He said calmly, "Are you carrying a gun in your purse?"

"No," she lied.

"All right. Let me see it then."

Livy hesitated. She didn't know what to say. But she couldn't look dodgy. That would blow it all. She had to keep him here. The words came out quickly. "*I* still don't trust *you*, Peter."

A slight smile creased his lips. "Well, that is at a premium in our line of work. Always has been. So, I propose an experiment. You want to see if you can trust me? Give me your purse."

Livy felt the ground shift beneath her feet. The dynamic between them had changed from last night's old friends/lovers reunion to one of mutual distrust. She'd thought she could orchestrate this, but control seemed to be slipping through her fingers.

"You want me to put myself under your protection, is that it?"

"I want you to give me the purse, Livy."

His brown eyes held her face like a spotlight. He hadn't superseded Valentine by being careless. Livy realized he'd get the gun one way or another, and hoped time was on her side.

"Fine. You're the boss," she said, and popped the snap on the purse. Peter reached in and pulled out the Beretta. He held it by the grip, studying it.

"Ah yes, Italian. Who gave you this? One of your boys at Six? Who do they have in Paris now? Probably some of the geezers from the old Firm, I'll bet. Dunbar? Is he around?" Peter held the gun at his side, his finger on the trigger. He had the power now, and Livy could see he didn't like being slapped and pushed about by the help. He stepped in closer to her, but Livy didn't move, allowing their bodies to nearly touch. The gun hung limp in his right hand.

"You do know Nathalie meant nothing to me. She was— useful, that's all," Peter said, his voice low and soft. He leaned in closer, almost as if to kiss her, but stopped. "Tell me what really happened when you gave them my offer." As he spoke, his lips moved to within an inch of hers. He traced the curve of her hip with the Beretta's barrel, moving up her body. "Or did you lie about that as well?"

Livy placed a hand on his chest, and he stopped. A flash of anger crossed his eyes.

"What?" he snapped, sounding like a hungry animal interrupted midmeal.

"Two men. Walking this way. The other side of the bridge."

Peter froze and slipped the Beretta into his coat pocket. He took Livy's hand.

"Ignore them and smile at me. We're lovers, out for a midnight stroll. Don't do anything stupid."

Livy glanced over his shoulder again. The men were about fifty yards away. The moonlight behind silhouetted them, and she couldn't see faces yet.

"Talk to me," Peter said, his body still against hers, so close she could feel the Beretta through his coat.

"They're not police," she said, smiling. The smile came easy. "Other than that, I can't tell anything." She put a finger to his lips as if wiping away a lipstick smudge, and then she giggled. Her hands moved to the lapels of his coat—she straightened them, and then picked an imaginary thread, flicking it away as she laughed again. Livy played the moment. The loving woman, taking care of her man.

The two approaching them had reached the bridge now. They walked side by side, unspeaking. Both wore long coats and fedoras. Livy recognized one of them.

She put her arms around Peter's shoulders and looked into his eyes. She smiled sincerely. So much so, he appeared to flinch.

His back remained to the approaching men, and that must have caused him more anxiety. Livy excelled in her role as attentive, coquettish girlfriend. She knew it was a limited engagement.

The men would be upon them in fifteen feet, so now their performances had to be in close-up. Two lovers sharing a private moment. She held his face in her hands and pulled him near to her.

"I want you to know I loved you, Peter," Livy said. She couldn't help the tears pooling in her eyes. God, how she'd have liked to stay in character. But she couldn't. The curtain was about to come down.

Something passed between Livy and Peter in that instant. The emotion landed, but left Peter confused. Then the moment passed, and they both became aware that the two men had stopped just behind them.

"Excuse me, please."

Livy recognized the voice. Slowly Peter turned, his arm at Livy's waist, still playing his part. The two men had looked very similar from a distance, but this near, they couldn't be more different. The man on the right was an inch or two taller than his counterpart. He had a wide face and wide chest. Livy thought he looked like a brick wall.

She had expected the man on the left. They'd met only twice, but she'd never forget the boxer's nose, the thick upper lip, the drooping mustache that framed his mouth and the noxious smell of his cigarettes.

"Do you have match, please?" Levchenko said. "My friend, he leave his lighter in restaurant. He drink too much, you know."

Peter broke into an easy smile, but Livy felt tension in the arm that still clung to her waist.

"Please, we do not mean to disturb. Just a light and we will go," Levchenko said in flat, heavily accented French. The man beside him poked a cigarette between his lips and grinned.

"Look, I'm sorry, but I—we don't smoke. So no matches. Sorry," Peter said.

Levchenko turned to the wide man and spoke quickly in Russian. When he finished, the bigger man shrugged and pulled the cigarette from his mouth.

"I see. No problem." The Russian grinned, his mouth twisting into a parody of a smile. Then he stepped away from them, followed by the larger man. Peter's arm didn't relax. His eyes remained on the two men as he said, "*Au revoir.*"

Levchenko stopped and pivoted. "I am sorry again. But we do not have francs for match. Maybe you could help us? Maybe?"

Peter nodded and jammed his left hand into his pants pocket, searching for change. His right hand hung just above his coat pocket and Livy's Beretta. As he drew out a handful of coins from his pants, his hand slipped into his overcoat for the gun.

But as he did that, the big man's arm shot out and pinned Peter's arm to his side. The two men stared at each other for a second, a contest of wills and strength. Then Peter's left hand flashed forward, chucking the coins at both men, sweeping the big man's hand away. Peter spun and the Beretta fell from his coat. It skittered across the walkway, nearing the stairs.

Peter ran. His long legs carried him toward the bridge in the direction from which the two Russians had come. The big man fell in right behind him, his speed surprising Livy. Before Peter could even reach the other side of the bridge, the large man fell on him, flattening him to the hard concrete.

Levchenko stood at Livy's elbow, watching. Livy shook. Like a fever had taken her.

The bigger Russian pulled Peter up by his shoulders and wrenched his arms behind, causing the tall Englishman to moan. The Russian dragged Peter by his coat as they turned toward the bridge girders.

"Livy, please," Peter begged. Tears rolled down his face. His teeth gritted in pain. His arms were pinned behind his back at unnatural angles. "Please, Livy, for God's sake."

She had to look away. Her stomach heaved. She couldn't lose it now.

Levchenko's partner took Peter down to the under-girder of the bridge, a big mass of steel that supported the *pont*, running deep down into the Seine. The great river flowed just feet away.

Livy had to watch now. It was her duty.

Levchenko went to stand in front of Peter. "I have been looking for you. The one they call Marcel," he said, pulling what looked to be a sepia-faded photograph from his coat. Livy couldn't see the picture from behind. But she knew what it was.

"This man—you know him?" Levchenko said to Peter.

Peter cringed, sobbing from the pain in his arms. The big Russian grabbed his thick hair and hauled him upright so he could see the photo.

Levchenko continued, "Do you know this man? No? He was my uncle. When I was little boy my father took me to Uncle Andrei's dacha in the country once every month. I was happy there. Do you understand?" Levchenko held the photo closer to Peter's anguished face.

"I beg you," Peter cried, his voice painful to hear. "Livy, please."

"Do you know him now? Andrei Ivanovich Mirov? You shoot him from behind. You did not even give him chance to die like a man." The Russian's voice was calm. He replaced the photo in his coat and squared himself to Peter. "I will give you more than you gave my uncle. I give you respect."

Levchenko nodded at the bigger Russian, who released Peter's arms. Peter gasped. One of his arms hung limp at his side. Peter tried to straighten up, prepare himself, but Levchenko moved quickly.

A knife flashed in the approaching Russian's right hand. Levchenko crashed into Peter, burying the blade deep in his midsection. Livy heard a sickening gulp. Then another as Levchenko twisted the knife, ripping it upward. The attack was savage and quick. Peter didn't scream. He gasped without sound, and a sickening gurgle rasped from his throat. Blood sprayed from Peter's lips as Levchenko shoved the blade even deeper.

The bigger Russian slapped a dark rag over Peter's mouth to stop the free-flowing carmine fluid from staining the concrete.

Finally, Levchenko stepped back. Livy saw a splash of red on the Russian's coat.

Levchenko pushed Peter against the railing of the bridge girder with his left hand. Peter's body teetered there for a few seconds, as if he were a child's toy or a gymnast warming up. Then he went limp, his shattered arms trailing out at his side. Peter's body tipped over the girder and almost gracefully slid into the Seine.

Livy watched the dark water accept her dead lover and sweep him downstream before pulling him under, little by little. She'd visualized this moment since her meeting with the man from the Soviet Embassy at Allard's flat. This drama had no other possible ending.

The man she'd loved had died long ago.

The Russians worked with efficiency. Levchenko took a handkerchief from his breast pocket, wiped the blade, and put it in his coat while the big man soaked up the blood Peter had spat up with the same rag he'd used to cover Peter's mouth. He threw the bloody cloth into the river, and moved with speed to pick up the Beretta where it had fallen from Peter's coat.

Livy still hadn't moved.

"We have to go," Levchenko said. He registered Livy's shock and barked an order at his companion. Livy felt the big man's hand on her elbow, and suddenly the three of them were walking together up the stairs, away from the river.

On the landing, the wind hit her face. The cold shook her enough that she realized two MGB agents were leading her away from a murder scene. Ripping her arm out of the big man's grip, Livy stopped at the top of the stairs.

"We need distance from river, yes? Sasha," he called to the big man. Livy swatted the Russian's mitt of a hand away.

Levchenko turned and sauntered up to Livy. He seemed so calm after having just butchered a man. "This man," the Russian said, nodding toward the river. "He was British. But you wanted him dead?"

Livy tried to speak, but she had no more voice. Peter was gone. Just as she had planned it. She cleared her throat and tried again. "He—he deserved exactly what he got."

Levchenko grinned. "I did what you ask. You say that no one know the body. The blood will draw fish. They will finish job. Now, we are finished too."

Having spoken his piece, he turned, and the two Russians set off quickly in the direction of the Eiffel Tower.

*   *   *

Thirty minutes later, Dennis Allard eased his gray Renault to a stop on a side street off the Champs-Élysées. Exactly one hour had passed since he'd dropped Livy off.

She sat on the curb, tapping her right foot. When the car stopped, Livy got in the passenger side. She didn't look at Allard. Twice she'd watched Peter Scobee die. This time it was for keeps. She collapsed back into the seat, suddenly feeling more drained than ever in her life. She wanted to sleep for days. Weeks. And never speak to another person again. But she wasn't done.

"Everything all right then?" Allard asked.

"The list," she said. "I know how to get it."

Chapter Thirty

❧

Two days later, Livy sat on a bench in Greenwich Park about a hundred yards away from the prime meridian. The line, little more than an interruption on the cobblestone entranceway to the park, marked the basic reference point for Greenwich Mean Time. It also happened to be a block or two away from the safe house where MI6 kept the uncooperative Nathalie Billerant.

Complaining the whole time, Allard had agreed to serve as intermediary between Livy and Henry Dunbar. After much negotiation, Allard had managed to secure Livy ten minutes alone with the Frenchwoman as she took her daily constitutional through Greenwich Park.

Like many of the commons in London, Greenwich was lush and green, especially after the recent rains. Today a morning shower covered the grass and cobbled pathways with a sheen of moisture. Livy opened that day's *Times*, keeping one eye on the newsprint and another on the strollers out for a walk in the misty morning.

The minders from Six were easy enough to spot. Brown suits. Mustaches. Creased papers tucked conspicuously under their arms. Livy had sussed two so far. They'd keep an eye on their prize French asset during the brief meeting. Nathalie couldn't be far behind.

She wasn't.

The Frenchwoman trudged slowly alongside a matronly sitter who looked like every other middle-aged woman in Greenwich. Raincoat. Bonnet. Shopping bag. Another housewife out for a little walk to the co-op for the weekly rations.

Nathalie had altered since Livy had last seen her. Her black eye had healed, but stooped shoulders and a slow gait replaced the glamorous, sexually confident physicality she'd displayed in Paris. Despite the transformation, Nathalie had enough sophistication in reserve to attract the attention of every man and woman who passed her.

Nathalie didn't see Livy until they were almost beside the bench. When she did, she turned to the matron as if to protest.

"Ten minutes," the older woman snapped at Livy. Then to Nathalie, "Sit."

The matron waited until Nathalie obeyed and took her place on the bench beside Livy before shuffling off toward the Royal Observatory.

Livy put down her paper and remembered what Nathalie had said to her at the Gare du Nord the night Valentine and Mirov were killed. *You and I—we are more similar than you would like to think.* Livy knew what she'd meant now.

But Livy hadn't pleaded for this meeting so she could be empathetic.

"Peter's dead," she said, without emotion.

An electric spark surged through Nathalie's body. Her back arched as she searched Livy's face.

"No," she said, finally. "You're lying."

"I saw him die. No magic trick this time. He won't be coming back."

Nathalie's face fell, and for a moment, Livy thought she would break down. But the stoic mask snapped back into place and the Frenchwoman turned away.

This one's got it bad. She felt pity for her. Treated like property by Valentine and Peter too.

"He didn't care one jot about you. I was with him before he died. All he wanted was to sell your damned list. He wanted the money. He didn't even ask how you were being treated. It was always the money for him."

A tear escaped Nathalie's right eye, but she wiped it away quickly. Livy knew her pain too well.

Livy went on. "Peter. Valentine. They're dead. The Americans have Jabot. You'll be tried as a war criminal here. To a British court you'll just be some tart who betrayed her own country to the Nazis."

Staring out into the park, Nathalie shook her head as if processing the idea of Peter's death.

"You have one, and only one, way out of this. It's the list. You told me you had it back in Paris. The full list. Well, that's your ticket out, don't you see? I know what you had planned with Peter. Sell it to us or the Yanks, maybe? Then the two of you would go somewhere fancy and live off the money? Well, that's over now. But you can trade the list for leniency. Cooperate and they'll go easy on you. You don't have to spend the rest of your life in a prison."

Nathalie fidgeted with a button on her coat, appearing unmoved by Livy's rhetoric.

"Fine," Livy said. "Your babysitter will be here in five minutes to take you back to your little room. You can wait for them to decide what to do with you. I don't really care. Although, Peter did say one thing about you before he died."

Nathalie stopped fidgeting and raised her head.

"He said you were useful. That was the word he used. *Useful.*" Livy let the word land before going on. "You don't have to sit in that little house and take the fall for what he did. You're a tough one, and you're nobody's fool."

Staring toward the town, Nathalie didn't move. "So we are friends now?" she said, scoffing. "Is that it?"

"No," Livy said. "I'm not your friend, luv. But we both thought Peter Scobee was something he wasn't."

Nathalie leaned back, refusing to look at Livy.

Livy put one hand on the Frenchwoman's elbow. "Nathalie, it doesn't have to be like this. Give me that list and I'll see to it."

Out of the corner of her eyes Livy saw the matron trudging back from the observatory. Nathalie turned. She wiped her cheek and smoothed her skirt. As the matron approached, she finally looked Livy in the eye.

"Go to hell," she said.

Livy didn't know how to respond, nor had she time.

"Let's go," the matron said to Nathalie. She looked at Livy. "Your time's up."

Livy figured that was just about right.

Epilogue

One week later

Livy Nash had a long journey ahead of her. Her train didn't leave for another half hour, but she wanted to find the platform, put her bag down, and sit quietly.

London's Euston station seemed like another world compared to the Gare Du Nord, but she still felt anxious. Perhaps it was the sound of the engines, the echo inside the terminal, or the particular smell of the exhaust that made her jittery. Or maybe it was the still-damaged roof of the Great Hall, bombed during the Blitz, and the grime and soot that seemed to cover the platforms—all reminders of her war and its aftermath.

She walked past the other commuters, not making eye contact. One bag over her shoulder. Two others at the counter. All felt as heavy as a load of bricks. Whatever a load of bricks felt like. The last week had been hard.

Livy was back at square one. No job and no prospects. Livy couldn't bear going back to the P&J. Fleming hadn't been in touch. That hurt most. She saw her life now. What it should be. She'd made mistakes, sure. But this shadow war—as

Mrs. Sherbourne called it—needed soldiers, and by God, she didn't plan to sit on her arse and let someone else do the fighting.

She'd spent much of the week sleeping. At least that came easier. Now she had a place to put Peter and that part of her life. Their "reunion" in Paris—as painful as it was—had made it clear to her that the Peter Scobees of the world only wanted to profit from the war, from the pain and the past. Livy was done paying.

The decision to leave should have been difficult, but instead was quite simple. She'd enough money to go back home for a week. So home it was. She'd go, stand on a hill somewhere amid the nettles, and figure out what was next.

At last, the platform loomed ahead. Mercifully, only one other passenger sat in the waiting area. The air from outside the tunnel felt crisp but not too warm. The great black engine lay still, waiting. A porter hurried past her.

The sun broke through the default overcast London sky, illuminating the track by increments as it led away from the station. She took the bag off her shoulder and sat on the bench farthest away from the other passenger, a small square man in a sweater vest and tie who looked to be somewhere between forty and seventy-five.

Livy stretched her legs and looked at her watch. Half an hour and she would be gone.

After five minutes of peace, he showed up.

He looked out of place on this particular platform bound for points north. He was dressed for summer in a khaki linen suit with a pressed white shirt and navy tie. He carried a folded copy of a newspaper, probably *The Times*, under his right arm.

He walked past the free benches and stopped near Livy. He smiled, and the lines at his mouth creased.

"Is this seat taken?" he said. His voice like honey.

Livy shrugged, and Tom Vance sat next to her.

"You know, most women I know wouldn't get in a car with another man and leave me in an alley," he said.

Livy considered her riposte, but realized the banter exhausted her. She wanted quiet.

"I'm sorry, Tom. But I did what you would've done had the tables been turned."

"I really oughta hate you, but that's not how my mama raised me." Vance reached into his jacket pocket. He handed Livy a silver-and-enamel cigarette case. "Going-away present."

"Tom, I don't—" Livy began. But something clicked and she recognized the art deco styling and the French proverb inscribed on the edge. L'HABIT NE FAIT PAS LE MOINE.

"Actually, the gift's from Mr. Fleming."

Livy shot him a look, unsure whether she should trust the American.

"Don't worry, Livy. Proper colleagues, remember? Anyway, two days after your chat with Miss Billerant, she had a change of heart. That case had been stowed away with her other belongings. 'Course it had been searched before, so she had to show us the trick to getting inside."

A smile spread across Livy's features as she cracked open the case.

"A false bottom," Vance said. "On the right there."

Livy's fingers traced the right inside edge of the case until she found a slight indention. So small it could have been a scratch. She pushed at it and the panel shifted to reveal another just like it underneath.

"Another magic trick," Vance went on. "The entire list was written on very thin silk paper and hidden there. I don't know what you said to her, but looks like Miss Billerant listened. You should've seen Henry Dunbar. He almost smiled."

Livy should have laughed at the joke, but instead she felt the emotion catch in her throat. *God, what a long road*, she thought.

"Your boys had a go at the list first, and then they brought us in," Vance said. "Once they get it through encryption, then the real work begins: converting these agents into assets."

"And what about Nathalie?"

"Her only condition was she wanted to go home. To Paris. I think Fleming would have married her, but she was determined to go back. She must have left something, or maybe someone, very dear to her there."

Livy looked at her watch. Fifteen more minutes. Time and distance could be very painful. She couldn't explain to Vance why Nathalie had gone back. How could anyone understand the obsession of chasing a dead man unless they'd been through it themselves? For the first time she felt real sadness for the Frenchwoman.

Vance lit up a Camel and exhaled smoke as the platform became more crowded with passengers bustling around, pushing baggage carts, checking tickets.

"You know, your little escape back there in that alley in Paris just might get me sent back to work in the family tobacco fields. And let me tell you, you do not want to work tobacco in North Carolina in summer. Fortunately, Fleming wants me to be the American liaison for the Mephisto list, so there's a chance Gray might take pity on me since it all worked out. Sort of. But let's forget all that for now. Cards on the table here, all right? Here's my proposition. Let me exchange your ticket for a sleeper car for two to—wherever it is you're headed."

"Blackpool. Up north. Home."

"Okay. Blackpool huh? Doesn't exactly sound like the Riviera, but I'm game. You can show me the sights. Have a few laughs, maybe."

Livy studied his face. It was a good face. Open and kind at times like this. "I could use a laugh," Livy said, and meant it.

Vance's smile expanded. She could see what he would have looked like as a boy. "Let's just go and put everything else behind us. The past is the past, right?"

The whistle on the engine blew twice. Ten minutes to board. Livy looked around, surprised by how many passengers had boarded while she listened to Tom's pitch.

She wanted the past exorcised from her life. Maybe a week in Lancashire with Tom would be just the thing. But wouldn't that be just another temporary salve for a pain that went deeper? Besides, every time she looked at him she'd be reminded of the Grand Guignol, the Pont Alexandre. All that death.

"I can't, Tom," she said finally. "I haven't been back home since the war really. I guess I just need the comfort. For a little while. By myself."

Vance nodded and took a deep breath. Then, with a bit of effort, his smile returned. "Well, Olivia Nash, you owe me one."

The quip brought an involuntary smile. She wondered if she'd made the right decision. Knowing she might never see Tom again, Livy didn't have the wherewithal to dive into whatever a romantic getaway with this man might bring. So she stood, slinging the bag over her shoulder, and said, "I really should be getting on board now."

Vance hopped up, hand in his coat. "Almost forgot. Fleming also sent you this." He handed her a note. She recognized the crisp vellum from the Gray's Inn Road office and the distinctive signature in the black ink from Fleming's Montblanc pen.

She unfolded it.

My dearest Spitfire, the Kemsley News Service needs you. You know the number.

His business card slipped out of the note. She remembered the first time she'd seen it in that pub during the parade. She clutched it in her hand.

The engine bell rang. Time to board. Tom Vance held out his hand.

"Let's not make a scene," he said. "This isn't the pictures, after all."

A broad smile broke out on Livy's face. A smile big enough to make her, for a few seconds, forget the pain and tears of the last few weeks. But only a few seconds. She stood on tiptoe and kissed his cheek.

"You're a good 'un, Tom," she said. "Do you have a light?"

Vance pulled a silver lighter from his coat and flicked it once. Livy held Fleming's note to the flame and watched it burn down. She blew out the flame and dropped the ash in a waste bin.

Fleming's card she carefully placed in Nathalie's cigarette case.

Then she joined the other passengers boarding the train, leaving London and heading for all points north.

Acknowledgments

Although my name is listed on the cover, so many people have given their time and expertise in the creation of this book.

First, I'm beyond lucky to have such a skilled and clever editor as Chelsey Emmelhainz. She has made every page better.

Also to my fabulous agent Carrie Pestritto, who has kept the faith and been a tireless advocate. I need more space here to convey adequate thanks.

Thanks also to Beatrix Conti, as well as to everyone at Laura Dail Literary and Crooked Lane Books.

I could post a lengthy bibliography of the many books I relied on for research, but I would like to recommend two especially: *A Life in Secrets: Vera Atkins and the Missing Agents of WWII* by Sarah Helm is a great story as well as a perfect primer on SOE's F Section. Also, Andrew Lycett's biography of Ian Fleming illuminates a complicated man who had a golden imagination.

My profoundest thanks go to my dear friends Dr. Sally Barbour and true French hero André Roche. Their patience with my questions about all things France helped bring 1946

Paris to life for me. I also seem much smarter thanks to the kindness of friends in the UK—Anthony Coppin and Russell Brown.

Thanks to Rosalind Tedford, Philip Powell, and Carter Smith—generous souls who read early drafts and offered words of encouragement as well as editorial support. Also to Charlie Lovett, Janice Lovett, Reed Johnson, and Megan Bryant for their advice and unwavering kindness.

This book would not exist without the help of my late friend James Dodding, who took me to Blackpool and showed a Yank true Lancashire hospitality. I so wish you could read this, dear friend, and that I could say thank you.

Finally, to Ian and Lucy, who inspire me in so many ways. Ian—thanks for encouraging me to "do something with this one," and Lucy—maybe you can read the rest of the book when you get to high school.

Any inaccuracies in this work are solely the fault of the author and not the lovely people listed above.